The Florida Keys.
Ninety Miles from Cuba.
For Some, a Final Destination Resort . . .

Tony Harwood: He liked being a cop, but the cops didn't like it when he roughed up a suspect. So now he's on his own, tracking down missing persons, dead or alive, and wondering which category he fits into . . .

Ramon Marquesa: A first-generation Cuban-American "entrepreneur," he's got a lust for the high life, a talent for taking what he wants, and a temper that unnerves his enemies. But his latest tantrum took things too far—and now he's in troubled waters . . .

Luis Marquesa: Ramon's Cuban-born big brother. He's got powerful connections, and big ideas about heading back to his homeland, with the backing and firepower to stage an anti-Castro coup—and seizing the commander's spot for himself . . .

Kay Fulton: A young, idealistic, fast-lane attorney, she's having serious thoughts about taking the first exit out of the heat and hustle of Key West corruption. She's got a young daughter to think about, a coked-up, abusive ex-husband to worry about—and Tony Harwood to wonder about . . .

Angel Lopez: Ramon Marquesa's slavishly faithful right-hand man—and the one man who can bring Ramon to his knees, if he can be found. Ramon just wants him under wraps. But if necessary, he'll put him under-ground . . .

Books by John Leslie

Havana Hustle
Damaged Goods
Blood on the Keys
Bounty Hunter Blues
Killer in Paradise

Published by POCKET BOOKS

HAVANA HUSTLE

JOHN LESLIE

POCKET BOOKS

New York London Toronto Sydney Tokyo Singapore

This book is a work of fiction. Names, characters, places and incidents are either products of the author's imagination or are used fictitiously. Any resemblance to actual events or locales or persons, living or dead, is entirely coincidental.

An *Original* Publication of POCKET BOOKS

POCKET BOOKS, a division of Simon & Schuster Inc.
1230 Avenue of the Americas, New York, NY 10020

Copyright © 1994 by John Leslie

ISBN: 1-416-59869-3   ISBN: 978-1-416-59869-5

First Pocket Books printing April 1994

10 9 8 7 6 5 4 3 2 1

POCKET and colophon are registered trademarks of Simon & Schuster Inc.

Cover art by Broeck Steadman

Printed in the U.S.A.

In memory of
Scott Sommer

"It ain't a fit night out for man or beast."

—W. C. Fields

HAVANA HUSTLE

RAMON

A golden snake hung from Ramon Marquesa's right ear. The snake, made more noticeable by the absence of hair on Ramon's head, was squiggly, with two small inlaid rubies for eyes. As Ramon spoke the snake shimmied and the rubies picked up the light from the candles on the table, dazzling Ramon's dinner companion, Angel Lopez.

Ramon took a long drink from his cocktail, a tequila sunrise, his third since he and Angel had come into the restaurant. Ramon leaned across the table trying to talk to Angel above the music. An American show tune that was vaguely familiar, but one he couldn't put a name to, was being played on a piano in the lounge. It was loud, louder than usual, and people were actually singing along around the bar.

"What is this shit?" Ramon asked. "I want to go to a Broadway musical, I'll go to New York." He looked around the restaurant. Everybody seemed to be getting into the act.

"Bloody Mary!" came a shout from the bar. And an answering chorus: "Now ain't that too damn bad!"

A couple of people were actually beating on the bar as if it were a bongo drum.

Was there a message here, a sign that he could interpret? Ramon believed in signs, a belief that went beyond mere superstition. He had a destiny, a link with the cosmos, and stuff like this could be a direct signal for him, his own message—he just had to figure it out.

Ramon had no sooner finished his drink than their waitress, a girl in a slit skirt with flowers painted all over it, was there to ask him if he would like another cocktail.

Ramon gave her the look. "I'll tell you the tail I like." He reached out to put his hand on her leg, but she sidestepped him and carried his glass back to the bar. Grinning, Ramon watched her retreat.

"Look at that," Ramon said.

"Jus' another *chica*," Angel said.

Ramon studied him across the table, feeling a rush, his eyes slightly out of focus. Angel had worked for him for twenty years, running the island transportation that Ramon and his brother, Luis, owned.

Angel was organized, good at keeping track of shit, stuff that Ramon—who was a thinker and destined for greater things—had no skill for. Angel frequently bored Ramon.

"You miss Cuba, Angel?"

"*Como mi corazón.*"

A heart attack a few years ago had left Angel dependent on a pacemaker. His heart and his country were like one.

Angel Lopez had come from Havana in 1960, when he was sixteen years old. Ramon, though he was of Cuban descent, was born in Key West and until a couple of weeks ago had never set foot in the country of his ancestors.

Ramon couldn't understand how anyone would want to be anywhere, no matter where they came from, but here. But Cuba was going through changes, and all the signs indicated Fidel might be on his way out. Ramon wondered if Fidel saw these signs, if he had the same sense of destiny Ramon felt.

"The place opens up, you wanna go back?" Ramon asked.

Angel smiled, showing a mouth full of bad teeth. "Yeah, sure, I go back. Even if is in a box, I go back."

Ramon smiled, shaking his head. "What about Oreste, he feel the way you do?"

Oreste Villareal, Ramon's business rival, was also Cuban. Both of them, Oreste and Angel, saw themselves as exiles, Ramon thought. Something he could never understand.

2

Angel lifted his hands. "Why don' you ask him?"

"Yeah, I will," Ramon said. "I'll ask him the next time I see him."

The *chica* brought Ramon a fresh drink, and moments later their dinner arrived. Prime rib hiding a platter big enough to skate on for Ramon. Angel had a whole fish smothered in tropical fruit.

Ramon cut off a slab of the prime rib and dipped it in horseradish sauce before plunging it into his mouth. "You know, Angel, we got to be prepared. Cuba opens up, somebody's gonna make a lot of money."

Ramon's brother, Luis, who saw his destiny in political terms, was, of course, already staking out a foothold in any future government that would be established in Havana. Luis talked with the Florida governor, even the Secretary of State in Washington—shit, maybe even the president, for all Ramon knew. Luis was definitely carving himself a niche, his own manifest destiny.

Ramon had no political interests and no desire to live in Cuba. His destiny was going to be to carry all those Cubans and gringos ninety miles across the water and make a fortune on the explosion of tourism that would come once Havana opened its doors.

"You know about the hovercraft?" Ramon asked Angel.

Angel neatly severed the head from his fish, removing the bone and leaving fossillike indentations in the flesh. "Is *rápido,* no?"

"Faster than piss going through snow."

Angel said something that Ramon missed. Was it his imagination, or was the music getting louder?

"I hear Oreste's talking about buying one," Ramon said. "Starting a ferry service to Havana when it opens up. You hear that?"

Angel nodded. So delicate, Ramon thought, watching Angel eat; the guy was like a doctor doing exploratory surgery.

"I hear something like that," Angel said. "But with Oreste, sometimes, is jus' talk. You know?"

"Huh-uh," Ramon said. This wasn't talk. Ramon was in

3

touch with an outfit that sold these things. Oreste was making inquiries, too, jockeying for position at the starting gate.

"Huh-uh," Ramon said.

"Anyway, he says he wants to talk," Angel said.

Oreste Villareal owned the other cab company in Key West. Number two and trying harder, Ramon always said. Ramon had offered to buy him out more than once, but Oreste wouldn't have it. Now, with a recession, the paying tourists on their way to classier resorts, and the possibility of competition from Cuba nearing, two cab companies made about as much sense here as central heating.

"Talk about what?"

"I don' know," Angel said. "He'll be at Bubba's tomorrow night."

The waitress was hovering around the table.

"The music's too fuckin' loud," Ramon said.

"We turned it up just for you," she said, smiling as she turned and walked away.

"I like her," Ramon said. He and Angel ate in here at least once a week. Business dinners.

Angel shrugged; just another *chica.* "Jimmy comes in from the island this weekend. You wanna go out there?" Angel asked.

"What?" Something about Jimmy, who was the caretaker on Ragged Key, the island the Marquesas owned a few miles out from Key West.

"I said you wanna go out to the island this *fin de semana?*" Angel couldn't speak without alternating English and Spanish, which always pissed Ramon off. Ramon almost never spoke Spanish unless he had to.

"Yeah, maybe the *chica* wants to go." Ramon mocked Angel, even though Angel would never understand that he was being mocked.

"Ask her," Angel said.

"What?" Ramon took another drink. Jesus, he couldn't have a simple conversation. All the money he'd dropped in this place. He stood up. "Fuck this," he said. He walked into the lounge and stood by the piano. The guy playing looked up at him and smiled. Ramon saw that this was a bad omen, that he was being tested and had to take charge.

Ramon smiled back. "You know 'Melancholy Baby'?"
The piano player shook his head.

Then Ramon slammed the keyboard cover down on the guy's fingers. "Well, now, ain't that too damn bad," Ramon said, and he walked back to Angel, who was still sitting at the table. Leaving a wad of money, Ramon walked out with Angel following him.

ONE

Two men with shovels turned the damp earth beneath bald cypress trees on a knoll thirty miles south of Tallahassee. Six others stood huddled in the cold wind, watching. Tony Harwood, wearing a black-ribbed roll-neck sweater, stood apart from them, leaning on a cane, his other hand shoved in the back pocket of his black jeans. His eyes followed the progress of the diggers as he unconsciously kicked at the dirt, scuffing the toe of one of his flat-heeled western boots.

It was not a happy morning. Tony sensed the mood, the hostility of the others, especially the cops, who were here at his bidding. He kept his distance and listened to the wind as it whistled through the tall trees, glancing up now and then at the gray sky as if expecting rain; all morning it had threatened, but the clouds ran fast and dry.

Two black Labradors sniffed and pawed the ground, occasionally whining nervously as they, too, watched the diggers, whose shovels broke, sifted, and turned the earth in easy, regular beats. Two uniformed officers, the Leon County sheriff and one of his deputies, who held the dogs on tight leashes, stood as grim-faced as statues. A photographer and two reporters were present—one from Tallahassee, the other from Miami.

Tony turned and looked back fifty yards to their vehicles. Wayne Costa sat in the Ford Taurus, the rental car Tony had driven here. Wayne's head leaned against the headrest as though he were asleep.

"Got something," one of the diggers said.

They had dug a rectangular hole less than a foot in depth, ten feet long and five wide around the base of several cypress trees.

The sheriff stepped closer to the diggers, who had put their shovels down and with gloved hands were scooping the dirt away with the care of archaeologists working on a dig. The dogs began to bark. The photographer snapped photos, using a flash in the overcast light.

Tony didn't move. From where he stood he could watch everything, could see the latex gloves the diggers had donned, blackened by the loam, could see sweat glistening on their shirtless bodies even in the cool March air.

One of the men stepped from the grave; the other had uncovered a remnant of cloth, and, using his hands to scoop more dirt, he began to unearth the skeletal remains; the bones appeared bleached clean, and as the work of uncovering them slowly progressed, Tony Harwood saw why. When the skull was uncovered the eye sockets were filled with maggots, a white mass of moving larva swelling over the area where the nose would have been, filling the mouth cavity.

There was a tangle of dark, matted hair, long fibers that reached the skeletal shoulder blades. A simple examination of the bones by an expert would determine the gender of the skeleton, but Tony was certain it was a woman.

"Jesus God!" the gravedigger said, and he stepped from the grave.

For a moment no one moved, standing transfixed, watching the disturbed maggots reclaim their territory.

The dogs crouched, tense, sniffing tentatively at the outer edges of the grave, whining.

Tony, pulling on a pair of gloves, walked over and, hooking the crook of his cane in his back pocket, bent to lift the skeletal hand as if to help it from the grave. He had seen something when the body was exposed. He now heard the click of a camera. The bones grated where they touched. There was a distinct rattle.

7

Something recoiled in him, some horror at what he was doing and seeing, at the same time that he felt a surge of anger. He held his breath. What he had seen was a piece of metal that glinted, a bracelet encircling the bones of the wrist. Tony carefully worked it over the bony digits. Was it his imagination, or did the finger bones seem to be turned inward, as if in the process of forming a fist? Or had she been buried alive, trying to claw her way out of the grave?

He stood up and started to walk back to the Taurus, breathing deeply, the bracelet clutched in his palm. The man who'd been sitting in the car was now walking slowly toward him. When they met, Tony put his hand on the man's shoulder and said, "Wayne, I think we've found Nicki." He held out the bracelet. Wayne took it, turning it over and over in his hands before looking up. "It's Nicki's," he said. "She wore it on her left wrist."

Tony took off his gloves, and ran his hand through his dark hair with its short ponytail. He'd grown his hair longer when he'd begun this investigation almost a year ago, the hair becoming a sort of talisman that he vowed not to cut until he'd found Nicki Costa. Someone once told him that he looked like a young Al Pacino, with the actor's dark, brooding looks and slightly skewed features. Tony seldom went to movies; he wasn't sure he'd ever seen Al Pacino.

Wayne was looking beyond him, toward the men who stood around Nicki's grave. His eyes were bloodshot, beneath them deep, wrinkled pouches that had not been there when he'd hired Tony to find his daughter.

"I wouldn't go over there," Tony said. "It isn't a pretty sight." Wayne Costa paused, his shoulders slumped. "The medical examiner will take it from here. If he moves on this, you'll probably be able to take her back to Miami tomorrow and bury her properly."

They walked back to the car.

Wayne had first come to him nine months ago and given him a picture of Nicki, explaining that she was a sophomore at Florida State University in Tallahassee. No one had seen her in three months. Her room in the sorority house where she lived contained all her things. Friends had last seen her leave class one Friday afternoon. A nationwide search followed. Photographs of her appeared in papers and on television news for a couple of months following her disappearance. The police indicated they were following leads, but as the weeks went by it became apparent that it would take a miracle to find her.

Now, after the miracle, Wayne sat in the passenger seat, and Tony walked around and got behind the wheel. He didn't start the car, just sat there. Finally Wayne said, "You know, I was sitting here thinking a minute ago. All these months we've talked about Nicki, about her life, people she knew, our family. You know us inside out."

It was true, but Tony said nothing, waiting, staring out the windshield at the men in the distance.

"And now it's over. What's left?"

Tony started the car. He had no answer. He turned the car around and drove back toward the highway.

"All I know about you is that you were once a cop," Wayne said.

Tony began talking, knowing it was simply a distraction for Wayne. "I was with the Miami Police Department for nearly ten years until I muscled a suspect a little too hard. I was suspended from the force. After the suspension was lifted I decided not to go back."

He didn't bother explaining that once he'd turned his back on the fraternity, giving credence to the charges brought against him by choosing not to rejoin them—the brotherhood could tolerate anything but rejection—he had become a pariah.

"Why didn't you go back?" Wayne asked.

It was a question he'd asked himself repeatedly. He had a reputation for going his own way, for independence, often running afoul of his superiors. The bureaucracy, the paperwork bored him; the structured methods and the failures that went with the job quickly discouraged him. But when he was out on the streets, working, he felt good, happy even. And he knew he'd been a good cop.

His fingers drummed against the wheel. "I don't know, maybe because it was too slow. I wanted to get things done."

Now here he was getting things done, doing a job the cops

9

had been unable to do, and rubbing their faces in it in the process. It was considered indecorous, to say the least.

If he had failed, there would have been the usual grumbling about wasted time before this was quickly forgotten; by succeeding he would remain a pariah.

None of that mattered. He had always been a renegade, even as a kid—especially as a kid—and he understood punishment. He was immune to the usual need for commendation. He formed deep attachments slowly. What mattered most was not that he was always right, but that he was not betrayed by his instincts. He trusted what he knew of the streets.

What he had wanted most here was to succeed—yes, for personal satisfaction, but also for the man sitting next to him who had hired him, a man with all the money he would ever need, but whose domestic life had been sullied by divorce, and now tragedy.

He tried to explain some of that to Wayne on the drive back to Tallahassee. When he finished Wayne said, "No kids, family?"

Tony shook his head, not mentioning his stepfather, Jack Dowd, who had suffered most by his decision not to return to police work. He didn't say anything because there was nothing in it that Wayne could relate to that would ease his own pain.

He thought of the picture he still had of Nicki and decided that now would not be the right time to return it.

The suspect who was responsible for Tony's suspension was a drug dealer named Ricky Lee, whom they'd been after for months. At his trial Ricky was convicted and given a two-year sentence. Tony was thirty-four when he was suspended, thirty-five when he moved to the Keys and into an Airstream trailer with a collection of Shaker furniture that seemed to suit his personality. He'd bought the furniture, most of it used, on a trip to upstate New York, and had it trucked back to the trailer. The idea was to reduce his needs, get back to a simpler life.

The trailer had a screened-in room on the back side overlooking the channels and mangrove islands, part of the backcountry that led to the Gulf of Mexico. The town of Big Pine Key in which he lived was thirty miles up from the southernmost city and resort capital of Monroe County, and a hundred-plus miles below the mainland and Miami.

After Miami he'd first gone to Key West, where he lived for six months before tiring of the hubbub of a tourist town and looking for something more isolated. He found the lot on Big Pine and an Airstream trailer to go on it all in the same week.

Then came a succession of women. He holed up in the trailer except to make nightly raids on a few of the blue-collar bars in Big Pine and nearby Marathon. It was a kind of delayed penance, using sex and alcohol in place of religion to atone for his misconduct in the arrest of Ricky Lee. The atonement finally came in the form of a big blond dyke who believed she held some property rights on Beth, one of the women he'd scored with. The dyke camped out in front of the trailer the night he and Beth were inside, and when they emerged the next morning she shot Tony in the leg with a .22 hollow-point that had shattered bone in his calf.

When Wayne Costa knocked on his door Tony Harwood discovered that he was all too happy to get back to work. The simple life had grown complicated and simply wasn't enough.

He ate alone in his room in the downtown hotel in Tallahassee to avoid questions from the media and went to bed at ten-thirty. After lying awake for half an hour he got up and went for a walk around the nearly empty streets of the capital for an hour. He scored a joint from some kids on the street and went back to his room and smoked it. When he got to bed he fell into a troubled sleep and awoke the next morning to find himself famous.

The phone rang at seven, just as he was about to leave his room. It was Jack Dowd. "You see the papers yet?"

"Not yet." Tony sat down on the edge of the bed.

"A wire service called me yesterday looking for a story. It'll be in every paper in the country, and that picture, too."

"What picture?"

11

"You standing in the grave holding a skeleton by the hand."

"There was a bracelet I wanted to recover before Wayne got there."

"Well, you've made a name for yourself," Jack said. "You solved a case that was destined to go on ice in the police files."

Along with the praise Tony thought he heard a note of alarm in Jack's voice. He pictured his stepfather, a cop for forty years, sitting now in his kitchen in the old apartment building near Lummus Park, where he lived within walking distance of the Miami Police Department.

"It'll blow over," Tony said.

"I wouldn't count on it. You know the success rate the police have finding missing persons."

Tony knew too well. It was all part of the frustration he'd felt as a cop—the procedural entanglements, the caseload that made it impossible to devote full attention to any one case. It was all part of his reason for leaving the force, even without the problem of Ricky Lee.

In addition, he had learned something in the past year about himself: He loved the excitement of the job while hating the cop image. Even though it was Jack Dowd, a lifelong cop, who had taken Tony off the streets when he was just a kid, a runaway headed for a life of trouble. Along with his wife, Beverly, who had died five years ago, Jack had given him a home and an education and guided him into this work. Jack had been devastated when Tony was suspended from the force.

"I'm flying down this afternoon with Wayne," Tony said. Wayne owned and piloted a Piper Cherokee. "I'll stop in and see you."

"You staying over?" Jack was sixty-eight, his health failing. Though he was still gruff and independent, Tony knew he took pleasure in these brief visits.

"I'll see how late it is," Tony said. In the past six months he had spent less than two weeks on Big Pine Key. He looked forward to the seclusion the Airstream and the Gulf of Mexico in his backyard afforded.

RAMON

When Ramon came into his brother's house Luis was in the living room with three or four men. Ramon walked past them, down the hallway past the paneled rooms on either side with their modern furnishings, to the kitchen in the back of the house where Lourdes, Luis's wife, was preparing coffee.

Ramon had a thing for Lourdes. She was small, dark-haired, with a certain vitality about her. Bouncy. Always trying to please people. He had never understood what she saw in Luis, who was so solemn Ramon half expected him to crack someday. Mr. Cool. Ramon supposed what Lourdes saw was the big house, two kids, and plenty of money. Still, he enjoyed flirting with her, mischievously teasing her.

"What we got, a cabinet meeting in there?" Ramon said.

Lourdes handed him a cup of coffee, and he sat at the table in the center of the Cuban-tiled floor of the large kitchen.

"Very important men," Lourdes said. "From Miami."

"Fuckin' terrorists," Ramon replied. Passing the living room, he had recognized two of the men. Juan Cabrera, a Miami developer, had fought with the CIA–trained 2506 Cuban brigade during the Bay of Pigs alongside Armando Rodriguez, who many years ago had been a busboy at a big hotel on Miami Beach before working his way up to director at one of the leading Spanish-language radio stations in Miami.

Rodriguez had been arrested several times, accused of terrorist crimes in anti-Castro demonstrations, but never indicted.

Like Luis, Cabrera and Rodriguez had Washington connections, lobbying for a strong anti-Castro policy among congressmen there. It seemed understood, at least among South Florida Cubans, that the next administration in Havana, once Fidel was gone, would be made up mostly of exiles from Miami. Cabrera was rumored to be the administration's choice to replace Fidel.

Ramon couldn't give a shit. These yo-yos sitting around in a cloud of cigar smoke and politics over a half-assed country ninety miles from here. *Patria.* The long, moony faces made by guys like Angel Lopez every time the subject of Cuba came up made him sick. This was home right here, and the only interest Ramon had in Cuba was in whatever wealth he could take out of there.

Ramon studied Lourdes's spectacular ass bound by a criminally tight black knit skirt as she stood on tiptoe to reach something from the cupboard.

"Tell me something, Lourdes," Ramon said, grinning when she looked around at him. "What does that old man do for you, talking politics every night?"

Luis was approaching fifty, fifteen years older than Ramon. Lourdes was thirty-three, his second wife. She and Luis had been married for ten years.

"Shush," Lourdes said. "You're bad."

"Yeah," Ramon replied. "I know." Lourdes smiled. "You ready to live in Cuba?" he asked. "Raise your kids there?"

Lourdes turned her back again, busying herself at the sink. She was like Ramon, American born; she knew nothing of Cuba except what she was told or read in the media.

"I don't even think about it," she said.

"Think about what?" Luis was standing in the doorway. He wore black slacks and a white *guayabera.* Tasseled loafers on his feet. Mr. Cool.

"We were talking about Cuba," Ramon said. He wondered if Lourdes ever told Luis what a flirt his brother was. Probably not. Lourdes was in awe of Luis, and Luis, Ramon knew, had never known what to make of his brother, always keeping a certain distance between them, maybe even a little afraid of Ramon.

"Our friends are ready for you now." Luis always referred to this crowd as "our friends."

Ramon grinned and stood up. Next to Luis, Ramon knew, he looked like a peasant. Short and stocky with the shaved head, wearing gray spandex shorts that hugged his meaty thighs and a T-shirt with a picture of Jesus on the front and SAVES written across the back.

Ramon winked at Lourdes before following Luis into the front room, where he was introduced. Along with Juan and Armando, Luis introduced Felix and Eduardo, conspicuously avoiding last names. Ramon barely stopped himself from laughing at this needless subterfuge. Who was Ramon going to talk to? He didn't give a shit if the ayatollah were reborn in this room.

Lourdes carried in coffee on a rattan tray, setting it on a sideboard where there were some brandy snifters and a bottle of Fundador. Once she was out of the room Luis got up and invited the others to help themselves to the coffee and more brandy.

Ramon sat down in a wing chair and knotted the laces that had come untied on his scruffy sneakers. When the others regathered Luis gave a summary of Ramon's trip to Cuba last week.

Ramon had taken Luis's Bertram Flybridge Cruiser across the Florida Straits ninety miles one night last week. The boat was loaded with consumer goods for families who had remained behind at the time of the revolution. Now, with no Soviet support, they were running out of food and fuel. It was ironic, Ramon thought, these Miami Cubans breaking the embargo they all had supported since 1960 to get supplies to their relatives.

Jimmy Santos had gone with him, despite the fact Jimmy was on parole and wasn't supposed to leave the county. Ramon said fuck it, he'd pick him up at Ragged Key, where Jimmy was caretaker, and drop him back there when they returned. Who was going to know? Jimmy agreed. It had taken them just over six hours to make the crossing, and they were there by midnight, tying up at a dock at a private home in Santa Fe, half an hour's drive from Havana. They were guided in by torches burning along the beach. With a shortage of fuel, the Cuban gunboats rumored to cruise offshore had restricted their patrols, and Ramon's arrival was without incident. In an hour the boat was unloaded, and by sunrise they were back in the Keys.

When Luis finished with his summary Armando looked at Juan Cabrera, who sat staring impassively at Ramon. Ramon stared back. There was discussion back and forth between Felix and Eduardo, directed primarily at Cabrera. They spoke Spanish. Talking about Kennedy and the Bay of Pigs. Kennedy, who had established the brigade that would invade Cuba, started the training in the Everglades that was going on to this day but then had abandoned the case the way every American president since Kennedy had done— rhetoric, and unfulfilled promises.

Ramon tried to tune them out.

"It's up to us," Armando said. "We can't depend on nobody but ourselves."

Armando asked Ramon about the men who had unloaded the boat.

The next president of Cuba, Ramon thought, the cabinet right here in this room? Asking about some laborers who had unloaded a boat. It was enough to make you laugh.

Cabrera said, "You want to go back?"

"To Cuba?" Ramon asked. And he laughed. "Fuck no. I like it just fine right here."

The others exchanged looks, took a sip of brandy, then swallowed their coffee in a gulp.

"We'd like you to make another trip," Luis said.

Ramon frowned. He was about out of patience and didn't like being bullied.

Luis must have picked up on that. He said, "You'll meet someone who can help set up a ferry service between here and Havana when Cuba opens up."

Now they were talking about something that made some sense. Ramon massaged the lump of muscle in his calf and said he'd think about it.

16

* * *

"You want some bump?" Ramon asked.

"What?"

"Bump. You want some?"

Oreste stared at him, said, "Yeah, sure. *Cómo no?*"

Ramon stood up from the bar in Bubba's, and Oreste followed him to the back and went into the men's room across from an office. Ramon locked the door and went into one of the stalls, where he laid out a couple of lines on the porcelain top of the water tank, then invited Oreste in. Maybe the marching powder would pick up his mood, dampened by the time with Luis and that crowd of exiles who wanted to go home.

They squeezed into the narrow stall. He watched Oreste take the cocktail straw, lean over the toilet, and suck up one line, dividing it between his two nostrils. Then he handed the straw back to Ramon, who filled his right nostril with the remaining line and laid out another one for the left nostril.

"More?" Ramon offered the straw to Oreste, who shook his head.

Oreste Villareal was no more than five or six years older than Ramon. Forty, forty-one maybe. Ramon remembered him from school when Oreste had first come to Key West from Cuba, a skinny, brown-skinned kid with a big nose and peasant clothes who spoke hardly any English. He got the nickname Pancho, Ramon remembered, from kids who didn't know the difference between Cuban and Mex. Pancho Villa.

Ramon said it. "Pancho."

Oreste smiled sadly. He was still skinny. Taller than Ramon. Deep furrows etched along his face on either side of his long nose and curving outward to the edges of his thin-lipped mouth. Something about him Ramon had never liked. The kind of weak, sad look the guy had without even trying. Wimp.

"You remember that," Oreste said.

"Yeah, I remember," Ramon said. Almost twenty-five years ago. Ramon was ten, and his daddy, a state senator, had helped Oreste's daddy get a start in his new life. Oreste's father was a car mechanic. Before long he had a couple cars

17

hat he'd put together to begin a taxi service. When Oreste got out of high school he ran the taxi business, built it up after his father died, and without competition.

Until Ramon came along a few years later.

Funny, Ramon thought. His own father, the senator, was dead by then, and it was Luis who got Ramon into the business. Ramon thought he could compete with Oreste, thought he could ruin him, in fact.

But Oreste was still here.

"What keeps you going?" Ramon asked.

The sounds from out in the bar assaulted his senses. The clinking of glass, the laughter, deadened music. Unintelligible conversation. It had always been there, but he was more aware of it now. Standing here staring at Oreste.

"The same thing keeps you going," Oreste said. "Keeps us all going."

Ramon shook his head. Someone banged on the door. People were marching to the toilet. Marching. They had been in here awhile. Been in the bar for a couple hours, since he'd left Luis.

Angel was waiting back at the bar, probably wondering what the hell was taking them so long. He looked at his watch. It was one o'clock in the fucking morning. They still hadn't talked.

Ramon whiffed another line of nose candy. "Time to go," he said. He unlocked the door to the men's room. A guy he'd never seen before was standing there. He looked at Ramon, then Oreste, lifting his eyebrows in a way Ramon didn't like. "You two having fun in there?" he asked.

Ramon jabbed four stiffened fingers into the guy's belly, just below the sternum. The guy doubled over and stumbled into the restroom. As the door closed Ramon could hear him upchucking in the sink.

"Teach the fucker," Ramon said.

Oreste didn't reply. They got back to the bar, and Angel was talking to two girls Ramon didn't recognize. He spoke to Angel. "Get rid of them."

Angel said something to the women, who got up. One of them stood next to Ramon and put her arm around him, running her hand over his head. "Is it true what they say about you bald guys?" she asked him.

"Every word," Ramon said.

She lifted his hand and put it on her breast. "Maybe I'll get a chance to find out for myself."

Ramon raised his hand to her face. "Maybe," he said.

She twisted slightly, keeping her eyes on him, and took his index finger into her mouth.

The din in here was deafening. It seemed like everyplace he went lately was so fucking noisy. Ramon was aware of Angel and Oreste watching him; the other girl had disappeared. This one sucked his finger, rolling it back and forth in her mouth.

What was this shit? This girl he'd never even seen before starts sucking on his finger. He should be getting a message here, a clear signal of something, but it wouldn't come. She kept looking at him all the while, her eyes cocked oddly, as if she were smiling.

Then she bit him. Hard. Her teeth grinding into the bone above the middle knuckle. Ramon raised his other hand against her face and pried her loose from his finger.

"Shit," he said. "You fuckin' bitch."

But she was already moving away from him, out of his grasp, grinning. He thought he heard her say something about a piano, but with the noise in here he couldn't be sure.

Ramon rubbed his finger—she hadn't broken the skin, but the bone was bruised. He sat down between Angel and Oreste. "What the hell was that about?"

Angel shrugged. "Jus' another *chica*," he said.

All the late-nighters were rolling in for the last rounds. There was high energy. "Fucking woman," Ramon said, practically shouting in Oreste's ear.

"What?"

"You want a woman?" He'd go find her, bring her back here and let her gnaw on Oreste's finger.

Oreste laughed. He was married; Ramon knew that.

So?

Oreste shook his head.

Still a wimp, a nerd.

19

"Ramon," Oreste said, "you and me, we oughta get together."

"Get together?" Ramon shouted. Angel was looking at him, looking at Oreste, Ramon caught in the crossfire.

"Join up." He pronounced *j* as though it was *y*. Yoin.

"What the fuck you talking about?"

Oreste went on a talking jag, the coke talking. Ramon only got bits and pieces of it, leaning in, staring at the bar, his ear close to Oreste's mouth. How times were bad. They needed to do something, pull things together. With Cuba opening up they could make some money.

Cuba. That was all anybody talked about anymore.

"Let's yoin up," Oreste said.

He was talking merger. The dumb shit. Ramon couldn't believe it. Oreste went back and forth between English and Spanish, mixing the two, just like Angel.

Ramon looked up, and there was a fresh drink in front of him. He knocked back half of it, high, but with that kind of coke-clear awareness, his finger still throbbing. Pissed.

And now the dumb shit, Oreste, a fuckin' mechanic, thinking he could move up in the world. He'd read the business page of the Miami *Herald,* read about a merger and thought he could talk this shit.

"Pancho!" Ramon cut him off midsentence.

Oreste looked perplexed. What? What'd he do?

Ramon held out his hand. Oreste took it, smiling now as though a deal was going down.

Ramon grasped the Cuban's thumb and wrenched it back. Oreste winced with pain. "Get the fuck outta here," Ramon said, releasing his grip.

Holding his hand, Oreste stood up. Pain, anger showed in his face, but Ramon had turned back to the bar, paying no attention. Angel saw it but was unable to do anything but watch as Oreste suddenly reached down, picked up his drink, and poured it over Ramon's bald head. Ramon jumped as if he'd been scalded.

"Don't call me Pancho!" Oreste said.

The din suddenly stopped. "I'll fuckin' kill you," Ramon said, standing up. He grabbed Oreste by the shirtfront, pulling him to within inches of his face. "You understand me, Pancho? I'll fuckin' kill you."

Ramon felt someone's arms wrap around him, pulling him away from Oreste, whose shirt was ripped. Ramon threw an elbow, and whoever was holding him gasped but kept the grip.

"Not in here," a voice said in his ear. Ramon recognized the voice as belonging to the bartender. A circle of people had formed, watching. Oreste was leaving, going out the front door.

"All right," Ramon said. "It's okay."

The bartender released his grip. Ramon shrugged, flexed his arms, and went back to the bar. Angel was there, standing beside the seats where they'd been sitting seconds earlier. Things went quickly back to normal. Angel wouldn't have pulled him off Oreste, Ramon knew. Ramon grinned. Picked up his drink. "Finish your drink," Ramon said, "and let's get out of here."

Angel drove. Ramon was wired, everything kicking in now, and he talked, talked, talked. About Oreste. Once Angel said, "Forget it." And Ramon blew. "Fuck forget it. Drive by his house, and I'll forget it."

Angel drove down the residential street where Oreste lived alone with his wife. The street was quiet at this hour, dark, no traffic, stop signs at each intersection. Impatient, Ramon told him not to stop, so Angel slowed, then sped through the intersections.

Brake lights blinked in the distance. In Oreste's driveway. They were half a block away.

"That him?" Ramon asked.

"That's his house," Angel said.

"Drive by slow, don't stop. I'm going to scare this skinny fuck so bad he hears a loud noise he'll be dribbling in his pants the rest of his life."

Angel drove slowly, coming up on Oreste's parked car. Oreste was just getting out when Ramon hit the button for the passenger side window, which hummed down. Ramon reached under the seat, bringing a gun back up, pointing it out the window. Angel punched the accelerator just as Ramon fired.

Turning around in his seat, the snake's ruby-red eyes dancing in the dash light, Ramon saw Oreste Villareal crumpled beside his car. "What'd you speed up for?" he asked Angel.

Angel looked confused. "I don't know . . . I saw the gun."

"You thought I was going to kill him?"

Angel nodded.

"You dumb fuck," Ramon said.

TWO

Kay Fulton, her head tilted back, her face only inches from the bathroom mirror, penciled dark liner above her thick eyelashes. In the next room she could hear her six-year-old daughter Patty telling Pooh Bear, her constant companion, how to behave while Patty was away at school. Kay recognized the tone of voice, the words, as her own, a simple repetition of the countless times she had admonished Patty herself before leaving her in the company of others while Kay went to work. Stepping back from the mirror, she smiled with quiet satisfaction at her daughter's mimicry.

"Are you ready for school?" Kay called as she walked from the bathroom into her bedroom.

A moment of silence before Patty said, "Yes, except for my shoes." There was a slight pout in her voice as she was pulled back to the reality of her role in life as a child.

"I'll help you," Kay said. "Bring them in here." She looked at the clock on the bedside table. It was seven-forty-five. They would have to leave here in half an hour for Kay to drop Patty at the Montessori school and get herself to work at the state attorney's office by eight-thirty. Patty still hadn't had her breakfast. No matter how early they got up, there never seemed to be enough time to do everything that had to be done just to get the day started. She checked herself before beginning to feel sorry about her status as a single parent.

Until six months ago she had been married, and the idea of raising Patty alone had never entered her head. They had come to Key West as a family when Patty was a year old. Kay, only a couple years out of law school, had seen an ad for prosecuting attorneys with Monroe County, had an interview, and was hired a few weeks later. Brad, also a lawyer, had been able to get into a small law firm, and their life seemed to be going in a very positive direction. They got a deal on two recently renovated houses side by side on Frances Street, using one as income property that nicely offset the balance of their mortgages.

For a few years everything was perfect. They had a boat, friends, and a comfortable life. Brad gained a considerable reputation as a defense attorney and began to command sizable fees, although—more times than Kay was happy about—he was defending local people who lived marginal lives. Her worst nightmare was that they would someday have to face each other in court in adversarial roles. Worse, however, than Brad's controversial defendants was his almost imperceptible lapse into recreational drug use.

There had been the usual round of cocktail parties on the weekends at which they both drank. Drugs were available, though not usually openly on display. They had both shared a joint with friends a few times and tried a line or two of coke on occasion. Kay didn't like it. Thinking it made her falsely chatty, after the first couple of experiments she declined further offers. She was also keenly aware of her professional position and indulged in these occasional forays only privately or with close friends.

Brad had less at risk. He also had no aversion to the Colombian marching powder, and as he was frequently keeping company with clients who used, she had no way of knowing how often he was indulging. Until he began to change. His temperament, the mood swings, the increasing number of weekends when he would be high most of the time, their declining sex life—all began to erode what had begun as a wonderful life. It took its toll. She let things slide

24

for a couple of years, being uncomfortable with confrontation and hoping Brad would come out of it. He didn't. Six months ago she had become so worried about the effect this was having on Patty that she recommended he move into the other house.

There were quarrels, bitter fights as everything came to a head. Then, as if to demonstrate his power, he became vindictive. He began partying at the other house with people she distrusted. The parties went on into the early hours, when she was often awakened. She knew he was sleeping with other women. Finally she'd had enough. She asked for a divorce. Brad said he would fight her in court for shared custody of Patty.

Patty, who was now standing in the doorway, one arm around Pooh Bear's neck, holding her black patent shoes with the straps that were too stiff for a six-year-old to buckle in her other hand.

Kay looked up, smiled, and wondered if she had learned anything from all this. Anything that would help her, relieve some of the pressure from her responsibility as a mother. She'd never had great ambitions, wanting only to do her job and raise a family.

She smiled at Patty, finished dressing, then helped her daughter into her shoes. Orange, the neutered tomcat they'd had for ten years, padded into the bedroom and rubbed himself against the backs of Patty's legs.

Patty leaned down to pet Orange as Kay was kneeling, threading the hook into the tiny hole in the stiff strap. "Mommy, will Daddy ever live with us again?"

"I don't think so, honey."

"Why not?"

Kay stood up. "Because he and Mommy don't get along." She'd gone to a therapist for a few months to deal with her stress and anxiety and Patty's questions. She had learned that she should be honest and direct, but without saying anything that might divide the child's loyalty. Patty's questions, though, could be endless.

"Let's get some breakfast now," Kay said, cutting Patty off and leading her into the kitchen. This day was getting off to a reasonable start. She hoped the rest of it would go as well but knew better than to hold any expectations.

There was a message for Kay to see Randall Welch, the state attorney for Monroe County, when she came in. Her office, barely larger than a cubbyhole, was in the cement building behind the old courthouse and jail. Nine other attorneys worked in the same building, in similar cramped offices. Window air conditioners wheezed and left the air cool but stale and with a faint odor of musty papers and old cigarette smoke and coffee. Filing cabinets filled every available space. Carpets were threadbare. The waiting room, with its uncomfortable seats, candy and gum vending machine, and victim's rights pamphlets had more the appearance of a social services office than a law office.

Kay looked over her desk calendar, then picked up a file folder and her personal cup before going to the hallway, where there was a card table that held a coffeemaker and a coffee-stained economy-size jar of Coffee-mate. She poured a cup of coffee and walked down to Welch's office.

Randall's door was open, and she stopped before entering. He was on the phone. When he looked up he called her in with the beckoning motion of one hand. He was a big man in his late fifties with a Karl Malden–like nose above a thick salt-and-pepper mustache. He wore a button-down pale pink oxford shirt, the sleeves turned up over hairy forearms. His colorful tie, whose design looked as if it had been taken from a Jackson Pollack painting, was pulled askew at the neck.

Randall was either gruff or jovial, depending on his mood and how many rum-and-Cokes he'd had at lunch. Among the office staff he was viewed as a capable administrator whose singular flaw was his penchant for cozying up to Key West's power brokers. The fact that he was on his third four-year elected term suggested that the cozying had been successful.

Kay did not socialize with Randall beyond a couple of large seasonal parties each year and had no feelings about him one way or the other. Like everyone else in the office, she almost always had a heavy caseload. Her loyalty was to

26

the job, however, not to the man, and she'd never had a confrontation with Randall Welch.

His office was twice the size of the others but was equally cluttered. She put her coffee on his desk and sat down on one of two brass-studded burgundy leather seats in front of the desk. She glanced through her file folder, waiting until he was off the phone.

When he hung up Randall said, "Morning, Kay. What's your calendar looking like?"

Kay sighed. "The usual. I've got forty-seven cases this month. I'm going to trial tomorrow and have two more court appearances scheduled next week." Nothing out of the ordinary. Of the forty-five to sixty cases she handled a month, only three or four of them went to trial; the rest ended in guilty pleas or continuances.

Randall leaned back in his swivel chair and clasped his puffy fingers, making a steeple of his two index fingers. It made her think of the game she used to play with Patty when she was younger and they were a happy family. Here's the church, here's the steeple. Go inside, see all the people.

"I'm thinking of giving you Marquesa. You hear the news?"

She hadn't, in fact, listened to the news this morning, nor had she seen the papers or had a chance to look at the Key West *Citizen* yet, so didn't know what Randall was referring to. The Marquesa family was often in the news.

"What's happened?"

"Ramon was arrested last night."

Randall tapped the tips of his fingers together, apparently waiting for a response. Kay only shrugged.

"Oreste Villareal is in the hospital. In a coma. He's not expected to live."

Her mind automatically began to sift information. Villareal owned one of the two cab companies in Key West, Ramon Marquesa the other one. It was well known in the community that the two men didn't get along. There had been an ongoing feud, with fights and threats over the years, to the point where it had become a joke. No one took the feud seriously anymore. Except apparently Oreste and

Ramon. The difference between them was that Ramon Marquesa had an influential family behind him, clout.

"Ramon was arrested and released on bail early this morning," Randall said, affirming the Marquesa family clout. "Half a million dollars."

Which meant someone in the family had written a check for fifty thousand dollars, ten percent of the bail bond, and still a tidy sum.

"I assume Ramon isn't going to enter a guilty plea," Kay said.

"I would assume so, too," Randall replied. He remained still, his hands in the same prayerful poise.

"What details are there?"

"Sketchy. There was a witness. Angel Lopez."

The name rang a bell, but she was unable to process it right away. She made a note even as Randall leaned forward and pressed a thin file folder toward her, a folder that would grow fat as information was gathered.

"He'll go before Judge Grabill today. I'm guessing arraignment will be set sooner rather than later. Be prepared to present your charging document within a couple of weeks."

She thought about the cases she was trying the next couple of weeks. She had two days, possibly three in court this week. Next week she'd be there most of the week. Which meant working late, less time with Patty, and less time to deal with her own disorder. There was also the spotlight that would be turned on the Marquesas and, consequently, her. It would not be easy.

Randall seemed to sense her concern. He said, "Can you handle it?"

She wasn't sure what he knew about her personal life, but she didn't want to appear as if she were seeking excuses, or even to discuss her domestic affairs. She didn't want to be given special treatment because someone felt sorry for her. Ultimately, it was always easier to avoid conflict by simply taking on whatever responsibility was handed her without complaint.

"No problem," Kay said.

Randall smiled. "That's what I thought," he replied.

*   *   *

28

Back in her office, Kay read through the file Randall Welch had given her. It contained the police report of the incident. Oreste Villareal had been shot once in the head at approximately two-thirty A.M. as he stepped out of his car after spending the evening in a local bar, where witnesses saw him argue with Ramon Marquesa, who was heard to threaten Villareal. Shortly before Oreste left the bar at approximately two-ten in the morning Marquesa, according to the same witnesses, departed along with his drinking companion, Angel Lopez. All three men were said to have been drinking heavily.

Villareal's wife was awakened by the sound of a car pulling into the drive. She got up to look out the window, just in time to see him shot as another car drove away; she identified it as Ramon Marquesa's. His name, Ramon, was on the vanity license plate. At six A.M. the police went to the Marquesa home with a search warrant and found a gun that matched the caliber used to shoot Villareal. Marquesa was placed under arrest.

It all seemed so deceptively straightforward, so easy, that even Kay, who had always accepted things at face value, who among most of the other attorneys in the office had a reputation for still having a degree of innocence about her, even gullibility, had trouble believing this was all there was to it.

As Randall had said, Marquesa would probably come up for arraignment quickly, at which time a trial date would be set if there wasn't a plea and her charging document was in order; she could be going to trial as early as six weeks from now.

And from the looks of it everything was going to turn on one key witness, Angel Lopez. Also as Welch had predicted.

Kay checked with the Cuban office receptionist, who told her that Lopez was Ramon Marquesa's right-hand man at the cab company. Kay called there for him and was told he wasn't in. She found his number in the phone book and spoke with his wife. Angel wasn't at home, either; his wife didn't know where he might be or when to expect him.

A tingle of apprehension surged in her, and Kay pawed through her Rolodex looking for the number of one of the

29

investigators employed by their office to track down witnesses for depositions. She came across the number of Colin Barker, with whom she'd worked in the past. An answering machine picked up the call, and Kay left a message.

After hanging up Kay went back to work on the case she was preparing for trial tomorrow.

A few minutes before noon Barker returned her call.

"I've got the Marquesa case," Kay told him.

"Lucky you."

"I need to talk with a witness, Angel Lopez," Kay said. "Could you track him down and get a statement as soon as possible? You can even call me at home." She gave Barker her home number.

At twelve-thirty Kay went out and picked up a salad at the deli and brought it back to eat at her desk. At one-thirty she went to the restroom, and on her way back to her office the receptionist said there was a call waiting for Kay from the Montessori school.

Kay felt a sense of calamity, of things going to pieces. She charged back to her office and picked up the phone. A teacher's calm voice said that Patty had fallen on the playground and broken her arm. It was not a serous break. She was at the hospital right now, and she was going to be okay.

Some of the tension drained from Kay's body. A broken arm she could deal with, but it served to bring back the guilt she felt at her inability to give her daughter the time and attention Kay would have liked to give her. The inability to be both father and mother to her. It was at times like these that she blamed herself for the failure of her marriage. Perhaps she should have tried harder with Brad, not been so hasty to separate.

She stuffed the papers she was working on into her satchel, left a message at the front desk as to where she was going, and drove to the hospital.

When she walked into the emergency room Patty had her left arm in a cast, her hair damp and tangled, but there was a smile on her face.

"Mommy," she said when she saw Kay, "I broke my arm, and it doesn't even hurt. Do I get to stay home from school tomorrow?"

Relieved, Kay smiled and hugged Patty while guiltily beginning to think about finding a baby-sitter to stay with her tomorrow. She drove Patty home, distractedly listening to her daughter's chatter.

Shortly after four o'clock Barker called her at home and said that Lopez wasn't around, no one knew where he was, and this might take some time.

Kay sighed. This was definitely not turning out to be the day she'd hoped for. "Please keep trying," she told Colin.

THREE

‗‗‗‗

Jack Dowd was shrinking. Tony could see it in the stooped shoulders that he remembered having been as square as planks. When Jack was sitting with his legs crossed, his ankles and a portion of his once-meaty calves exposed, Tony saw how shriveled they had become. The flesh, once hairy, was now almost as smooth as the skin of a plum.

Tony knew that these were subtle changes, ones that he could have watched over the years if he'd been paying attention. It was the sort of thing you only noticed after a long absence. Somehow he'd always taken Jack's massive size and vitality for granted. Of course, he knew Jack would die someday, but he supposed he had believed, or wanted to believe, that he could be spared this evidence of his stepfather's decline.

Jack himself would never discuss his own health. As far as Tony could tell, he had maintained the familiar lifestyle even into his third year of retirement from the police force. Except for cooking, he had no hobbies; he detested boats and fishing and got no pleasure out of working with his hands or collecting things. He swam nearly every day, either doing laps at the pool reserved for police officers or going over to the beach and swimming in the ocean. He played cards one or two evenings a week with cop friends, both active and retired, but he played more for the gossip he picked up than out of any interest in poker. Metro-Dade had a hold on him that he wasn't inclined to give up. He remained active in the Police Benevolent Association and as a liaison with the city in an effort to improve community/police relations.

Jack Dowd was also capable around the house, and though he had a Cuban woman come in only four times a year to clean, the two-bedroom apartment was always neat. He'd moved here five years ago after Beverly died, carting most of his personal belongings from their home in Miami Shores. The walls were plastered with photographs, and with various trophies and plaques Jack had collected over the years from the department. He was no stranger to the kitchen, either. He'd always taken an interest in cooking, an interest he'd passed on to Tony, and the death of Beverly and his retirement had only reinforced it.

The evening Tony returned from Tallahassee Jack prepared linguine with clam sauce made with littleneck clams he'd gotten at the fish market. There were thick slices of Italian bread that he'd put under the broiler with garlic and butter on top. After the meal they sat around the kitchen table drinking bottles of ice-cold Rolling Rock and playing cribbage. Twice Jack was able to muggins him when Tony's concentration slipped while counting points. Jack was already twenty points ahead.

"Your mind's not on the game," Jack said. "You still thinking about the Costa girl?"

"Yes," Tony said. After so much time and energy had gone into that case it was hard to accept the conclusion. "I'll be okay after a week in the Keys."

"Then what will you do?" Jack was shuffling the cards, making a bridge of the deck in his large hands and releasing them as though they were spring-loaded.

It was a subject Tony had hoped to avoid. His future. "I don't know," he said, trying not to sound defensive.

"I had another couple of calls today, people who would like to hire you."

Jack had been mentioned in the story the paper had done

33

on Tony and the Costa case. Some background bio. Since Tony chose to live without a phone, messages were often relayed through Jack for anyone knowing the connection and who needed to get through to him faster than the mail or a trip to the Keys could provide. Jack didn't seem to mind. It was a way of staying in touch.

Tony picked up the five cards Jack dealt. "I'll have to think about it," he said. In fact, he wasn't sure what he wanted to do, if he could ever put himself through this demoralizing process again.

He understood Jack's concern. He was only trying to get him settled, get the pieces put together so that Jack could stop worrying. The worry, of course, being that Tony was directionless, easily headed back to the life he'd known as a kid before Jack had rescued him from the streets at the age of fourteen. Jack took rightful pride in that, and Tony felt indebted to his stepfather.

He had drifted into police work—after losing interest in law school—both as a means of appeasing Jack and because he thought he might be happy with it. It was an acceptable way back to the streets. And for a while it had worked. Everything seemed fine until one day he snapped, lost it. But even through the suspension, the censure, Jack had stuck with him, never a question, not even a probing look.

Tony took a hit of the cold Rolling Rock and studied his stepfather, who was ticking off points on the cribbage board. In the shrinking flesh of his father's face he saw Nicki Costa's skull in a rictus grin, felt her bony fingers, and wished there had been some way to save her. Save Jack. And save himself.

The next morning, after a restless sleep, Tony was up at six o'clock. He found Jack dressed, sitting at the table over a cup of coffee, reading the paper.

Jack had always been an early riser. He would get up in the mornings, make sandwiches that he brown-bagged to the office, and have breakfast alone while looking over the morning paper. Then Jack would drive Tony to school on his way to work. It was a twenty-minute ride during which

Jack would relate the details of what he would be working on that day. Sometimes those details would be grim, and Tony understood that they were meant to be a reminder of the life he had barely escaped. But they were also exciting stories that had gradually bonded them.

Although still rebellious, Tony Harwood had been smart enough to see that he was viewing the same world he'd inhabited for the past couple of years, just from a different perspective. Initially, in his fourteen-year-old eyes, it seemed the only difference between the players was that one group had society's consent. On the weekends he and Jack would often go to the police shooting range, where Tony learned to fire a handgun, or to the gym, where he could learn martial arts. His personality began to be forged here as he gained some self-confidence and an ego that wasn't constantly under attack by the physically and emotionally abusive family he'd run away from.

It was Beverly who, after time and in her own quiet way, was able to instill in him some forbearance, to get him to see the advantage of patience. By the time he was fifteen and had to go back before the juvenile-court judge who had remanded him to the custody of the Dowds, Tony Harwood was a different kid. No longer sullen, he stood before the judge, answering his questions in a positive way and smiling confidently when the judge lifted Tony's parole.

It was an unusual success story of a troubled youth turned around. There was added poignancy in the fact that he learned from Beverly a few years later that she and Jack had had a child, a son, who had drowned when he was eight years old. He and Tony would have been the same age.

"Coffee?" Jack asked.

"I'll get it," Tony said. He went to the cupboard, took down a mug, and poured from the electric coffeemaker. He carried the mug back to the table and sat down across from Jack.

"I was thinking," Jack said. And Tony knew the previous night's conversation was about to join the cards and the cribbage board, which were still on the table.

"You know, I've still got connections with the department, access to files, information."

"Jack, I don't know if I want to keep doing this." He knew only too well about Jack's connections; he had made use of them while tracking Nicki Costa's killer.

Tony had roamed the state following some of the earlier police leads, but mostly relying on his own instincts. He worked among immigrant pickers around Florida City and hung out in the bars frequented by cane cutters in Clewiston and Belle Glade. He went to Key West and talked casually among the commercial fishermen there. And everywhere he went he listened, eavesdropping on conversations, taking notes on seemingly irrelevant chatter.

The break came months later in an unexpected quarter. Tony was having lunch with Jack Dowd one day at a Cuban place near Jack's apartment in downtown Miami when two Cuban businessmen sat down at the table behind them. He listened to the men speaking Spanish, missing some of the words but able to pick up the gist of their conversation about someone they knew who had recently been released from jail and the horror stories he had to tell.

At that moment it occurred to Tony that Nicki's abductor could already be in jail, a habitual criminal who could be doing time for something that had nothing to do with Nicki Costa.

He mentioned it to Jack, who suggested they spend a few hours going over records at Metro-Dade, singling out perpetrators of violent crimes who had been arrested since Nicki's abduction.

It was a daunting task. There were hundreds of names and arrest dates to be paired. They had to read enough of the information contained in the rap sheets to determine which ones deserved closer scrutiny and which could be eliminated. Even with Jack's influence and some assistance from a loyal network within the department it took four days before they had a complete list of names.

Tony thought about getting himself arrested, booked, and placed in cells where he could question the men who had turned up in their research. But it could take months, with more paperwork, more bureaucracy, and the possibility that he might be recognized. It would be easier and certainly faster just to walk in cold, a visitor, identify himself, and ask questions. He divided the names into the locales where they were incarcerated and, starting in the northern part of the state, began working his way south, crisscrossing east and west to Florida's jails and penitentiaries.

He questioned dozens of men a day, asking the same questions, getting a litany of similar responses. When he wasn't sitting in the visitor's seat across the Plexiglas from an inmate, he was sitting in his car driving to another jail in another town. The hours, the days began to merge, a blur of highways and faces. He was sleeping only three or four hours, often in his car.

The men he talked to had little to lose and much to gain if their information proved useful in solving the mystery of Nicki's disappearance. He made that clear. Leads had to be verified or dismissed. He kept in constant contact with Jack in Miami, who was often able to run down those leads using the services of Metro-Dade.

Nothing came of anything for the ten days he was on the road. Convicts were suspicious by nature, always wary and seldom dumb when it came to protecting their own interests. Then, one evening when he called Jack from a motel, his stepfather told him to drive over to the state pen at Raiford and talk to a prisoner named Willis Wendell. Tony had already visited Raiford. From Gainesville, where he was now, it was about an hour's drive—one that proved worth making.

Willis was twenty-nine years old and up for armed assault, his third conviction in ten years. He was looking at middle age before he would get out. Willis had heard talk. There was a guy on death row, Carl Finley, convicted of killing a gas station attendant he'd been trying to rob. Although there were no similarities to Nicki Costa's abduction, Tony's source said he'd shared a cell briefly with someone who had shared a cell with Finley.

Willis Wendell was small, with tiny hands and distinct, fragile-looking features. His hair was gray with tightly curled natural ringlets that might have given him a feminine appearance if it hadn't been for his eyes. They were the same color as his hair but didn't reflect light. Tony was given permission to question Willis in a special office. Wendell came in in leg irons, then he was handcuffed to a steel ring at the end of a chain embedded in the concrete wall.

He never changed expression nor took his eyes from Tony's.

There was a rumor Finley had killed others besides the gas station attendant. Tony asked Willis about that.

"I heard talk," Willis said.

"What kind of talk?"

Willis stared at him. "Finley killed a college girl in Tallahassee," he said in a flat voice.

"How do you know?"

Willis shrugged without shifting his gaze.

"What do you want?" Tony asked.

"I come up for parole in ten years. I want that cut in half. In writing. And I want to serve the rest of my time in another pen."

"I'll see what I can do," Tony said.

Two days later, after conferring with the state attorney and Wendell's attorney, Tony returned with a written statement. Willis talked.

Fragile links began to appear with the time and place of Nicki's abduction. Blood and hair samples were taken from Finley in an effort to match those found in Nicki's apartment; corroborative evidence began to pile up. The authorities tried unsuccessfully to coerce a confession.

Tony went back to Willis. Without a confession or a body there was no deal. It took two more weeks, but finally Willis came through. Nicki Costa's body was buried on a knoll beneath a stand of cypress trees thirty miles south of Tallahassee off the main highway.

Two days before he was to be transferred Willis was killed—stabbed to death with a spoon handle that had been sharpened to a point.

After months of an intense, bizarre investigation the whole thing had unraveled as the result of an unrelated conversation overheard in a Cuban diner. So often that was the way it happened; a chance remark, a seemingly unrelated

38

random event that could not be forgotten. Everything had to be scrutinized and double scrutinized.

Now, sitting across the table from Jack, it all seemed so useless that he wondered whether everyone might have been better off not knowing the truth.

"You're at some crossroads in your life," his stepfather said. It was rare for Jack to preach or to make judgments, and he was seldom angry. It did not seem to be a deliberate behavior pattern on Jack's part, but simply the way he was. Now he just sipped his coffee and looked at Tony.

Tony put a teaspoon of sugar into his mug from the sugar bowl on the table and stirred. "I need some rest, a chance to lay low for a while," Tony said. He knew it was a lame excuse. He'd spent a year laying low after the suspension. Were these the storm clouds of a breakdown, was he on the verge of mental collapse? Or was it simply the expected depression at the end of a particularly gruesome case that he would soon shake off?

"All I'm saying is don't burn your bridges," Jack said. "You don't have to. I'm willing to deal with the people calling here looking for you. I can get the preliminary stuff out of the way, talk to them, run information through the computer at Metro-Dade. If it looks like something you might be interested in, I'll let you know. A little teamwork." Jack smiled.

Tony acquiesced. "I won't burn my bridges," he said. "Just give me a little time."

As Tony was leaving, Jack brought out the cane Tony had been using the past few months. "You forgot this."

"I'm done with it," Tony said. "I'm leaving it here."

"I'll hang on to it, use it when I get old," Jack said.

Tony suppressed a nervous laugh. He was already thinking too much of Jack's approaching infirmity. Was that why he'd left it, some subconscious thought that Jack might soon be needing it? He didn't think so; it was more that he'd outgrown his own dependence on the cane and had simply put it out of his mind. Now it served to remind him, however, of their individual frailty. How much interdependence existed on some unspoken level between them; how much they propped each other up.

"Just don't get stuck with it the way I did," Tony said.

Jack waved his hand in front of his face as if he were slapping at a fly. "Pshaa," he said. "Don't worry."

Tony wasn't sure if Jack was embarrassed or amused to be reminded that his stepson had been shot in the leg by a jealous lesbian.

FOUR

═══

For three days Tony Harwood fished from the skiff he kept tied to the rickety dock ten steps from his trailer. He caught red snapper in a deep hole near a clump of mangroves out in the bay a short distance from his dock. In the evening he would pan-fry or broil the fish, spicing them with his own tangy remoulade sauce, adding capers and garlic to the basic ingredients. For three days he saw no one; sleeping, fishing, or making repairs to the Airstream, putting his life in order while he tried to forget the details of the death of Nicki Costa. He went to a barber and had the ponytail cut.

But forgetting wasn't so easy. Several times he found himself standing beside the water watching the huge black frigate birds, their wings motionless, soaring on thermal currents high above the Gulf. When he looked at his watch an hour **might** have gone by, and he'd realize he'd been thinking about her. In the months he had talked with her friends, visited the places she frequented, listened to the details of her life, she had become real to him.

What had happened to her would remain with him forever. Gazing at the sky or walking along the beach in his T-shirt and shorts, he thought about her constantly.

The flight back to Miami was depressing. The coroner's report in the cockpit console lay between him and Wayne like an unwanted passenger. Nicki had been drugged, it was determined, and probably raped. The medical examiner also thought she had been buried alive, choked sufficiently to immobilize her. Her final moments left nothing to the imagination.

And all for nothing. Just another sicko getting his kicks.

Wayne Costa had paid Tony $750 a week plus expenses for nine months, and when they arrived in Miami with Nicki's body Tony took Wayne's final check for $5,000. Carrying the image of Nicki Costa in her grave was not something he wanted to be paid for. He had thought about refusing it, offering it to charity, but in the end he took it for what it was: payment for a job completed. When he shook hands with Wayne for the final time, then watched as he drove away, Tony wondered how a father would cope with this loss.

There was no telephone or television in the Airstream. Tony relied on newspapers purchased at a convenience store two miles up the road and on his shortwave radio for news of the outside world. A neighbor, Tom Knowles, a Conch who had left the glitter and development of Key West ten years ago for a simpler life, lived with his wife, Nan, and a variety of tame but undomesticated animals, including a raccoon and a couple of the miniature key deer who still eked out an existence here, in a house Tom and Nan had built themselves on two acres of land within walking distance but not sight of Tony's Airstream.

If he wanted company, the Knowleses were happy to see him, but they each respected the other's privacy, and days, even weeks, would go by without their seeing one another. Whenever Tony was away for any length of time Tom would keep an eye on the trailer. Since he and Nan had a phone they had let Tony give out their number to anyone who might need to reach him for emergency reasons, knowing he wouldn't abuse the privilege.

Only Jack Dowd had the number, and he used it sparingly.

On Good Friday, nearly a week since Tony's return, Tom walked over to say that Jack had called, leaving a message for Tony to return the call. "Not urgent," Tom said. "This evening or tomorrow will do, Jack said to tell you."

Tom Knowles was a thin, angular man who had gray hair, even though he was still in his early fifties. He reminded Tony of pictures of New England preachers from the previous century. While the features of his face were stern, Tom's blue eyes twinkled with undisguised humor.

Their conversations had to do with the daily mechanics of living back here, the water and the best places to catch fish, and the threat of development overtaking them. Tom talked about the past and gave Tony insights into the people and geography of the Keys, invaluable local knowledge.

He had also helped Tony install the solar panel that heated his well water, and he willingly offered any requested advice on making repairs and keeping up with maintenance on the trailer.

"Nan wants to know if you'd like to come by for dinner this evening. Thought you might be getting tired of those snapper we've seen you pulling in the past few days."

Tony stood in the doorway, holding the aluminum door open with one hand. "Shrimp or chicken?" he asked. They raised chickens and occasionally hand-netted small shrimp. They lived as close to the land, and sea, as was possible anymore, eating what they could catch, raise, or grow.

"Neither," Tom said. "Crawfish."

"That'll do." Tom had a secret rock hole in ten feet of water where he usually found lobster several times a year. He shared the lobster, but not its habitat.

"About seven, then."

Tony nodded. "I'll bring some wine."

Tom waved. Tony watched him walk across the yard and into the trees.

Tony drove his Chevy S-10 pickup to the supermarket on Highway 1, where he bought several bottles of wine, two of which he would take to the Knowleses tonight.

It had skipped his mind that Sunday was Easter. Since Beverly had died it had become a habit bordering on tradition that Tony took Jack to dinner Easter Sunday. Which was probably why Jack was calling. The thought of driving

43

back to Miami, a couple hundred miles there and back, so soon after he'd just been there was not appealing. He would do it, though, because of the deterioration he'd seen in Jack; he needed to confront him, force him to talk about his health.

Tony's own depression seemed to be lifting. After nearly a week of rest and solitude he was beginning to feel better, human again. He was even thinking of driving into Key West to pick up some items he needed that were unavailable in Big Pine. Perhaps he would go to lunch, maybe take in a rare movie. Come out of his shell and take a peek at the world.

He'd lived in Key West for six months after leaving Miami, renting a house from a married couple, both lawyers. They were the only people he knew in Key West. The Fultons. Kay—he remembered her name, having seen it occasionally in the paper—was a prosecutor with the state attorney's office. She had been friendly, taking some interest in his suspension from Metro-Dade, even offering some legal advice. He had not seen the Fultons since he left Key West nearly a year ago to come to Big Pine. He thought about calling them.

After picking up a few basic provisions Tony loaded the grocery bags into the pickup, then stopped at a pay phone to call Jack.

When he heard Tony's voice Jack said, "Ricky Lee's out of prison."

Ricky Ticky. Rick the Tic. Tic Tac. Street names by which Ricky Lee was known. An animal, a crack addict who had haunted the streets of the Liberty City and Overtown ghettos, selling drugs to kids. In police bulletins he was always described as armed and dangerous. But when Tony smashed Ricky Ticky's face while making the drug bust that would take Ricky off the streets for a year, it was described as "overzealous use of force."

Before going to jail Ricky had publicly vowed to take care of Tony Harwood.

"When?" Tony asked.

"Last week."

The sun was beginning its westward slide, sending up a

heat haze over the asphalt as Tony looked down the highway, the weekend holiday traffic moving steadily in both directions. It was exceptionally warm for the end of March.

"Well, he's somebody else's problem now." Tony knew Ricky would be back on the streets, going through the same motions. Guys like Ricky Lee didn't remember faces; he'd probably even forgotten Tony's name. It was the uniform, the badge that was the threat.

"I just thought you ought to know. What are you doing for Easter?"

Was there an appeal in Jack's question?

"I thought I'd drive up. We could go out to dinner."

"Good," Jack replied. "By the way, there have been more calls," Jack said.

Tony felt the tingle of apprehension.

"Fifteen people who are looking for someone who is missing. Most of them old cases that have been forgotten or put on the shelf by the various investigating bureaus."

He was still not ready for this. He had deliberately kept a low profile in the Costa abduction, refusing to talk about the case or himself to the press. That hadn't stopped them, however, from getting their story.

"What did you tell them?"

"As we discussed, I talked with a few people and took phone numbers," Jack said. "Except for one woman who came here all the way from Kansas."

"Kansas?"

"Yes, her son's missing. She's here with her daughter, who had to come to Miami on business. The mother thinks the boy might have come to the Keys with a friend on spring break. She hasn't heard from him in more than two weeks."

Another college student; another distraught parent. No, he definitely wasn't ready. "The kid's probably just partying, afraid to call home."

"Maybe." There was something in Jack's tone, some awkwardness.

"What did you tell her?"

"I told her I would talk to you, that if you came up perhaps you would meet her."

"Jack."

"I know. But she came all the way from Kansas."

RAMON

===

Jimmy Santos had another couple of appearances before his parole officer, after which his debt to society would be paid in full. After a year of subjecting himself to a urinalysis each week to test for drugs, Santos would soon be able to resume a life free of surveillance.

On the boat back to Ragged Key with Jimmy, Ramon Marquesa thought he would be as glad as Jimmy to see the end of these weekly excursions.

Ramon had given Jimmy Santos the job of caretaker on Ragged Key, the Marquesa family-owned island six miles offshore of Key West. For a year now Ramon had paid Jimmy to make needed repairs to the house and maintain the grounds, which had been neglected for almost a year prior to Jimmy's arrival. It was a modest salary, including room and board, but the island was not overrun by vandals, and during his parole it served to keep him out of reach of temptation.

There was something about Jimmy Santos that Ramon liked. Santos, who was only twenty-five years old and had had only the one unfavorable incident with the authorities, still had some innocence, a belief in his own incorruptibility. Ramon took a certain pleasure in that thought, since his own tastes ran to corruption. Especially of the innocent.

Jimmy had everything he needed out here on the island,

46

including his girlfriend, who came out on occasional weekends to stay with him. Ramon didn't want Jimmy to feel too
isolated and had suggested the idea before Jimmy had to
ask. As a result Jimmy had shown his gratitude through
loyalty. He did everything he was asked to do on the island,
and often more, to protect Ramon's privacy.

When they landed at Ragged Key Ramon jumped onto
the dock. The dogs—two Dobermans—bounded down to
meet them, barking their greeting. Ramon cuffed them on
their snouts, pulled their ears, and waited for Jimmy.

After securing the boat Jimmy brought up a boxful of
supplies he'd purchased with money Ramon gave him in
Key West following the appointment with his parole officer.

"How's our guest?" Ramon asked as they walked along
the path to the house, the dogs running ahead.

"Just fine, Mr. Marquesa. Except he wanted some different coffee from the instant stuff I drink."

No one in Key West called Ramon mister, but here on
the island Ramon took a certain pleasure from it, never
suggesting that Jimmy refer to him in any other way.

"You don't have to worry about Angel's coffee, Jimmy,"
Ramon said. "Soon he'll be able to get all the Cuban coffee
he wants."

Angel Lopez was in the upstairs bedroom with his own
bath and a hot plate so that he could make coffee if he
didn't feel like coming down to the kitchen. A large generator supplied the house with electricity. Communication with
Key West was maintained by marine radio.

The door to Angel's room was locked, as Ramon requested it should be when Jimmy wasn't on the island. The
key to the door hung from a hook in the kitchen, and
Ramon carried it up and went in.

Angel was lying on the bed, reading a magazine. He put
the magazine on his stomach when Ramon came in. Angel
looked gray, thinner. He had not shaved in a couple of days.

"Cuánto tiempo más? How much longer?" Angel asked.
He'd been here almost a week. It was the first time Ramon
had been out since the night Oreste was shot.

"Not long," Ramon replied. "You complaining? You
know what people would pay to come to a private island?"

47

"To be locked in a fuckin' room?"

Ramon brushed off the question with a wave of his hand. He wasn't going to argue with Angel. He was trying to keep everything together here until they saw which way this thing was going to go. But if necessary, he could deal with Angel in other ways, and he figured Angel must know it.

"What's happening in town? They looking for me?" Angel sat on the edge of the bed facing Ramon.

"A few questions. Nothing too serious," Ramon said.

Angel nodded. "You been to court?"

"Next week."

Angel nodded again. "Who's running the office?"

"Datilla." Don Datilla was the night supervisor at the cab company. Ramon had told him to take over the day-to-day operations until Angel got back, making it sound as if nothing was out of the ordinary. Routine. When Angel was away Datilla ran the cab company.

"What about Maria Elena? You talk to her yet?"

Maria Elena, Angel's wife, had called Ramon once wanting to know where Angel was. Ramon told her he didn't know. She badgered him until he'd finally hung up on her. She never called back. Ramon had heard that Angel's cousin, Mingo, was now spending time with Maria Elena.

"She's fine," Ramon said. "Let's take a walk."

Angel sighed and stood up. Ramon went downstairs with Angel following him. Jimmy was putting out food and water for the dogs. He nodded at Angel, who didn't speak. When they were on the other side of the house Ramon said, "You and Jimmy get along okay?"

Angel shrugged. "I get more conversation from the dogs."

It was true that Jimmy Santos didn't talk much, another attribute that appealed to Ramon.

They stood beside a small arena Ramon had had Jimmy build for cockfights. Once every month or so Ramon would have a party and invite some guys out with their fighting birds, matching them against the half-dozen birds he raised here.

"Jimmy bought you some Cuban coffee," Ramon said. "Says you don't like the stuff he drinks."

Angel stared at the dirt floor of the arena. "You think

48

I'm a *boca ratón?* A rat? I'm going to say anythin' about that night?"

"No," Ramon said. He put his hand on Angel's shoulder. "I don't think you're a rat. But people are asking questions. They're going to pressure you. This'll blow over. In a couple months—"

"A couple months! I've got to live like this a couple months?"

"I didn't say that. But look at it this way." Ramon squeezed Angel's shoulder tendon. "There are worse places you could be right now." Dead was one of them that went unspoken. The other place, of course, was Cuba. Maybe Angel would be happier there, a returning exile.

FIVE

===

Nan Knowles had a freckled face, smooth and dark as the inner shell of a coconut. Short, sunbleached hair framed her face in an oval. In her forties, six or seven years younger than her husband, Tom, she had a youthful presence, something of a pioneer look about her, Tony Harwood thought, watching her open one of the bottles of cabernet sauvignon he had brought, her knuckles white against the dark bottle.

"You want to call your father?" Nan asked, popping the cork and picking up a wineglass from the table.

"I called him from town," Tony said. "Since the Nicki Costa story he's been getting calls from people with missing family."

"Who want to hire you?" Nan carried a glass of wine to Tom at the stove, where he was cooking.

"Jack wants to see me working again."

"It must have been horrible," Nan said innocently. "Finding that girl."

Tony didn't say anything.

Tom turned from the stove and said, "Ready to eat?"

It was a large kitchen. The long pine table that Tom had made was set with mismatched plates and silverware that he and Nan had purchased over the years from various yard sales and flea markets. Everything in the house was either made or purchased secondhand. The rooms were filled with

functional objects as well as bric-a-brac peculiar to the
Keys—old bottles, ship's lanterns, shells and pieces of drift-
wood they had collected along the beach.

Tony sat at one side of the table opposite Tom, with Nan
at the head. On the table were a platter with the lobster
tails, deep-fried in a golden batter, a clay crock filled with
rice and vegetables, and a salad bowl containing a simple
mixed salad. Except for the rice and wine the meal had been
caught or grown by Tom and Nan. Tony admired the simple
affection they communicated to each other and the control
they seemed to have over their lives, the way they seemed
to live in harmony with nature.

He knew he would always admire their life even though
he could never hope to emulate it. He was too much at war
with himself, too restless, too needy. This life required a
kind of acquiescence, an acceptance he wasn't ready—and
maybe never would be ready—to make.

"We're thinking of moving," Nan said.

Tony bit into the light, tender flesh of a lobster tail and
stared from Nan to Tom, stunned by this admission.

Tom smiled. "Nothing concrete yet."

"But why?"

"The place is changing too fast," Nan said. "Developing.
That dreadful word."

"When we first came here," Tom added, "there was just
a gas station, a couple of convenience stores along the highway. People didn't even slow down on their way to Key
West or Miami. Now there's a supermarket and a traffic
light on U.S. 1. A traffic light, for God's sake!"

"Next there'll be an antique store." Nan made a disgusted
face and drank some wine.

"You know it's all over when the antique stores move
in," Tom said. "All this junk we've been getting from yard
sales suddenly appears in a shop at ten times what it's
worth."

It was true. Tony had seen changes, too, in the short time
he'd been here. Still, they were almost five miles from town;
he'd always thought they were remote enough to be able to
ignore the development.

"But you have your own life back here," Tony said.

51

"There are other things," Nan said, glancing at Tom.

"Two murders in the past year," Tom said. "Neither of them solved."

"And both women," Nan said. "I don't feel comfortable wandering around here alone anymore."

Tony knew about one of the murders, committed six months ago. A woman's naked body found near a desolate road not far from here. She'd been stabbed several times. There was the usual problem—lack of police resources and so many drifters coming down in the winter that the authorities had difficulty establishing any links. The dead woman wasn't from here either, and she'd been walking alone in an untrafficked, unpopulated area.

"Where would you go?" Tony asked.

"That's the problem," Tom replied. "We don't know where to go."

"It's got to be warm and not in a city. We've been thinking about some of the islands around Sanibel. Or Captiva."

Tony couldn't believe what he was hearing. They finished the meal, talking about other things, Tom explaining the intricacies of Tony's malfunctioning water pump. He promised to come by and take a look at it.

Nan uncorked the second bottle of wine, which they drank with cheese and fruit. It was hard to imagine life here without Nan and Tom nearby, however infrequently he saw them.

Tony looked at his watch. It was nine-fifteen. They sat around the table for another quarter of an hour before Tony left. After saying goodnight to Nan he walked outside with Tom.

"I didn't want to say anything in front of Nan," Tom said as they stood in the damp grass in the dark, a few feet from the house, "but I found a dead deer today."

The key deer, an endangered species, were the subject of some debate as development eroded their natural habitat. And several of the animals were killed each year, struck by cars as they tried to cross the roads and highway.

Tony shook his head. "On the road?"

"It wasn't a car. It looked like somebody had used a club or a board or something to beat its head in."

52

A feeling of anger rushed through him, then a deep sadness—everything he'd been trying to get out of his system.

"I buried the deer," Tom said. "I didn't report it. Nan is more determined to leave here than I am. This could have been the last straw."

Tony said, "Who would do something like that? Do you have any ideas? A kid, maybe?"

"I don't know, but keep your eyes open. Let's hope it's an isolated case, somebody's perverse idea of a prank."

Disturbed, Tony set off into the darkness.

It was a ten-minute walk back to his trailer. The beam from the flashlight he carried stabbed at the pathway between the trees. A breeze carried the rattle of palm fronds from a thick stand of fan palms and a few Jamaica talls that had proved resistant to the blight of lethal yellowing that had destroyed many of their species in the Keys the past few years. Everything existed, or didn't, in some precarious balance, he thought, even without man's intrusion.

He could hear the scuttle of small animals, lizards, palmetto bugs, maybe some tree rats over the dry, dead leaves that had dropped to the ground, and he could smell the sea that was tinged with sulfur, a smell like rotten eggs that came from the thick piles of damp seaweed washed on shore. He shivered as a sudden cool breeze came out of the north, where it was still winter, across the bay. The wine had affected him, and the conversation, usually uplifting, had left him feeling agitated, nervous.

Tony awoke at six after a restless sleep. Images from his dreams crept in the shadows of his consciousness without fully revealing themselves. Somehow he knew they were related to the conversation of last evening and Tom's disclosure about the battered deer.

He put on the coffeepot, then, barefoot and wearing an old pair of khaki shorts, walked down to the skiff and worked his way out into the bay, where he fished for half an hour just as the sun broke above the line of palm trees. He felt the recognizable peck of a yellowtail on his bait, waited a second before setting the hook, and reeled in the fish that he estimated would weigh close to a pound. He stuck his rod in its holder and turned the skiff toward the dock.

The dreams, however insubstantial, had awakened old fears. The propensity for violence that smoldered just below the surface and erupted in odd ways bothered him. A cop's overzealous use of force, a man clubbing a deer—was there something that linked them?

After cleaning the fish and throwing the guts to clamoring pelicans, he washed down the dock, took the fish up to the trailer, and poached it in milk and fresh garlic, serving it to himself on a bed of parsley.

Then he drove into town, bought the Miami *Herald*, came back and, with a second cup of coffee, went out to the screened-in room off the side of the trailer facing the bay. He sat down on a redwood couch with plaid cushions, part of a fifties outdoor furniture set that he'd picked up second-hand for this room.

He went through the paper by reading the first two paragraphs of each article, then skipping to the end. If something caught his attention, he read the entire article; otherwise he only scanned the pages. Knowing the media's own limited attention span, he was surprised to find continuing stories on, and references to, the Nicki Costa case. Interviews with police authorities and legislators on how the system had failed, how a man working alone without the benefit of high-tech equipment available to the authorities—and paid for with taxpayers' money—could succeed where they had failed.

Tony started to turn to the comics section when his own name caught his eye a few paragraphs into the article. The reporter, doing more research, had dug into the cause of Tony's suspension from Metro-Dade, revealing that "Tony Harwood was living somewhere in the Keys like a hermit, without a phone, without known employment, an apparent dropout."

Tony dropped the paper and sat staring out at the bay. The light reflected off the water was almost perfect at this hour. The bay, glassy calm at dawn, was beginning to kick up some wavelets. Two sparrow hawks, locally known as klee-klee birds, chased each other, screeching.

Tony felt a wave of irritation, like the onset of a headache one knew would only get worse. He understood the media. They were pursuing him in their own way. He'd done something, he'd made news by beating the cops at their own game, but instead of talking about it, giving the papers something to do, he'd retreated. Because of that they wanted to turn him into a freak. A crazy loon who lived alone in the wilderness but had a talent for solving crimes the cops couldn't solve. He objected to the characterization, just as he would have objected to their portrayal of him had they been able to get the story they wanted. They would have gotten it wrong, the emphasis in the wrong place, and he would still have come out looking like a freak.

But it was only a matter of time before they tracked him down, if that was what they wanted, and he was sure it was, screeching after him like those damned klee-klee birds.

He decided he had to do something before this got out of hand. He went out to his truck and drove into Big Pine, where he got a roll of quarters from the convenience store and called the Miami *Herald* at the pay phone outside. After five minutes and $1.75 in quarters he was told by a woman that the reporter was not at her desk. Did he care to leave a message? No, Tony said. He would call back.

By this time some of his anger had subsided, which, he reflected, was probably a good reason for having to travel to get to a phone. A forced cooling-off period. So he used a couple more quarters and called Kay Fulton in Key West.

SIX

═══

It was Saturday. The end of a week, thank God, that she'd just as soon forget. Two weeks, in fact. Last week she'd spent two days in court trying a child abuse case. She'd lost. She'd had to put a seven-year-old girl on the witness stand with an anatomically correct doll, but in the end the jury chose to believe the girl's father, who was answering charges brought by his wife. They were going through a divorce, and the girl was the subject of a custody dispute.

Kay did her best to keep her emotions in check, to keep it impersonal. She had steeled herself ever since she'd been assigned the case to avoid this, but try as she might when the girl was on the stand, all Kay could see was Patty.

Brad had picked Patty up this morning to spend the day with her. They'd agreed on the time several days earlier. Tomorrow was Easter, and Kay was flying with Patty to St. Petersburg this evening to spend Easter Sunday with her parents. Patty didn't want to go. She wanted to go to the Easter egg hunt in Bayview Park with her friends.

Kay tried to reason with her that she could do that next year when she didn't have a broken arm and that it had been almost a year since she'd seen her grandparents, and wouldn't it be fun to see them? As a last resort she said that maybe her grandmother would know where there was an Easter egg hunt in St. Petersburg.

But her friends wouldn't be there, Patty had argued.

But she could make some new friends. Patty had pouted for a few minutes, then began to show some enthusiasm, talking about the things she could do at Gramma's.

By the end of the day, yesterday, Patty was looking forward to the trip more than Kay. In fact, Kay probably wouldn't have gone at all if it hadn't been for the fact that she'd decided that Key West might not be the place to bring up a child, especially as a single parent. She was going to check the paper in St. Petersburg and talk with her own parents about moving. And though she didn't relish the idea of being that close to her parents, who lived in a small two-bedroom condo in a retirement complex, Tampa, across the bay from St. Petersburg, was a booming city where she could have her own life. If she could find a job.

And if she could get through the Ramon Marquesa trial. No foregone conclusion. Ramon had come up for arraignment last week. As expected, he pleaded not guilty to attempted murder.

In the charging document that she presented to the judge, Kay went over the available evidence. Of the dozen witnesses in the bar the night Ramon Marquesa and Oreste Villareal had argued, only two were willing to testify that they had been aware of an altercation between the two men, and neither of them were sure they had heard Ramon threaten Oreste. Oreste's wife would testify, but what she saw followed the attack on her husband, and Kay knew what a good defense attorney would do with her testimony. What she saw had been seen from a window, at night, by a witness who was half asleep.

Judge Grabill was in his early fifties, black, with straightened thin black hair always shiny with grease that held it slicked across his scalp. He wore half glasses over which he stared in an attempt to intimidate attorneys who got on his bad side. He was noted for his sexist attitudes. Grabill was also up for reelection this year.

He had studied the file Kay had handed him and then, his eyes downcast, rustling the papers in his hands, said, "You mention this Angel Lopez in your charging document, but you don't have him listed as a witness. Was that an oversight, Miss Fulton?"

"No, your honor. We intend to present Mr. Lopez as a witness for the prosecution."

"I see."

She was aware of Ramon Marquesa, sitting at the defense table in a whispered conversation with his high-powered Miami attorneys. She did not look over, but she thought she heard Ramon snicker.

"So it was an oversight then," Grabill said. He finally looked up from the papers and fixed her in his sight, leaning forward, his forearms on the rostrum, waiting.

Kay swallowed. "Judge, we have not been able to speak with Mr. Lopez up to now."

"And why might that be, Miss Fulton?" He pronounced her name so softly it sounded like he was calling her "missy."

She stood in the middle of the room and stared back at the judge. "We haven't been able to locate him, your honor."

Judge Grabill didn't speak for a moment. She stood there waiting. Finally he said, "So for all intents and purposes your case rests on the recovery of the alleged weapon used in the shooting?" He gave strong emphasis to "alleged."

She was about to speak when the defense attorney stood. "Your honor, we made a request yesterday to examine that weapon and were told that it could not be found. It was not with the evidence the police are holding in this case."

"There is no weapon?" Grabill demanded.

"It appears that way, your honor."

Kay was stunned. Why hadn't she been informed that a piece of evidence was missing? She watched in dazed silence as Grabill leaned back in his chair and, speaking to the ceiling in a monotone, asked, "Would it be fair to say, missy, that the key to the prosecution's case rests with this piece of evidence the defense now claims is missing?"

"Your honor, I'm sure there has been a mistake, that this can be—"

"And that Angel Lopez is your key witness?" Grabill interrupted. "Who is also missing."

"We regard him as an important witness," Kay replied.

Grabill suddenly reached forward, grabbing his gavel, and aimed it at Kay. "Important, shportant," he thundered. "Without him, without the alleged gun, you don't have a case. Now you've got two weeks to produce them. I'm not going to waste the court's time hearing cases based on hearsay and circumstantial evidence." He banged the gavel.

Kay felt Ramon's eyes on her as she gathered up her papers. Her legs trembled as she walked from the courtroom.

When she got back to the office she called the police and found that, yes, the gun taken the morning Marquesa was arrested was missing. More than once evidence had come up missing, often recovered later and charged to an oversight. She had the distinct feeling this wasn't an oversight.

Two days later a typewritten note came in the mail, addressed to her at home. "Angel sends his best wishes," the message inside read. No date, no name where there should have been a signature. The postmark was Key West, two days earlier.

She took it in the next day, yesterday, and showed it to Randall Welch.

Randall grinned. "Looks like the boys are having some fun with you."

"You think it's funny?" She was indignant. She'd had just about all the sexist innuendo she was going to take. An anonymous note in the mail about a case she was trying—coming to her home, no less—had the effect of scaring her. It was like a threat. And the state attorney was laughing.

"Well, Grabill's denying the case anyway, isn't he?" Randall tried to recover.

She recognized what Welch was trying to put her at ease. "What's that got to do with it?"

Randall just shrugged. She put the note back in her bag and started to leave.

"I take it you've had no luck finding Lopez?" he asked when she reached the door.

Was he trying to be cute, some more humor at the expense of little missy Fulton?

"No. I haven't found him yet, but I haven't stopped looking," Kay said, and she went back to her own office. She was angry. She called Colin Barker and got him at home. The last time she'd spoken with him, two days ago, he said he was following a couple of leads.

"Forget it," Barker said when she asked if he had turned up anything on Angel Lopez. "The guy's vanished. He'll never be seen again."

"No hope?" Kay asked, dispirited.

"None that I can see," Colin replied.

Kay hung up. She was angry and tired, and she had the sense everyone was just as happy to see this case forgotten before it even went to trial. It was possible, from what little she knew about the Marquesa family, that no one wanted to go up against them, that they had a lock on the entire criminal justice system. Possible only. But in a town this small she could never risk making such an assertion.

More and more she was convinced that she was merely being used as a foil, lending credibility, showing that she had done her best to see that justice was served. Well, to hell with that, she thought. She would just have to see if she couldn't approach this from a different angle. See if she could put together enough evidence in the next week to build a case that she could take to Judge Grabill. One that he couldn't dismiss.

If she failed, at least then, she thought, she would have done her best.

She was up until nearly three in the morning after spending the day Friday on the phone and going to the bar where Oreste and Ramon had argued, trying to find someone who could shed more light on this, bring out a new angle. She read the police report over and over, went over the report that Colin Barker had filed, went back through old files on Marquesa, everything they had in the office, everything she could find after poring over newspaper articles on microfiche in the library.

She'd gotten up at seven-thirty to get Patty ready to go off with her dad at nine. More worry. What if he didn't bring her back? It had happened. When Brad showed up she got close enough to smell his breath but didn't detect

any alcohol. His eyes were clear. He wasn't constantly pulling on his nose, which she'd come to recognize as a habit after he'd been snorting lines of cocaine. He seemed fine. Patty went off happily with him.

She had to relax, stop worrying.

She made herself an iced tea and sat down with a book. Her undergraduate degree was in English, and she seldom had time to read for pleasure anymore. She picked up the book of poetry and stretched out on the couch, the sunlight coming in the east windows muted by the blinds.

When the phone rang she came awake, realized she'd been asleep, and looked at her watch. It was only ten o'clock, so she must have just dozed. The book was open on her stomach. She got to the phone on the fourth ring.

"Hello."

"Kay?"

"Yes."

"Tony Harwood."

A hesitation as her mind started to track. She hated it when people didn't identify themselves on the phone or expected you to know them.

"I stayed—"

"Yes," she said. "I remember now." There had been something in the paper about him not long ago. He had found a missing girl. Yes. "How are you?"

"I have my days," he said. "I'm driving into Key West today, thought we might get together, you and your husband, for a drink, possibly lunch?"

"Yes," she said. "I'm glad you called. I'd like to. Lunch would be fine."

"I'll be there by noon. Where can we meet?"

"Louie's? At, say, twelve-thirty?" she asked.

"See you then."

Tony Harwood. An ex-cop. A man who had a reputation for finding people. She remembered him. He was troubled, but he'd been a good tenant when he was here. Yes, she thought again. Yes, maybe he could help her.

SEVEN

The streets of Key West were filled with the buzz and beep of hundreds of rented mopeds ridden by college kids wearing ACA Joe and Gap-labeled clothing or, in some cases, nothing more than a bathing suit and a sunburn. They darted the wobbling mopeds in and out of traffic, screaming and hooting as if they were on carnival rides. It was spring break. And it was noisy, not to mention annoying and dangerous. Tony turned off Truman Avenue onto a side street, trying to avoid the adolescent mayhem.

Key West was a chameleonlike city. It changed its spots to accommodate whatever flow of lucre came its way, whether fashionable or filthy. In the little time Tony Harwood had spent here he had come to understand the Knowleses' push northward. He had read some of Key West's history, and Tom had given him even more colorful details.

The island city, like most sea towns in the last century, had opened its arms to any immigrant hardy enough to withstand the mosquitoes, the endless days of sun and heat, and the threat of storms; their only compensation was whatever they could haul from the sea. They came from the Bahamas with English names like Knowles, Pinder, and Russell. They were fishermen and ships' carpenters, and they built their houses the way they built their boats: to withstand the elements.

HAVANA HUSTLE

Shortly after mid-century, by 1880, Key West was the richest city per capita in America, but its wealth was ill-gotten, derived from wrecking—salvaging the cargo from ships that had foundered on the deadly reef that lay, and still lies, in wait like a saw-toothed yawn ready to snap shut on unwary vessels that ventured into the shallow waters around the Keys. False lights were even erected by the Key West tycoon-pirates, luring sailors to their death and riches to the shores—until the first of the reef lighthouses was erected and the salvage industry itself foundered. In the early part of this century cigar makers and spongers kept the city alive, but only briefly, and by the 1930s Key West was the poorest city in the country, finally bankrupt in 1934.

It took the navy and tourism to pull the place from the doldrums, until during the winter season the town came to be filled mostly with American tourists who came from the mainland looking for some distant dream of adventure. And a few weeks each year college kids on mopeds. Not exactly progress, Tony Harwood thought.

As he wound through the backstreets giving passing admiration to the homes, some of which had survived a century or more, he began to change his mind. Maybe Key West wasn't so much chameleonlike, but more a grande dame whose face had had a few tucks taken here and there, adding another layer of cosmetics, primping and preening for yet another evening on the town.

He squeezed the pickup into a space between a Rolls Royce and half a dozen mopeds at Louie's Backyard, where Kay Fulton had suggested they meet for lunch. He walked onto the afterdeck overlooking the Atlantic, feeling some anticipation in seeing Kay again, but also a strange awkwardness about being here.

The last woman he'd been with was Beth, whose lezzie lover had ended his philandering ways a few weeks before Wayne Costa hired him. The bullet had left him with a permanent limp and the belief that vengeance, like love, was a basic emotion that never really explained anything and was not to be trusted.

*   *   *

Kay Fulton was sitting on the deck at a corner table, one sandaled foot resting on the wooden rail built around the deck. She wore jeans and a coral cotton sweater that matched the polish of her toenails, which peeked from open-toed leather sandals. Her sorrel hair was straight and fell in a soft wave along the side of her face. She was attractive, missing real beauty only by eyes that were a little too wide-set. She was staring out across the water, and until she turned when he touched her shoulder, Tony had forgotten the intensity of those wide-set green eyes.

As she stood up he saw that beyond the superficialities of grooming she appeared tired, tense. Tiny half-moon wrinkles stretched around the corners of her mouth when she smiled. He extended his left hand, which she clasped, then they touched cheeks as a sort of afterthought. Tony stepped back, and they both sat down.

"Well," Kay said, "you've made a name for yourself since I last saw you." Her voice was resonant, confident, full of husky promise—suited, he'd always thought, both to the courtroom and the bedroom.

"It seems a long time. What was it, six months ago?" he asked.

"I think so. I've lost track of time. It's been an abysmal year."

A cocktail waitress came by and took his order. Kay was drinking a beer, Amstel Light, which she poured from the bottle into a fluted glass.

"Sounds familiar," Tony said. When the waitress had gone he said to Kay, "Tell me about your abyss."

She shook her head and ran her long fingers with their clear clipped nails through her hair. "I'm going through a divorce," she said.

He felt his earlier awkwardness begin to dissolve. He had been expecting to see Kay's husband, then agreeably surprised by his absence. Brad, also a lawyer, was a man Tony had considered too short for Kay. Which wouldn't have been important except that Brad had apparently compensated for his lack of physical stature by being a tyrant. Tony rented the house next to theirs and—as was the case with most Key

64

West properties, because of their proximity—he knew more
of his neighbors' private lives than was comfortable.

"Do I offer congratulations or condolences?" Tony asked
after the waitress had brought his beer.

"Neither," Kay said. "We're in a custody dispute."

Of course. There was a five-year-old daughter—six
now—a sweet, contented kid he remembered seeing at play
in their backyard for hours without fussing. He pictured her
now, caught between adversarial parents who also happened
to be lawyers.

"Good luck."

"Brad is living next door, the place you rented. It should
be easy. Patty sees both of us all the time, but he wants
papers drawn up and he wants to divide the custody."

"Messy. But working for the state attorney, I'd think
you're probably used to messy situations by now."

Kay sighed. "This is Key West. It's a small town, but it
isn't like any other small town." She paused. "That's my
personal life. Work-wise it isn't much different. In fact, I
was surprised when you called."

"Why?"

"The timing. I need to talk to you. You may be able to
help me."

Tony felt an odd frustration. "What do you need with
me?"

"A witness in a case I'm preparing to prosecute has
disappeared."

Tony took a drink and poured the rest of the beer from
the bottle into his glass. Though he'd had no formal excuse
for seeing her other than renewing a social contact, he began
to feel he'd made a mistake. "You don't have someone in
your office who does that kind of work?" he asked.

"Not for this case. I'm prosecuting Luis Marquesa's
brother."

Tony shrugged. He'd heard the name, but it meant nothing more to him than many other names that were common
to the life of this city.

Kay apparently saw that and launched into an explanation. "Luis Marquesa practically runs Key West," she said.
"I mean that literally. Downtown businesses, residential

property. I checked the tax rolls. He's probably the biggest individual taxpayer in the county. Up until ten years ago, when Key West became more cosmopolitan and outsiders began running for office, the Marquesa family had controlled politics here for as long as anyone can remember. Rumor has it that he still does, but from the sidelines."

"I get the picture," Tony said. "You're being stonewalled, and you don't know who to trust."

"Exactly."

"Who's the brother? What did he do?"

"Ramon. He's in his thirties, fifteen years younger than Luis, and he's been in trouble all his life. Each time Luis has been able to bail him out."

"And this time?"

Kay looked out across the ocean. "He's doing his best, but Ramon is under indictment. Attempted murder. The guy he tried to kill is a vegetable, and he'd be better off dead. Ramon did a number on him. If you want the details—"

"Spare me," Tony said. "I've had my share of violent death recently."

"Good. I've been working on this case for almost three weeks, trying to get a judge to grant a trial. I've got a good case, but a lot of the evidence is circumstantial. The gun that was used is missing from the evidence room. I have to believe that none of this is coincidental, that Marquesa's fingers reach into every segment of this community. What I've got won't hold up in court if I ever get there. And Ramon has got the best defense team in Dade County down here representing him."

"And one witness can bring him down?"

"Maybe bring the entire Marquesa empire down. That's what this trial is going to be about."

"Who's the witness?"

"Angel Lopez. He's a pal of Ramon's, one of his flunkies, but he was with Ramon the night Oreste Villareal was shot. Angel was probably drunk, panicked, and he made a statement before anyone could shut him up. Who knows, Ramon might even have tried to frame him. In any case, the arresting officer got enough out of him before he disappeared that we know Lopez is the key."

"He's probably dead, then."

Kay shook her head. "I don't think so. If he turns up dead, then there's another murder investigation leading back to the Marquesa family. I don't think they're ready for that. Luis has too much respectability at stake. I think Angel Lopez is cooling his heels somewhere, waiting for this to blow over."

"And you want me to find him?"

"One of our investigators has spent two weeks looking for him and says he's vanished. But I don't know anymore who I can trust. It won't be easy." She finished her beer. "I need an outsider. Yes, I would like you to find him."

"I'd need information about Lopez and the Marquesa family. Detailed information."

Kay smiled. "I brought all that with me." She picked up a satchel from the deck.

"Who would be paying me?"

"That's more difficult. We will, but we'll probably have to do some finagling."

"The last job paid seven-fifty a week plus expenses. I wouldn't work for less. And what kind of a time frame are we looking at?"

"Two weeks."

No time at all. They both turned and looked across the water. Tony finished his beer. Jack Dowd, at least, would be happy.

They had lunch on another deck, beneath the large fanlike leaves of a sea grape tree. This was not what he had come here looking for, though truthfully he wasn't sure anymore why he had come, except that he had wanted to see Kay Fulton again; perhaps she was a way back from this dead place he'd been inhabiting the past year. He wasn't sure. But she was smart and attractive. He liked the connection. Working with her might not be such a bad prospect, he thought.

"What happened with the Miami police?" Kay took a bite of grilled salmon, its inside flesh the color of her tongue.

"The suspension was lifted, but I decided not to go back. I don't think it was much of a marriage."

She nodded understandingly. "I don't remember you limping."

He told her the story of Beth, which made her smile. "Teach you to mess around with other women's women."

"No, it taught me to be more suspicious of people's motives."

Kay frowned. "You think she used you?"

"It's possible, don't you think? Or maybe it just takes women longer to get over a broken relationship than it does a man. Before getting into a new one, it's a good thing to know."

"You weren't in love, were you?"

"No," he said. "I wasn't. But that isn't the point." He didn't tell her that he'd been using sex to expiate his guilt.

She was silent, finishing her meal, gazing into the distance while a busboy cleared the table and the waiter asked if there would be anything else. She shook her head. Tony took a credit card from his wallet.

"I enjoyed the break," she said, "but I've got to get back to work."

"Marquesa?"

She nodded.

When the waiter returned with his receipt he followed Kay out to her car, taking note of her slender ankles, the way the backs were dimpled just above her heels where the hem of her jeans ended. She had a smooth, fluid walk. When they got to her car, a 1966 Mustang convertible, its top down, he started to open the door for her, but she leaned against it.

"You don't seem happy," Kay said.

Tony shrugged. "I'm not even sure I know what it is. We've both been caught in the abyss this year."

" 'To think the abyss is to escape it.' Or something like that."

"It sounds awfully easy. Did you make that up?"

"I think it's from a poem by Conrad Aiken."

"You read a lot of poetry?"

"Not nearly enough. I studied it in college. After all the legalese it's the only reading that makes any sense." She got in the car.

"And how's your own escape coming?" He was stirred by tenderness and felt a loss at the thought of this woman driving away. He felt a closeness and wanted to get to know her more.

"I'm trying to think my way out," she said. "But I can tell you that I'm over the old relationship."

Tony touched her shoulder. "If you feel like it, drive up to Big Pine sometime. The spring breakers haven't discovered it yet." He closed her door as she started the car.

"Good." Kay smiled. "I may do that." Waving, she drove off.

EIGHT

———

"It will take fifteen, twenty minutes," Jack Dowd said. "She's here with her daughter, staying in one of the beach hotels on Ocean Drive. Right around the corner from the Strand."

They were driving up Biscayne Boulevard toward the MacArthur Causeway turnoff to Miami Beach. Easter Sunday. Tony had driven to Miami this morning. He'd made reservations at the Strand, the place that had become their restaurant of tradition—Jack's favorite.

"Jack, I've got a job." Tony had never called his stepfather anything but Jack. Jack had never encouraged him to call him Dad, knowing probably that Tony's age and difficult relationship with his biological father would make it hard for him. Occasionally Jack would refer to Tony as son, usually when he was trying to coax him in a direction Tony was reluctant to take. As was the case right now.

"The mother is anxious to meet you, son. She made a special trip with her daughter, who is here on business. They go back to Kansas early tomorrow morning."

It irked Tony that Jack had set up this appointment without confirming it with him even though he knew Jack had probably told the women it would have to be tentative. Tony did not relish the idea of spending the rest of the day with Jack if he did not meet with them.

"You've already met them, then?"

"I told you. I talked with the woman on the phone and met with her a couple of times. The mother's name is Helen. She's a widow in her early sixties. Her daughter Claire is a sales rep for a cosmetic outfit in Kansas City."

Driving over the corrugated bridge of the MacArthur Causeway, the tires whining, Tony glanced at Jack. He was wearing a new tropical shirt, one Tony had never before seen. There was something in Jack's demeanor, some of the familiar robustness that had not been there the last time he was here ten days ago. Once in a while Tony would get a whiff of Jack's after-shave.

"And the son—" Tony started to say.

"The boy's name is Wyatt Anderson," Jack interrupted. "He's nineteen. Helen thinks he came down here on spring break. She hasn't talked to him for more than a month, and he's been missing for almost three weeks. He was only supposed to be gone ten days, and it's been a week since he should have returned."

"He's in college?"

"Yes, also in Kansas."

"He's probably partying. Nothing to worry about."

"I'd like you to talk to Helen."

They were on the long four-lane stretch of road between the bay and Government Cut, where a cruise ship was docked, a thin wisp of smoke curling up from one of its stacks, the traffic really barreling along here.

He turned off on Ocean Drive and had to park three blocks from the hotel. By the time they walked back to the hotel Tony was beginning to regret that he'd so easily agreed to this. Jack smiled as they walked in the door and went straight to the elevator.

When the door opened it was immediately clear to Tony what Jack's urgency had been: the new shirt, the after-shave. Helen Anderson put her hand on Jack's arm and smiled. It was the deceptively simple smile of seduction. As Helen closed the door behind them Jack winked at Tony and shrugged.

Jack introduced them. Helen was medium height, brown

71

hair flecked with gray. She wore a long, full denim skirt and a blouse with a floral print. She had an open face, bright eyes, a perky, upturned nose. Her smile was brief but sincere.

"My daughter has gone to get us some coffee," Helen said. "Please sit down."

There were two twin beds. A pair of deco chairs flanked a small table. A TV was on a stand in front of the beds, and the two windows looked out across Ocean Drive to the beach. Tony and Jack sat down while Helen fussed around the room, getting a pack of cigarettes from her bag, then came and sat on the edge of one of the beds, facing them.

"I quit smoking a few years ago, but this has made me so nervous." She held her hand up in an empty gesture. "I'm sure Jack told you what has happened," she said to Tony.

He wished Jack had told him what *was* happening. There was more than just the tension of a nervous mother in the room.

"He mentioned your son is missing," Tony said.

"Yes." She paused, looking at Jack. "Claire, my daughter, thinks I'm overreacting. But it has been three weeks since I've heard from him, and he should have been back in school a week ago."

"It isn't unusual," Tony said. "Kids party too much and take extra time. Did you report him missing?"

"Yes, I called the police at Kansas State in Manhattan a few days before we came here. They haven't been able to turn up anything. Then when I called your father he—we— filed a report with the Miami police."

Tony looked over at Jack, who stared at Helen, his large hands clasped around one knee.

"Jack has been very helpful," Helen said. "My husband, Wyatt's father, was a trooper with the highway patrol before he died ten years ago."

Tony could see the trust and intimacy in Helen's eyes; she spoke more easily to Jack than she did to him. "Did Wyatt tell you where he was going on spring break?" Tony asked.

There was a knock on the door, and Helen went to open it. A younger version of Helen came in carrying a tray with a pot of coffee and some cups. "This is my daughter, Claire," Helen said. "Jack's son, Tony Harwood."

"Hi." Claire put the coffee on the table between Jack and Tony. She poured three cups and handed one to her mother, who was lighting her second cigarette.

"Mom!" Claire said.

"I know," Helen said. "I'll try to cut back. Where were we?" she asked Tony.

"Did Wyatt tell you where he was going?" Tony repeated.

"No. I heard from one of his friends that he and another friend, Roger Ansell, where hitchhiking, and they mentioned going to the Keys. It's a popular spot with the kids from there."

"Did you call Roger's parents?"

"Yes, of course. They aren't worried, or they weren't. They have money, and Roger is more independent than Wyatt."

"When did you last talk to your brother?" Tony turned to Claire.

"A couple of months ago, probably. I can't remember."

"Was he okay? Did he talk about any problems? School? Girls?"

"He sounded fine. He didn't mention any problems."

"What about drugs?"

"No, I don't think so," Claire said. "He drank beer, he might have smoked marijuana now and then, but I don't think he had any serious drug habit."

Helen shook her head. "He wasn't doing too well in school, but Wyatt's a good boy."

"Did he talk about quitting?"

"He never mentioned anything to me."

Tony looked at Claire, who shook her head.

"What about money? Would he have had enough to keep him going for a while?"

"He didn't have a lot," Helen said. "He was going to school on a government loan and working in the evenings and weekends at a lumberyard."

"Helen," Jack said, "why don't you show Tony a picture of Wyatt?"

Helen put her cup on the table and went to get her purse.

She took a photograph from her wallet and handed it to Tony. It looked like a high school yearbook photo showing a clean-cut kid in a suit and tie smiling into the camera.

"He has longer hair now, but that's the most recent picture I've got."

"May I keep it?" Tony asked.

"Of course."

"I'd like the names and phone number of Roger's parents. Also any other friends."

"I have some in my address book." She reached back into her purse. "Does this mean you're going to help?"

Tony looked at Jack. "I'll do what I can to run a check on him in the Keys," he said. "But my guess is that he's fallen for a girl, something like that." Another look passed between Jack and Helen. As they left Helen wished them a happy Easter, then said to Jack, "Please call me later this evening."

The Strand dining room was crowded, and Tony waited to speak until they were shown to their reserved table. Jack had offered nothing on the short walk over. "Well," Tony said when they were seated, "you want to tell me about it?"

Jack looked sheepish. "I talked to her a couple of times, trying to help her. She was nice, we got along, so we went out to dinner a few times. That's about all there is to it."

"About," Tony said. "Why didn't you tell me you had a personal stake in this?"

"I wasn't sure I could get you to meet with her."

Tony shook his head. "How serious is it?"

Jack shrugged. "I don't know. She leaves tomorrow, and she's got her mind on her son right now. We'll see."

"But how about you?"

"I like her," Jack said.

After Beverly died Jack had given even more time to work. Tony had never thought of him remarrying or having much of a romantic life. He'd been devoted to Beverly. Perhaps this was what he needed.

A waiter came to their table. They both ordered grilled lamb chops with mint sauce, creamed sweet potatoes, green beans, and a bottle of the Beaujolais nouveau.

"Why don't you look into this yourself?" Tony asked.

"What, track Wyatt down?"

Tony nodded.

Jack said, "I'm too old, not mobile enough."

"But you've got the contacts, and there's a lot you can do on the phone."

Jack seemed to mull it over. "You don't want to do it. You're too busy with this other work you mentioned?"

"I may be. I don't know yet. But you've got a personal interest here. I'll have a check run in Key West tomorrow, see if anything turns up. I'll bet, however, that Wyatt's back home, broke and embarrassed, by the time Helen returns."

"Let's hope so," Jack said. "But if he isn't?"

"Then I think you should take it on."

When their meals came Jack asked about the job with the state attorney, and Tony told him about Ramon Marquesa.

A real piece of work. Tony had spent most of the previous evening going over the file Kay Fulton had given him at lunch. There was the police report from the investigation of the attempted murder, depositions from various witnesses, and a personal profile that Kay seemed to have prepared especially for Tony with notes and background information, some of it purely subjective, on Ramon Marquesa. Her feelings about the man were unconcealed; she didn't like him. If even half the information in the report was true, it was easy to see why.

Ramon was Tony's age, thirty-five, with a history of drug- and alcohol-related incidents of violence. He had been charged with a few misdemeanors and brought to trial twice on felony charges—once for smuggling and a second time for rape. Each time he'd gotten off without a conviction. There were accusations of vote buying, of racketeering, and of tampering with a jury—all of which was speculation because he had never been charged.

Rumors, however, were abundant. Kay opined that Ramon Marquesa was running illegal cockfights on his private island. Marquesa was, according to Kay, little more than human trash who should have been behind bars years

75

ago and would have been if it weren't for family connections.

Ramon operated Key West's considerable transportation system, owned by the Marquesa family—all the taxicabs, the Conch train and trolley, a couple of tour boats, and most of the moped and bicycle rental agencies that kept the tourists moving, an operation that brought in hundreds of thousands of dollars a year. He was generally regarded as a tyrant, disliked by most who worked for him, and feared by everyone. He was quick-tempered and mean, and you only crossed him once. Which a guy named Oreste Villareal had apparently done. Villareal now lay in a coma in a Key West hospital.

Tony had scanned the report on the attempted murder until he picked up the name of the witness Kay was looking for—Angel Lopez.

Angel was Ramon's sidekick, the troubleshooter, the guy who did the actual grunt work of keeping Key West's transportation industry running smoothly while Ramon dabbled in his nefarious pursuits. Tony wondered who was minding the store with Angel missing and Ramon under indictment.

The sun was setting as he drove back down the Keys, a pink glow in the sky along the bay and over the distant islands. He stopped for a hitchhiker, a kid holding a piece of cardboard with Key West written on it. Tony watched in the rearview mirror as the kid shouldered his pack and ran toward the truck. He was eighteen, nineteen, and when he jumped up into the cab he looked even younger than eighteen. He said, "Thanks, man. I was afraid it was going to get dark before I got a ride."

Tony nodded and pulled onto the road. "What's your name?"

"Mickey. What's yours?"

"Tony." They shook hands. "You a student, Mickey?"

"No, I'm a faith healer."

Tony turned to look at him. Mickey stared at him a second in innocence, then his face broke into a grin. He said, "I just heard that one the other night. It's a good line, isn't it?"

Tony smiled and said yes, it was a good line. "I can get you to Big Pine, thirty miles from Key West."

"Thanks," Mickey said. "What about you? What do you do?"

"I'm a lost soul," Tony said. Deadpan.

The boy gave a nervous laugh, then rode in silence.

RAMON

Havana seemed to be melting, dripping into the sea under dense gray clouds that hung over the city like a bubble. They were trapped by a low pressure system that wouldn't move. A similar depression seemed to weigh on everyone on the boat.

Angel stood beside Ramon, his shoulders bowed, as the first glimpse of the city of his birth came into view at dawn. Ramon thought Angel was going to cry, and the poor bastard didn't even know he was on a one-way trip home.

The state attorney's office had hired an outside investigator to look for Angel. It was impossible to know what he would do or what he might learn; there were no reference points with a stranger—even with Franklin trying to monitor the investigator's progress. Ramon didn't like the feeling he had about this. It was a bad sign, and his instincts told him better to be safe than sorry. Angel was going home. At least it wasn't in a box.

Jimmy sat in the cockpit staring at the pitiful sky.

"*Mira,*" Angel said, holding a pair of binoculars to his eyes. "Look, there's the *malecón.* Nothing's changed. *Nada.*"

Ramon wanted to ask him what he had expected to change in a country like this.

They were a couple miles out; he could see the house on

the beach at Santa Fe, where they'd brought the stuff in the last time.

Ramon was irritable, doing Luis's chores for him, and if it hadn't been for Angel, seeing a way around the problem of what to do with him, he'd never have made this trip. They were carrying the usual items—soap and canned food, stuff that was being rationed in Cuba—but this time Luis had set Ramon up with a contact, Guillermo, some dissident who had a connection in the government.

Guillermo would come to the boat, and they would talk about the future, the possibility of running some hovercraft in here once Cuba opened the doors. Which was only a matter of weeks now, depending on who you talked to. But everybody was thinking about it, trying to make sure they would get some of the action. Everybody, that is, except Oreste Villareal.

Ramon tried to picture Lourdes coming over here to live and raise her family. It was bullshit, Ramon thought. She would never be happy, and Luis was an asshole for even considering it. Mr. Cool. Luis could be such a sanctimonius ass, getting under Ramon's skin to the point where Ramon sometimes just wanted to bust him in the face.

Luis had blown up over Oreste, lost his temper with Ramon, really blowing his cool. Had tried to pull the big brother act, but Ramon just laughed at him. So Oreste had been shot, so what? The dumb son of a bitch deserved it. Ramon wasn't going to jail.

Luis had said he was tired of bailing Ramon out of trouble. Ramon laughed and said, well, don't then. He could handle it himself. Which meant doing something about Angel and was why he'd agreed to this trip.

He didn't trust Luis. Not after the other night, when he'd met those Miami Cubans and seen their interest when Luis described Ramon's last trip across. Something was going on, and Ramon knew he was probably being used. Which accounted for his nervousness. He'd be glad when this was done and he could go home, take the Bertram back across the Straits. Minus some cargo and a passenger.

Ramon said, "Billy, I'm in the transportation business ninety miles from here. Just about anything people pay to ride in Key West, except for commercial airlines, I'm going to make a dollar."

"A dollar?"

"A figure of speech," Ramon said. "We can afford to joke about money in America."

Guillermo seemed to smile halfheartedly. He was skinny with dark hair and sunken cheeks from too many cigarettes and too little food.

"I think to start out, two departures a day, figure a couple hours for the crossing, one in the morning and another late afternoon. Bringing in a couple hundred people a day to walk along the *malecón* and sip cuba libres in the bar at La Bodeguita beside the ghost of Hemingway."

"How many dollars to come on this boat?"

"The hovercraft?"

Guillermo nodded.

Ramon thought about it. Billy was sharp, already figuring in his cut. Well, he would suggest a bottom-line price and watch the monkey's eyes light up. "A ballpark figure."

"Ballpark?"

"You know, baseball. Roberto Clemente. Approximate."

Guillermo nodded.

"Fifty bucks a head," Ramon said. And he watched Billy calculate. Ten grand a day. More money in one day than he saw probably in two years.

"Then there's fuel expenses and harbor fees," Ramon said.

Guillermo's expression remained stoic.

"And something for the guy who could set this up with the authorities. Grease the skids, you know what I mean?"

Billy said, "Skids?"

"I'm thinking at least ten percent."

Guillermo offered his sad, dog-eared smile once again.

Angel was standing on the dock trying to have a conversation with Jimmy Santos when Ramon and Guillermo came up on deck from the cabin. Angel looked good there, Ramon thought, the old houses and buildings of Santa Fe behind him, the narrow, broken road, and off in the distance Havana rising from the sea like some ancient beast. It reminded him of the photographs he'd looked at as a kid, the albums his daddy, the senator, had put together and brought out at least once a year to show the family their roots. This was where they came from. Ramon never said anything, but he didn't like the pictures, and the reality wasn't any better. It had the mark of the fucking peasant about it, and Ramon was no peasant.

Angel, now, looked like he belonged here. Back where he'd started—and where it looked like he was going to end. At least he wasn't coming back here in a box.

Ramon put his hand on Billy's shoulder, stopping him. "The skinny guy standing there talking to the kid," Ramon said. "He was born here."

Guillermo nodded. To be Cuban-born was to be Cuban forever.

"He's my manager," Ramon said. "He runs things for me in Key West."

Again Guillermo nodded.

"I want to leave him here with you for a while, let him get an idea of some of the problems we'll have to solve."

"Problems?"

"How many more skids there are to grease."

Guillermo shook his head. "Skids?"

"Forget it," Ramon said. He didn't feel like explaining anymore.

Two kids from the village had finished unloading the boat. It was still only eight o'clock in the morning. A breeze was picking up, and the clouds were beginning to shift and break up, scattered sunlight stabbing the water. Ramon wanted to be on his way. He didn't want to get socked in here or have to cross in rough weather.

Guillermo lit a cigarette from a match, cupping the flame in both hands. "Wha's the name of your friend?"

"Angel Lopez," Ramon said.

"Angel." Guillermo rolled it off his tongue, his eyes on Angel. "He doesn't have any papers."

"He's a Cuban. I told you he was born here."

"He needs some papers. The police ask for his papers, he goes to jail."

Better here than in Key West, Ramon thought. He said, "Then don't let him talk to the police."

Guillermo turned. He reminded Ramon of a puppy that had been hurt by the sharp tone of voice.

"Don't worry," Ramon said, "I'll be back for him in a couple of weeks." He wondered what kind of a hassle Angel would put up when he learned that Ramon was going back without him. It would be easier to leave here without Angel watching.

The kids who had unloaded the boat were standing off in the distance, kicking a ball along the beach, but glancing their way, keeping an eye on them.

"Whose house is this?"

"Mine," Guillermo said with some pride. "Is the place the *balseros* leave from."

"Who?"

"The people who go on the boats to America."

The rafters. Kids on dinky boats and rafts made from old inner tubes. Ramon wanted to get out; the last thing he needed right now was to be caught at a dissident's home.

"Why don't you take Angel inside for coffee? I've got some work to do on the boat."

"You want to take anyone back with you?"

"No," Ramon said. "No way." Guillermo was looking off at the two boys on the beach.

Guillermo shrugged and stepped off the boat onto the dock. Jimmy walked over, and Ramon told him to get ready to leave. Angel was following Guillermo along a path up to the house.

"What about Angel?" Jimmy asked.

"He'll be okay," Ramon said. "They got his kind of coffee here."

Twelve miles off the Cuban coast, into the Gulf Stream, seven-foot seas broke over the flying bridge of the Bertram. The boat would wallow in the trough between waves, then be scooped up onto the crests, where it would dance out of step with the sea for a time before being violently rejected and tossed back to the trough to wallow some more.

Santos was on his knees, sick. Drenched, he clung to a stanchion and vomited onto the deck, the yellow bile washing down the scuppers with each wave that overpowered them. His dark hair was matted against his head; water ran down the neck of the rain slicker and the life jacket he'd hastily donned when the seas came up.

Ramon watched the walls of water crash into the boat as he tried, and failed, to hold a steady course. On the crest of a wave, as the water drained from the windshield, he thought he saw a ship loom, only to be lost once they were slammed back into the trough.

The Stream would carry them northward, but if the front that was pushing against them continued, they'd be lucky to hit Key West, less than eighty miles away now, before midnight. They were struggling to make five knots.

Ramon thought about Lourdes, tucked up in the big house, and cursed Luis. Returning to Cuba would take only a couple of hours, but the hazard of running back through that tide of deceit held less appeal for him than being mauled twelve hours at sea. But there was the question of fuel. He had transferred over a hundred gallons from the fifty-five-gallon drums lashed to the deck, and with the fifty gallons that were still in the tank after the trip across he estimated that under normal conditions they had just enough to get back to Key West. But these weren't normal conditions.

Ramon switched on the weather channel broadcast from Sugarloaf Key, outside Key West. Turning up the volume, he listened to the crackle of static, then tried to dim it by twisting the squelch control to bring in a clear signal. Amid the noise of the laboring engines, the rattle of gear shifting with each buckling wave, and the roar of the sea as it pounded against them, Ramon had to strain to hear the monotonous broadcast.

The front was moving quickly, according to the forecaster, and could be expected to pass through the Keys by midmorning. Which meant it would be noon or after before it was across the Straits. They would have to turn back. He switched the radio to channel 16.

If it was a ship he'd seen—twice now he'd caught a glimpse of something through the mountain of water—he thought he should probably make contact and relay his loran coordinates. Just in case.

Before reversing course Ramon keyed the mike and made

a call to any ship in the area. Then he turned the wheel. They were in another trough, the Stream pushing them one way, the wind and waves another. At first the Bertram resisted, stalling, before he felt her begin to turn as a wave lifted them.

The radio suddenly squawked.

Ramon listened as an American voice said: "This is Coast Guard cutter *Cape Sable*. Repeat. Coast Guard cutter *Cape Sable*, over."

Where the fuck did you guys come from? Ramon wondered. The fuckin' Coast Guard. What were they doing, watching him, waiting for him to move out of Cuban waters? Or was it coincidence?

The Bertram crested the wave and began to surf, the props cavitating as they came clear of the surface for an instant.

Then he saw it coming, a fifteen-foot freak wave moving in at an angle to the boat, slamming them hard on the beam as they came down the crest of the wave they'd been riding. Ramon knew they were going to broach even as the Bertram began its crablike stutter step down into the trough, taking on more water than the boat could drain.

A thought zapped his mind like lightning: God, get me out of this and I'll do anything! He didn't think of it as a prayer and a promise, really, but an exclamation, an appeal in crisis that shot across his mind before he took charge and did what he could do in the here and now.

Ramon shouted to Jimmy, then keyed the mike three times, screaming, "Mayday!" before the wheel was ripped from his hands by brute force, and they were engulfed, as though they were being swallowed, the roar of the water closing over them like a noose around the neck.

Gasoline. It was like smelling salts. Ramon came to on the high, dizzying essence of gas. Must have banged his head when the boat went over; there was pain above the left eye, which was nearly swollen shut. Someone was holding him under the arms. He could feel the thick padding and rough texture of Jimmy Santos's life jacket. Opening his right eye, Ramon was greeted by the orange canvas. Jimmy the saint, the savior, ever-cautious Jimmy, who was terrified of the sea.

There was something peaceful, rocking here in the water, not so much noise, and they bobbed like corks, no longer fighting against the waves. The light was strange, the way it came through one section of clouds and seemed to shine directly on them. They should have been drowned men.

He was still groggy. "It's Easter," Ramon said. Just remembering; he'd never thought about this day one way or the other since he was a kid. He felt like he was letting go, just drifting; had never felt so peaceful, in fact.

"Yeah," Jimmy Santos said. "And there's a big bunny sitting about fifty yards away."

"What?" Something stirred in his consciousness, some dim knowledge.

"The Coast Guard's out there. I think they've seen us."

As Ramon tried to interpret this sign other things began to come back to him. He remembered now the ship he thought he'd seen and the radio transmission. This was heavy, man. Shipwrecked in a storm-tossed sea, and there's the fuckin' Coast Guard. It was a message, maybe the biggest message of his life, and he knew he was going to have to respond in some way, but what? On Easter Sunday. Was it a sign from God? Then he remembered his appeal just before they'd gone down.

"What do you think the fuckin' Coast Guard was doing out here?" Ramon asked.

"Saving your ass," Jimmy said.

Yeah, maybe. So it was a sign from God. Ramon began to tremble. A prayer and a promise. Was he being converted, baptized right here in the Caribbean on Easter? Suddenly there was a loud whapping noise, and he looked up and saw a helicopter with the Coast Guard's red slash, like a holy vestment, nosing down toward them; a rope with a rescue basket dangled from it. They were going to be saved, drawn up a little closer to heaven.

Knowing he couldn't be heard over the noise of the chopper, Ramon tried out his response to his rebirth. "Praise the Lord," he said.

NINE

The state attorney's office was in a building at the end of Fleming Street, behind the courthouse. At ten o'clock Monday morning Tony parked in one of several diagonal slots reserved for the office that faced a chain-link fence bordering a weed-covered lot on the edge of a development project.

Kay was in a meeting. Tony waited in the reception room with a blond woman whose bruised, swollen face looked like a piece of crushed fruit. She was cajoling the receptionist: "This is the second time they robbed me. They took my money, my clothes. All I've got left is my body, and God knows they've abused that enough. All I want is a bus ticket to California and money for food."

The receptionist, a Cuban woman, tried patiently to explain. "We don' have money for this. You got to go to the Health and Rehab agency."

Minutes later Kay appeared, looking harried. She was wearing a navy blue skirt with blue-tinted hose and a white blouse with a patterned scarf knotted loosely at the neck. He followed her to her office, which was small, crammed with file cabinets and boxes; the desk was littered with papers, legal pads, and typed depositions. The only personal things were a row of four framed pictures of Kay's daughter,

Patty, on the wall behind the desk and a vase filled with crimson bougainvillea.

"How was your weekend?"

"I took Patty to see her grandparents in St. Petersburg. She never let me forget that she was missing the Easter egg hunt here."

"Well, there's always next year to look forward to," Tony said.

"That's what I told her." Kay opened one of the file cabinets and pulled out a manila folder. "Did you read the reports I gave you?"

"Ramon Marquesa is some hombre," Tony said.

"You see the spot I'm in." She perched on the edge of her desk, the navy skirt riding up three inches above her knee. "Can you help?"

"I'll do what I can," Tony said. "But I need a favor from you."

"What's that?"

"I had dinner with my stepfather yesterday. He seems to have fallen for a woman whose son is missing, and she thinks he might have come to the Keys on spring break. I said I would look into it."

"We've had the usual drunk and disorderly arrests. A kid fell or jumped off the roof of a hotel and lived. I can check and see if this kid is among them. What's his name?"

"Wyatt Anderson." Tony handed her the picture Helen had given him with his name and particulars.

"I'm curious," Kay said, examining the picture. "Why are you asking me to do this?"

"I don't have much of a working relationship with cops anymore. I'm sure if I walked in and made this request they'd do whatever they could to delay getting any information to me."

"I see. Then we're going to be operating on a quid pro quo basis?"

"Hardly." Tony smiled. "You'd be getting a bargain. All you have to do is make a phone call to the right person and jump-start the process. I'll be putting in hours. I'm happy to sign a contract with you, but I won't work for less than seven-fifty a week no matter how many hours I put in."

"I don't know how we're going to handle this yet, but I'll promise you that much even if I have to make up the difference from my own salary."

Tony nodded. "It's that important?"

"It's becoming that important," Kay said. "Where will you start looking for Lopez?"

"Just jump in the middle and see where the ripples lead."

Kay smiled. Tony held out his hand. She shook it the way a man would. "You can call me here or at home. It doesn't matter what time you call if you have some news."

"How about for lunch?"

She shook her head. "I'll be lucky to get a sandwich at my desk this week." As if to confirm it, the phone rang.

Tony turned and went out the door as Kay picked up the receiver.

Leaving his truck parked in its slot at the state attorney's, Tony walked to the corner of Whitehead and Fleming streets. He hailed the first empty cab that came along.

"Just drive around," Tony said, getting into the back. "I'm looking for someone."

"Anyone in particular?" the driver asked. He was wearing shorts, a purple shirt printed with red hibiscus, and a bill cap with floppy wings attached.

"Angel Lopez," Tony said.

The driver turned half face and whistled. "Along with everyone and his brother," he said.

"I didn't know he had a brother."

"Everybody named Lopez has got a brother. And a sister. Several of them. You read the paper, you'd think the Cubans are the only people getting married and having babies these days." A grin crossed the driver's face.

"How long have you been driving?" Tony asked.

"Ten years, give or take a couple when I tried real work."

"When'd you last see Lopez?"

"A couple of months, maybe. I can't remember. I never saw much of him even when he was around."

"How's the business running without him?"

"As far as I'm concerned, better than it was with him. Angel could screw up a wet dream. What are you, a cop?"

88

"No," Tony replied bluntly, studying the driver's identification card with his picture—without the winged cap—attached to the dashboard. The name on the card was Malcolm Scott.

"Well, it doesn't matter. I guess they've already asked their questions. Anyway, Angel's gone, history."

"Dead?"

The cabbie hunched his shoulders.

"He have any spots where he hung out?" Tony asked.

"A few that I know of."

"Let's take a look at them," Tony said.

Damp air came in the open windows of the cab while a drier but only marginally cooler version was pumped through the car's air conditioner. The interior smelled of sour sweat and stale smoke and something else that Tony couldn't identify. He watched out the window the street scene that reminded him of an old Chaplin movie as it unfolded with irregular speed. An elderly black man, a cigar wedged in the corner of his mouth, slowly pedaled a rusted balloon-tired bike up the street while mopeds, bikes, and cars whirled around him; it seemed to Tony that there was less traffic now than when he'd come here two days ago for lunch with Kay.

He saw her sitting on the edge of her desk, her tight skirt riding up over one blue-stockinged thigh. He felt himself both irked and excited by her presence. He was still trying to get a measure of control over his life, and the inability to look at her without wanting her was annoying. She was a woman, a lawyer; she had a kid, a soon-to-be-ex husband, and problems. So who didn't? He wondered why he was fighting this. Was he trying to protect her, or himself? And what did it matter? She told him she was over the old relationship, her marriage, but otherwise her only interest in him seemed to be professional.

They were stopped at a light. A fight—more a shouting match—between two guys who looked like bums was in progress. Tony watched them. Back and forth, back and forth, insults as grimy as the squabblers themselves were hurled until one man jabbed his finger in the other's chest and a punch was thrown. They were drunk, weaving and staggering before eventually wrestling each other to the ground.

The cabbie turned around in the seat. "Key West," he said, lifting his hands from the wheel as if in explanation. He turned back and, when the light changed, jabbed the accelerator. Tony watched the guy's wings flapping on the inrushing breeze. Key West.

They pulled into the parking area of an open-air Laundromat. Inside, half a dozen women and two men were in some stage of doing laundry. A large sign on the wall announced: Dropoff Service Seven Days a Week. Not responsible for damages, loss, theft, or fire. Another sign proclaimed: Our Dryers Are HOT. Next to the Laundromat was a pet grooming shop.

The driver started out of the cab and, turning to Tony, said, "You coming?"

"Why, you need help carrying your laundry?"

The cabbie grinned. "First stop on the Angel Lopez tour."

"He hung out in a Laundromat?"

"The *buche* bar in front."

Buche bars where Cuban coffee was served from espresso machines were as common in the South Florida urban landscape as drugstores in northern climes. A place where deals were made throughout the day, information and gossip exchanged over short hits of the dark, sugary coffee. Tony had spent his share of time in Miami hanging out in similar places where the *buche* generally cost less than the information.

"Angel made the scene here and a couple other places at least two or three times a day."

The driver held the rear door while Tony got out of the cab. "Your name is Malcolm?" he asked.

"Yeah. You can call me Scotty, though," the driver said.

Tony handed him a twenty-dollar bill. "Point out any of Angel's friends to me, Scotty. Anyone he might pass the time with."

Scotty nodded and pushed the bill into a dirt-stained pocket of his shorts. "Follow me," he said.

90

*   *   *

"Yo Mingo."

"Hey, Scotty. Whatcha know?"

"Nada."

Tony ordered two *buches* standing at the counter. Scotty stood beside him, winked, and nodded toward the guy he'd spoken to, who was sitting on a bench talking to another man in a narrow-brimmed straw hat, a toothpick dangling from his mouth.

Mingo was a hawk-faced man with wiry salt-and-pepper hair that came to a widow's peak above his narrow forehead. He wore a pair of houndstooth checked pants that had gone shiny, an old pair of brown and white wingtips on his feet.

Tony picked up the small plastic cup of *buche,* and together he and Scotty stepped onto the sidewalk, Tony facing the *buche* bar and Scotty with his back to the two seated men.

"That's Charlie Mingo," Scotty said in a quiet voice, the traffic cruising by on the street muffling their conversation. "He's close with Angel. Distant relatives—cousins, I think."

"What's he do?"

Scotty shrugged. "What do any of these guys do? He hangs out here and around town. I think he worked for the city at one time. One of those cush jobs, you know the kind. Guy gets it because he knows somebody who knows somebody, but what the hell he actually does, nobody knows."

Tony nodded and downed the *buche* in one caffeine-laden gulp.

"Another?" Scotty asked.

"I want to ride, not fly," Tony said. "Where's the next stop?"

They got back in the cab, and Scotty zipped across town, whistling an unrecognizable tune as he drove. Tony took mental notes of landmarks and street names, most of them familiar from the time he'd lived here.

Moments later Scotty brought the cab to a stop at the curb in front of a small neighborhood grocery store. Two cops, one of them black, stood near a parked patrol car holding plastic cups similar to the ones Tony and Scotty had discarded moments ago.

"This place is a favorite with the cops, the firemen, and city workers. Angel hung out here, too. You wanna go in?"

Tony shook his head. "What about the cops? Angel know them?"

Scotty chuckled. "Angel knows them all. The black guy's Morris. He usually hangs out with a cop named Franklin. There are rumors about Franklin."

"What kind of rumors?" They sat in the car, the engine idling, the A/C spitting out warm air. The digital readout meter clicked over to $21.65.

"Look, man," Scotty said in a tone that was more wheedling than angry, "I don't even know who the hell you are. Twenty bucks got you a peek at Mingo. Don't press your luck." He was trying to sound tough, but there was also a hint of amusement in his voice.

Tony pushed another twenty across the seat and watched as Scotty slid it into his pocket without looking at it. "I told you I'm not a cop. I'm working for someone who needs some information. You're not involved, your name isn't going to be mentioned. I'm trying to put a picture together."

Scotty put the car in gear and pulled away from the curb. "Franklin is rumored to be in tight with Ramon Marquesa. Ramon needs something done on the inside, Franklin's the guy who gets it done. I don't know any specifics, so don't bother asking."

Tony said, "Is Angel married?"

"Yeah."

"Let's go by his house. Ramon's place, too. I want to see where they live."

When Scotty dropped him back at his truck half an hour later the fare was $37 and change. Tony left him a fifty-dollar bill and asked for a receipt. "Get a new set of wings," he said. Scotty flashed him a V. "Fly high," he said.

Tony Harwood had never understood what it was about surveillance work that appealed to him. It was certainly tedious, and for most of his colleagues it had been a bore. But for him there was something satisfying about watching people go about their lives, tracking them while picking up tidbits of information. But it was more than just voyeurism and the learning process that appealed to him. There were often hours when he just sat waiting, and even that time he didn't mind. It provided time for reflection, time when he could look inward as well as observe the passing human parade.

Maybe what it was—he was having this thought often—was that he was back out on the streets and on his own. The streets were his roots, his life.

The way domestic life was Kay Fulton's. He tried to imagine her at home with her daughter. Preparing dinner, talking about school, listening to the endless chatter of a six-year-old. It must be hard for her, having such a time-consuming profession and being a single parent at the same time. He couldn't imagine it, raising a kid, not even with two parents.

From a deli he had bought a couple of smoked turkey and provolone sandwiches, made dry to keep the bread from going soggy, and a thermos of coffee. He sat now on Riviera Drive, three houses down from Angel Lopez's place.

The house was brick, ranch style, similar to others in the neighborhood off Flagler Avenue and out of the old town district with its older wooden homes. He could see a canal behind the house. Angel's place had windows facing the street, but they were closed and covered by drapes. In the side yard he'd seen a compressor for a central air conditioning unit big enough to cool the entire house. A Cadillac was in the driveway, a late-model Coupe de Ville.

There was something about Kay Fulton, apart from the physical. Tough in a nonmasculine way. Putting everything between her and any intimate situation with a man. He was guessing. But she came across that way. Maybe she had somebody she was sleeping with and wanted to discourage any advances. He didn't think that was the case with Kay. He thought about asking her. But what for? Did he want to get involved with a woman with a kid, who if she was looking for anything was looking for a husband to play father?

At five o'clock, after a two-hour stint, Tony ate half of one of the sandwiches and drank some coffee. Twenty minutes later a woman came out and got in the Caddy. She was

93

dark-haired, probably in her early fifties, wearing cream-colored slacks and a frilly blouse. Her hair had recently been done. She backed the car out, drove to the next block, and turned left, which would take her back to Flagler.

Tony started the pickup, made a U-turn, then turned right at the corner a block back from where the Caddy had turned. He saw it coming in his direction and let it get half a block away, then pulled into traffic. Two blocks later the Caddy pulled into the parking lot of a small shopping center. The woman got out and walked into a grocery store. Tony parked and went in after her.

While she roamed the aisles he went to the magazine rack and thumbed through magazines. When she went to the checkout counter Tony carried a copy of *Esquire* and stood in line behind her, glancing at her purchases as they were rung up. Ordinary stuff. Shampoo, toothpaste, dental floss, nail polish remover. Two boxes of Kleenex. One Weight Watchers frozen chicken dinner. Half a dozen cans of Slim-Fast. And two bottles of wine. She paid, waited while the stuff was bagged, then left the store.

Tony paid for the magazine, dawdling in the store while the woman went out to the Caddy. He left and walked to his truck as she turned out of the parking lot, heading back in the direction of Riviera Drive.

He stopped at a gas station, filled his tank, and used the restroom. Then he drove back over to Riviera, approaching the house from a different block this time, parking several houses away and on the opposite side of the street. The Caddy was in the driveway. Tony settled back with his *Esquire.*

When it got too dark to read he ate the other half of his sandwich. Then, stretching one leg across the seat, he rested his head against the backrest. He thought about Jack Dowd, remembering, when he'd gone off to college to study law at the University of Florida in Gainesville, how proud Jack had been. He'd had a scholarship; it was almost like a tribute to Jack, who had turned Tony around.

After two years in college he knew it wasn't for him; he hated it. He came back to Miami and saw the disappointment in Jack's eyes. Which was only marginally relieved when Tony told him he wanted to get into police work. He felt he might fit in there, back on the streets, some excitement. He had taken some courses in criminology at Gainesville and was easily accepted at the police academy. A year later, almost fifteen years ago, he was at Metro-Dade, working his way up. Until he crashed. A burnout. And once again he'd seen the disappointment in Jack's eyes.

Now here he was on a side street in Key West, doing surveillance like a P.I. in a cheap novel. At nine o'clock he ate the rest of his sandwich and drank more coffee. At nine-forty-five the lights of a car hit his rearview mirror, and he watched as it cruised slowly past before turning into the Lopez driveway next to the Caddy. Tony sat up. He wrote down the tag number of the car, an older model Buick, saw its lights go out and Charlie Mingo get out.

Angel Lopez's wife, wearing a smile and a housecoat, opened the front door. Mingo went inside.

TEN

When Mingo came out two hours later Tony tailed the
Buick across the city into old town, to a house on Duncan
Street not far from the Laundromat where Tony had first
seen him almost twelve hours earlier.

On a corner lot was a modest two-story frame house that
had three individual room additions at the rear, each of
which had its own peaked roof. From where Tony sat across
the street, looking at the silhouette with its sawtooth
roofline, it looked as if the rooms had been added on at
different times. According to Scotty the cabdriver, Charlie
Mingo had one of those jobs—nobody knew what he did.
Working for the city. A friend of a friend. Kickbacks. Could
cousin Angel Lopez have provided some of those kickbacks?
It was possible. And with each kickback came a new
addition.

Maybe he should put a room addition on his trailer and
bring Jack down, Tony thought. Get him out of Miami. Jack
had been to Big Pine once or twice, but only for the day.
Big Pine wasn't Jack's environment. He needed the city, the
cops—his social nerve center. There was nothing for him to
do here unless he had decided to look for Helen Anderson's
son. Still, it would be good to have a place to come to now
that he was getting old. If something happened to him, who
was going to look after him? Helen? She was almost ten

96

years younger than Jack. At their ages, though, that wouldn't seem to make a difference. Jack seemed okay, not like he was going senile, getting Alzheimer's—old-timer's disease, Jack called it.

It was something Tony had to think about, though, to prepare for. He could probably get Tom Knowles to help with the addition.

A light came on in one of the downstairs rooms, and Tony watched as a shadow moved across one of the jalousie windows, its individual panes partially cranked open. A moment later the shadow passed across the window again, then the light went out. Another light came on upstairs, and moments later, when it was extinguished, the house was dark.

Tony opened the glove box and took out the stainless steel 9mm Beretta he kept there in its clip-on holster, and he tucked it inside his waistband, pulling his T-shirt out to hang loose over his jeans. He got out of the truck, quietly closed the door, and walked across the street onto the Mingo property.

The corner was darkened by an old sapodilla tree, its dense leaf-laden branches covering half the yard. He walked up three steps to a side door that gave access to one of the add-ons at the rear of the house. There was no porch light. He knocked on the door, stepped back, and watched as the light came back on upstairs. Tony stood off the porch away from the door. He heard slippered feet approach.

"Who is it?"

"Mingo," Tony whispered.

"Yeah, who's that?"

"Ramon sent me. I got to talk to you."

"At this hour?"

"It's about Angel."

From another room in the house a woman's voice spoke in Spanish. *"Quién es, Carlos?"*

Mingo said, *"Nadie.* I can take care of it. Go back to sleep."

Tony heard the dead bolt turn in the lock before the door opened six inches. Mingo's long, skinny nose slid out into the night. "Where are you?"

"Right here," Tony said. He stepped out from the side of

the house and put his hand on the door. Mingo was in pajamas and a dingy robe, a pair of slippers whose backs were caved in under his heels.

"Who are you?" Mingo asked, peering out in the dark. "I don't know you."

Tony moved up on the step and held the door to prevent Mingo from closing it. "You and your cousin's wife have a good time tonight?" he asked quietly.

Mingo's face registered his mistake. He reached out and tried to push Tony away, pulling at the door.

Tony got one shoulder between the door and the frame. "All right, we'll do this the hard way." He reached in, grabbed Mingo by the robe, and pulled him close. There was the smell of wine and peppermint on Mingo's breath. "We're going to talk," Tony said. "You and me. Or you and me and your wife. However you want it."

The woman's voice said, *"Carlos, qué pasa?"*

They stood there staring at each other. Finally the tension drained from Mingo. "It's Manny," he called to the woman. "Car trouble. I'll be back in a minute. Go to sleep now."

Tony stepped out, gripping Mingo by the robe, closed the door, and led him across the street to the truck. With Mingo in the passenger seat Tony got in behind the wheel. "I'm looking for Angel," he said.

"Look somewhere else. He ain't here."

Tony started the truck and made a U-turn in the direction of new town. No one spoke until they crossed Kennedy on Flagler. Then Mingo said, "Where you going?"

Tony took the next turnoff to Riviera Drive.

"Look, I don't know where Angel is," Mingo said. "I haven't seen him."

Tony parked in front of the Lopez home. The Caddy was still in the driveway. There were no lights showing. It was quiet. Tony shut off the engine.

"How's Angel's wife holding up?" Tony asked. "She unhappy, feeling depressed?"

"She's okay."

"You're keeping her spirits up, is that right, Mingo?"

Mingo ignored the question. He looked older in his grubby robe with ancient food stains on the front of it and his beaten-down slippers. He didn't look like a man who would be two-timing his wife and his own cousin. Looks could deceive.

"I'm not interested in busting up the fandango you've got going," Tony said. "Just tell me about Angel Lopez and you can get back to bed."

"Angel ain't around," Mingo said. "What is there to tell?"

"Maybe you've got some ideas where he is, what happened to him."

"Maybe, but I don't."

"When did you last see him?"

"I don't know. A month ago, probably."

"Where?"

Mingo hesitated a second. "We had a *buche* together."

"He seem okay? Anything wrong? He talk about leaving town?"

"I don't remember," Mingo said.

Mingo the mute. Tony thought about pushing his ploy to the limit. "How about we walk up to the house, push the doorbell, and talk to Mrs. Lopez? You think it would jog your memory?"

"I think you'd be in more trouble than you're in now."

"Who would I be in trouble with?"

"The wrong people," Mingo said.

"Ramon Marquesa?"

Mingo resumed his silence.

Tony turned the key in the ignition. He put the pickup in gear and drove back over to Flagler, heading downtown. He crossed the intersection of Duval and South streets and found a parking place on South just before the monument at the Southernmost Point, a garish concrete replica of a nun's channel marker used at sea. Ramon Marquesa lived in the house across the street from it.

Tony opened his door. "Let's go talk to Ramon, see how much trouble we can get into."

Mingo didn't move. Tony walked around to the passenger door and opened it. "Party time," he said.

"No," Mingo said. "I ain't goin' in there."

"I don't see you have much choice." He put his hand on

Mingo's skinny arm. "Here it is: Either talk to me, or we both talk to Ramon."

"Get back in," Mingo said. "I'll talk to you."

He drove through the nearly empty streets of Key West. It was almost two o'clock in the morning. Everything was in shadow; dark palm fronds like broken wings stood out against the old buildings. He thought about calling Kay. But what did he have, really? Nothing but a series of names, a few of Angel's hangouts to be checked out. Mingo knew nothing. He was an old man having a last fling with a girl he'd known in high school more than forty years ago. The fact that she was married to his cousin meant nothing. Mingo's indeterminate fear of Ramon Marquesa was greater than the specific fear of being caught screwing his cousin's wife. Which revealed more about Ramon, Tony thought, than it did about Angel Lopez.

Tony wasn't ready to head back up the Keys. He was wired. The hours of sitting in the truck under the stimulus of coffee, then the encounter with Mingo, had left him dissatisfied. He found the bar where Oreste Villareal had had his last argument with Ramon Marquesa, the last place Angel Lopez was known to have been seen.

Bubba's was outside the tourist district, a neighborhood bar favored by Cuban money crunchers and the guys who stuck to them like lice. The decor was a mix of luxury and license. Double-stitched leather and mahogany chairs surrounded the leather-bolstered bar. A large painting of a voluptuous nude, reclined and eating a pear, hung behind the bar. The bartender looked like a Spanish grandee, with a high pompadour of black hair and thick sideburns peppered with gray.

"Rolling Rock," Tony said, sinking into one of the leather armchairs.

The bartender shook his head. "Try again."

"Too proletarian for this establishment?" Tony asked.

The grandee managed a smile. "It helps keep the riffraff out."

"How about a Corona, then? Hold the cute lime on top."

When sideburns returned and put the bottle down Tony

declined a glass. "Want to stay in touch with my roots," he said. He pushed a five-dollar bill across the bar and saw less than half of it come back in change. "I understand even the aristocracy can get out of hand in here at times."

"Where'd you hear anything like that?"

"Idle rich gossip."

"A man of your social stature listening to them? Come on!"

Tony started to reply, but the bartender moved off to fill an order. In a couple of hours Bubba's, like all other bars in Key West, would be closing. There was a gentle ebullience among the small crowd, a bubble of energy carried by the alcohol and the hour. Tony watched as pairs of people made frequent trips down a hallway that led to the back of the building. Tony noticed that they were usually gone less than five minutes and seemed to come back happier than when they left.

Tony took a hit from the bottle of Corona and felt an insistent pressure against his bladder. It had been several hours and a thermos of coffee since he'd peed. He stood up and walked along the narrow hallway to the john. He stood at the urinal and relieved himself. When he was finished he walked out into the hall and saw the destination of the parade he'd noticed. A door to an office was partially open, and two people were snorting lines with a cocktail straw from a glass-topped desk. Someone saw him and pushed the door closed. Tony went back to his seat.

The bartender came over and asked if everything was all right in the working-class section.

"As good as it gets without any peanuts." Tony took his wallet and lifted a fifty-dollar bill out, placing it on the bar next to his change from the five. "Were you working the night Oreste and Ramon Marquesa had their blowup?"

"I might have been." The expression on the bartender's face remained aloof. "What are you, a cop?"

"If I was, I would close this place. The cocktails you're serving in the back office are a no-no."

"You don't seem to be having a good time here. Why don't you go down the street where you can find your own poison?"

101

Tony creased the fifty and held it between his first two fingers close to the back edge of the bar. "I'd like to take something with me, some information I'm willing to pay for. I'd like to talk to anyone who was in here that night with Oreste and Ramon. Maybe you could help me."

"I could, but I won't. I've got to live with these people, pal."

Tony shrugged, folded the fifty, and tucked it in his jeans pocket. He finished his beer and stood up, picking up a dollar and change from the five.

"Come back and see us when your fortunes improve," the grandee said.

Tony stood on the curb outside the bar. It had been a long night filled with empty promise. He looked at his watch. It was almost three o'clock in the morning. Half a dozen people came out of Bubba's, one of the girls with laughter as brittle as the rattle of dice in a cup. He watched the group weave its way up the street. Time to go home.

Tony walked to his pickup and drove through the narrow streets until he found a main artery that led to U.S. 1. He rolled the windows down, turned the radio on, and found a soothing jazz station for company on the half-hour journey up the Keys.

At this hour there was very little traffic, the highway a dark ribbon that monotonously unwound in the glare of his headlights; mangroves bordered the highway; occasionally a side road turned off into swamps or a development project.

He had just passed mile marker 17 when a flash of light caught his eye in the rearview mirror. Thinking it was an emergency vehicle, Tony slowed and eased off the shoulder, expecting it to pass him, surprised when it pulled behind him and stopped.

In his mirror Tony watched as a black man got out of the car and walked toward the pickup. He wore the uniform of the city police; his hand rested lightly on the holstered revolver at his waist. In his other hand he carried a long-handled flashlight. The car was not a patrol car, but the portable light attached to the top was still spinning.

The cop stopped just behind the driver's door and spoke

to Tony through the open window. "Your driver's license and registration." The voice was a slow, deep bass. The beam of the flashlight swept over the cab.

Tony reached for the glove box. The Beretta was there in its holster, where he'd put it after taking Mingo home. Beneath it was the truck registration.

The light stayed on the gun. "Lift it out with one finger and drop it on the floor," he said.

Tony did so, then got the registration and passed it and his license, which he took from his wallet, to the outstretched hand.

The beam of the flashlight retreated. Moments later the cop said, "Step outside, put your hands on the hood, and spread your legs."

Tony started to protest. "Officer, I—"

"Do it now!" the cop commanded.

Tony opened the door. The beam of the flashlight touched his face and held there as he got out, blinding him. He assumed the position, one that Tony had put others in countless times. The cop kicked his feet wider apart, just as he was trained to do.

"Aren't you a little out of your jurisdiction?" Tony asked. They were outside the city limits.

There was no reply as the cop frisked him, bending to pat his legs down. Tony had a glimpse of the black face as it was lit briefly by the flashlight tucked under the cop's arm. There was something familiar, some stirred memory. Presidents' names began to come to mind. Jefferson, Lincoln. Wilson. Black names.

A car passed.

"What's this all about?" Tony asked.

No answer.

He saw Scotty the cabdriver's wings flapping in the breeze. Ramon Marquesa. Angel Lopez.

Tony said, "You're making a mistake." Then he saw the light from the flashlight describe an arc and felt the blow to his head at the same time the name came to him.

He said, "Franklin!" But there was no answer.

103

ELEVEN

A TV commercial was selling an electric appliance that chopped and sliced vegetables and grated cheese, did everything but dance, and was dishwasher-safe. There was a picture of it at work, a pair of hands holding it over a salad as sliced radishes shot from its mouth. A singing jingle repeated itself; then the price flashed on the screen along with an 800 number voiceover repeated three times.

A noise woke Kay Fulton. She wasn't sure if it was something outside the house or the TV. She lay on the couch and stared in dismay at the stupid commercial. She wore a pair of men's purple cotton pajamas. A pile of papers surrounded her. She looked at the clock on the wall and saw that it was three-thirty in the morning. She had been working all evening, going over depositions, preparing questions for more interviews and depositions she had today. She remembered lying down on the couch around midnight, thinking she would work some more. An old movie on TV had captured her attention, and she had watched most of it. Later she masturbated. The tension of the past several days had knotted itself in her neck and shoulders, and masturbating temporarily relieved it as well as the sexual frustration she felt. She had not slept with a man since Brad moved out. In the office she knew that she was perceived as the ice queen by the young male attorneys who worked there, some of whom had asked her out. But the last thing she wanted was to get involved with another lawyer. Neither was she ready to introduce another man into Patty's life right now. So she lived with her reputation, and her tension, by trying not to think about it.

She got up and turned the TV off. Everything was quiet. One lamp was on beside the couch, the rest of the house in darkness. She tiptoed into her daughter's room and found her asleep on her back, clutching Pooh Bear, whose arm Patty had wrapped with white first-aid adhesive tape to simulate a cast. Patty's own cast was covered in children's drawings. Kay smoothed the damp hair on the child's brow and, leaving the door ajar, walked back into the living room, where she began picking up her papers.

She was going to get less than four hours of sleep tonight, including the time she'd slept on the couch. It wasn't enough. Especially when she was only getting five hours of sleep most of the time anyway.

Her parents were sending her ads from the St. Petersburg and Tampa papers, and she'd actually answered a couple of them and sent out her résumé. If she were hired, she didn't know what she would do. She hadn't mentioned to Brad that she was thinking of moving. She knew it would create a scene; he would hurl accusations at her, object to her moving and taking Patty away from him.

It was so preposterous, she thought, that a man could destroy himself with drugs the way he was doing and still be concerned about whether his daughter was living next door or four hundred miles away. Kay was sure Brad was only using Patty as a way of punishing and controlling Kay. But she couldn't talk to him about it. Which added another source of tension.

Thankfully, there seemed to be some good news in the Marquesa case. After all the hours of research she'd put in going over the documents in the case, reading and rereading the file that was building, she had uncovered names of other people—people who were not directly related to the Villareal incident but who might be able to shed light on it indirectly. She was in the process of talking to some of those people now. And yesterday she had come across one person she was hoping could help.

A waitress. A young woman who'd been in the Keys only a short time and who had not yet been intimidated by Ramon Marquesa. When Kay called her she seemed willing to talk. They made an appointment for today at nine o'clock in the morning, less than five hours from now. Her name was Coral, and she worked in a restaurant frequented by Ramon Marquesa.

Kay stacked the papers on her desk in the study and put the ones she would need this morning in her briefcase. She laid out Patty's clothes for school, looking to make sure she had something clean to wear herself, then went into the bathroom.

She came out, crossed to the living room to turn off the light, and realized she hadn't seen Orange. Normally the big cat slept inside at night, either in Patty's room or on paper bags that Kay put down on the floor for him, giving him a clean, flealess bed.

She checked Patty's room again. No Orange. She went around the house, wondering where the cat was. She had had to live with the awareness that he could be hit by a car any time now that he was getting so old, adding one more thing for her to worry about.

Kay walked to the kitchen and opened the French doors that led into a small patio deck and down to the backyard.

She called him. "Orange. Pusspusspuss."

There was no sign of him. She stood and listened, hearing nothing but the muted sounds of what little traffic traveled Truman Avenue a few blocks away. From somewhere downtown came the distant sound of a siren.

She walked back inside, went through the darkened living room, and opened the front door. Stepping out onto the porch, she once again called to Orange. Nothing. Brad was apparently home, his car in the driveway, the house dark. She stepped off the porch to give one last look for the cat, didn't see him, and was about to go inside when something caught her eye.

In the corner of the yard, next to the hedge of bougainvillea that grew around the porch, was something that looked like a lump of clothing. She walked across the lawn, her heart beginning to pound when she realized it was not clothing, but an animal.

Orange.

She knelt and touched the thick striped fur on the cat's back. Orange was dead, there was no doubt about that. She started to pick him up, thinking how this was going to affect Patty, wondering how she was going to explain this death. She would bury him tonight in the backyard.

As she picked the cat up it seemed that he was unusually light. Then she saw why. He'd been disemboweled; his guts lay damp on the grass like a pile of dog crap.

Coral lived in a two-bedroom apartment on Simonton Street that she shared with another waitress and Coral's seven-year-old son. Coral was twenty-nine but looked younger.

The apartment was a mess, kids' toys strewn everywhere over the floor and ancient furnishings; gray wadding was coming out of the ripped cushions on the couch. A broken leg was taped with duct tape to the coffee table. There was dust and termite droppings everywhere. Kay wasn't sure where to sit.

"I'm sorry," Coral said. "The place is a dump, but it's all we've been able to find, and we can't even afford this. Can you imagine? Six hundred dollars a month for this place."

Kay was very aware of the high cost of living here. If she moved to Tampa she thought she could cut her living expenses by a third.

"Sit anywhere," Coral said, cutting a path through the toys. "I was going to try to get the place cleaned up this morning before you got here, but getting Cory ready for school . . ." She sighed without finishing her sentence.

"I know," Kay said, smiling. "I've got a six-year-old daughter."

Coral nodded and lit a cigarette. An ashtray full of butts was on the coffee table. Kay sank down on the couch and felt the plywood beneath the cushion.

Coral took several deep drags on the cigarette, flicked ash in the general direction of the ashtray, and set about nervously picking things up only to set them down again in some other place without doing anything to relieve the clutter in the room.

Kay tried to picture her on the witness stand. Coral was pretty in a pasty, unkempt sort of way. She was small with uncombed blond hair; a cloth band circled her head behind her ears. She was barefoot, wearing a T-shirt and shorts. She smoked, made an effort to pick up the room, and talked all at the same time, going on about the difficulties of trying to raise a kid by herself.

Kay hoped that she didn't sound like this, and she didn't think she did, even if she sometimes had similar thoughts. Coral had a tendency to whine, but there was a potentially good witness here.

Finally Coral paused long enough to get a new cigarette, lighting it from the butt of the old one. Kay said, "I'd like to ask you some questions."

"Right," Coral said. She plopped down cross-legged on the chair opposite the couch. "Fire away."

"You understand," Kay said, "that these are just preliminary questions, that I may want to subpoena you as a witness against Ramon Marquesa? You might have to go to trial. Would you be willing to do that?"

Coral drew on the cigarette. "Why not?" she said.

Kay tried to smile. It was what she wanted to hear, but what she was thinking about was Patty's first question of the morning. "Where's Orange?"

"He got hit by a car last night and died." Kay had been painfully aware that she was lying to her daughter for the first time.

Patty didn't say anything, just stared at the kitchen floor, shuffling her feet back and forth like a tap dancer. Kay knelt down and hugged her. She had been up until four-thirty digging a hole in the backyard to bury Orange, then scooping the guts off the lawn into a plastic bag, which she sealed and put in the garbage. Then she stood in the shower and cleansed herself by letting cool water wash over her body, mixed with her tears.

"Will Orange go to heaven, Mommy?"

She had avoided discussing the concept of heaven and hell

with Patty, and this was the first time she'd heard her mention it. It must have been something she picked up at school.

"I'm sure he will." There. She lied again. It was so easy. She had a sense that things were suddenly snowballing out of control. She needed to talk to someone, she thought. See a therapist and get help in how to handle this. She needed also some time to talk to her daughter. But once again it was time to get her ready for school, get breakfast, and be at work in two hours, starting another twelve-hour day that could stretch into fifteen or twenty.

Coral reached for her third cigarette.

"All right, then," Kay said. "Let's get started."

Ramon had been a regular at the bar-slash-restaurant, the Bali Ha'i, with its South Pacific decor and waitresses who flitted back and forth in gossamery saronglike skirts that exposed as much leg as the management deemed discreet. During the dinner hour a piano player worked through a medley of show tunes from a baby grand.

The Bali Ha'i was pricey and had tried to cater to the gentility of Key West but quickly found that there wasn't one and learned to cater instead to anyone with money. At times the atmosphere could get down and dirty.

Ramon was among the worst. He liked Coral and when he could, which was almost always, would get himself seated at her table. The waitresses were usually tipped well here, but they put up with more hassles than did their counterparts at other places.

Ramon, drunk and high, would frequently attempt to run his hand up her skirt while she was going over the fish specials, telling about all the pineapple and cherry toppings. She would laugh out of embarrassment, push his hand away, step aside, and generally spend most of her time trying to dodge him.

He propositioned her. Right at the table. In front of everyone else there, sometimes even other women. He was gross and disgusting. When she complained to the management they only laughed and told her she was a big girl, she could handle it. Besides, she was getting big tips, wasn't she?

Ramon Marquesa left lousy tips. If she got ten percent, she was lucky.

Still, she couldn't afford to quit. Coral was pissed and began paying attention to what was going on at the Ramon Marquesa table, eavesdropping. He sometimes dined there two or three times a week. Over the months she'd heard some juice.

"What kind of juice?" Kay asked.

"I heard him talk about getting rid of somebody." Coral lit another cigarette.

"What did you think that meant?"

"I wasn't sure, but I paid closer attention."

"Did you think he was talking about killing someone?"

"After a while, yes."

"Did you hear him say who?"

"I never heard a name mentioned, but I know who it was."

"How do you know?"

"There are two cab companies in town, aren't there?"

Kay nodded.

"He was talking about the guy who runs the other cab company."

Oreste Villareal.

"How long ago did you hear this conversation?"

"About a month ago. I've got the date written down."

"You've got the date written down? Why did you do that?"

Coral shrugged. "I wrote the whole conversation down. Everything."

Kay was stunned. "Did you mention it to anyone?"

"No."

"So you could have just written it down from memory when you got off work, or on a break?" She knew that she was going out on a limb here, planting this suggestion, leading a witness, and if it ever came up under cross-examination, Kay was dead. Still, this wasn't a formal deposition.

"I suppose so," Coral said.

"Coral, why did you do that?"

Coral shrugged. "I thought I might be able to get something on the dink asshole to get him off me. That isn't illegal, is it? I mean, I wasn't going to blackmail him for money or anything."

"I don't know," Kay said. "But I wouldn't talk about it to anyone else. Do you know who Ramon was talking to by any chance?"

"Somebody called Angel."

"It was a long conversation?"

"Yeah. I only got bits and pieces of it, but I've got my notes if you want to see them."

"Yes," Kay said. "Yes. I would like that very much."

RAMON

—————

"Do you believe in God?" Ramon asked.

Lourdes laughed but looked puzzled. "I don't think anybody's asked me that since I was a kid."

"What did you say then?"

"I said yes."

"And now?"

Lourdes seemed to think about it. "I guess I don't know," she said finally.

Lately he'd begun to feel his destiny slipping away from him. After the rescue at sea and the interrogation by customs he was beginning to wonder about his conversion. Maybe he'd misinterpreted the sign.

The female lawyer at the state attorney's office was doing everything she could to nail him, and even though he was sure the weight of the court was on his side and he would not go to jail, there was always the possibility that the Fulton woman could turn up new evidence, or a surprise witness, and change everything.

Ramon was having a hard time believing that prayer was the answer; his faith was being tested, according to the priest he'd contacted early this morning. Ramon simply had to let Jesus into his life. Maybe.

But when he tried to question his brother about getting a tighter grip on the process, Luis, who was spending more and more time in Miami, had brushed him off. Luis had other things on his mind now and seemed more annoyed than concerned by this latest trouble.

Uncertain how much support he was going to get from Luis, Ramon began spending more time in the big house keeping Lourdes company. Hoping he could learn something, pick up some information that could be useful. Lourdes, however, seemed to know nothing.

There was a certain line that Ramon had never crossed with her; he had always kept the flirtation light, never pinning her down, although in his old life all he'd ever wanted was to pin her down. Now what he wanted was her approval, and someone to confirm his newfound faith.

Ramon had gone to see Luis a few days after his conversion. Luis wasn't home, but Lourdes asked him in, as she always did, offering coffee, and Ramon went with her into the kitchen.

It was ten o'clock in the morning. The kids were with the nanny. Ramon watched as Lourdes ground fresh beans and tamped them into the stainless cup of the espresso machine.

"What happened to you?" Lourdes asked. Her luxuriant hair was clipped loosely in back. She wore a pair of baggy shorts, and he could see the beginning swell of flesh on her ass as she moved around the kitchen. It was disturbing.

Ramon hadn't told anyone what had happened to him when he came to in the water. He wasn't comfortable talking about it, so he'd just gone to the priest. Now he felt the need to talk, and Lourdes was the only person he could think of to confide in.

"It's a miracle," Lourdes said when he told her what had happened to him.

"You think so?"

"Sure, look at you. You're a different man."

Ramon looked down at his hands, the thick, stubby fingers with almost no nails because he chewed them. That was a bad habit, one that belonged to the old Ramon, he thought.

He'd make a conscious effort to stop, he decided, and he offered up a silent prayer to give him strength to stop biting his fingernails.

"You think I'm different?"

"You're calmer, more relaxed," Lourdes said.

He didn't feel relaxed. The bartender at Bubba's had called Ramon a couple days ago to tell him about the guy who'd been in one evening asking about the night Oreste and Ramon had tangled. Then Ramon had run into Mingo at the coffee stand, and Mingo said he'd been harassed by the same guy. Mingo also remembered seeing him with a cabdriver at the *buche* bar one day.

Which cabdriver?

The guy wore the stupid hat with wings on it.

Mingo, however, had heard that Franklin had taken care of it.

Franklin! Jesus! And there was the other thing. He had to try and get a handle on his language. A man who had been born again couldn't go around taking the Lord's name in vain.

Who, Ramon asked Franklin, had called him in? Franklin couldn't remember, or was reluctant to say; just that it was an anonymous call, probably Mingo or someone at the bar.

Luis, Lourdes told him, wasn't home that day. But Ramon could imagine that Luis wasn't going to be pleased when he heard about this latest episode.

"Luis is still in Miami?"

"I think so," Lourdes said. "He didn't come home last night."

Yes.

"I wouldn't leave you home alone at night," Ramon said. And he regretted it as soon as he said it. This was the old Ramon. He couldn't believe how hard it was to change.

Lourdes laughed and turned the steam on for hot milk. She had been born in Miami to Cuban parents. Like most of the Miami Cubans, her parents were anti-Castro, always talking about returning to a free Cuba. But Ramon was sure that Lourdes, like him, had no desire to go to Cuba to live.

"You know what Luis is doing in Miami, don't you?"

"No," Lourdes said. "He doesn't talk to me about his business."

Just as Ramon thought.

"Well, he's working with guys who want to return to Cuba. Take over when Castro's gone."

This news didn't seem to affect her; probably she'd grown up listening to this stuff.

"And you're helping them? Is that what you were doing there?"

"I was looking out for myself." This, too, sounded strange to him in light of his new self-image. It was going to take some getting used to, being a nice guy.

"What do you mean?"

"If Castro is finished, then there's going to be opportunities over here for anyone smart enough to seize them."

Lourdes nodded. "Would you move to Cuba?"

Ramon scoffed. "Never!"

"Me neither," Lourdes said. He noticed how she ducked her head away as though she'd said something she regretted.

He wondered what she would do if Luis told her they were moving to Cuba. Leave him?

"I was thinking about you when the boat went over," he said. The temptations of the flesh; the smoothness of her skin drove him crazy.

"What were you thinking?"

"How Luis manipulates us all."

Lourdes didn't say anything. Ramon had never talked like this before. She wouldn't want to be drawn into finding fault with her husband in front of his brother; Ramon could see that.

"Luis doesn't go to church, does he?"

"No," Lourdes said. "He doesn't have time." She seemed to relax a little.

"Well," Ramon said. "I'd like to go with you and the kids on Sunday, if that's okay."

"Of course."

"I haven't been to mass or said confession since I was a kid."

Lourdes giggled stiffly. "It will come back to you," she said.

He hoped so. Where would he begin? The list of sins was long. Perhaps he would begin with the most recent and work back. Lust to murder. Attempted murder. Soup to nuts, Ramon thought, unable to take his eyes from the wobble of Lourdes's ass.

TWELVE

The Keys, in the language of the promotional ads, were a destination resort. A place where people believed they could go to get away from it all. Whatever *it* was. And life was meant to be a breeze in the Florida Keys.

Tony Harwood was reminded of that slogan when he woke up the next morning at nine. He had a knot the size of a golf ball behind his right ear and a headache so severe he was nauseated. He tried and failed to hold down some coffee. There was only a minor laceration of the skin where the flashlight had struck, so there hadn't been a lot of bleeding, but the pain was visceral.

He had come to lying beside the road no more than a few minutes after being clubbed. A civilian navy employee on his way to work at the Boca Chica Naval Air Station had stopped and was leaning over him when Tony opened his eyes, his vision fuzzy. "I was just going to call an ambulance," the navy man said. "How bad are you hurt?" Tony shook his head. "I'll be all right," he said. The guy helped him up, stayed with him while he walked around before getting into the pickup. The Beretta was still on the floor of the cab. Tony asked the Samaritan if he'd seen anyone else around, and the guy said, no, he'd just picked him up in his headlights lying there on the ground. Tony nodded, thanked him, and drove another twenty miles to Big Pine Key, where he kept ice wrapped in a towel on his head before falling asleep.

Tony had gone back to the ice packs when he got up. Unable to hold down coffee, he tried drinking small amounts of Coca-Cola until the nausea abated and he could eat some soda crackers and take aspirin.

By noon the headache was less intense, and he felt able briefly to face the world once again. He drove into Big Pine and bought the papers. In the event that he might have forgotten overnight, a story in the Key West paper reminded him of just the sort of world he was facing: a cabdriver, Malcolm Scott, was killed when his cab's brakes apparently failed and the taxi careened into the retaining wall as he was going around the curve on south Roosevelt Boulevard on his way to the airport at five o'clock, his first run of the morning.

Scotty, his wings flapping in the breeze. Life was a breeze. In the Florida Keys. Another front-page story recounted the discovery by boaters of a young male, an apparent victim of drowning, floating in the mangroves near the state park at Bahia Honda. The body had been taken to the county morgue at Fisherman's Hospital in Marathon. There was no identification, and anyone having any information was urged to contact the Monroe County Sheriff's Department.

Life was a breeze. In the Florida Keys. A final destination resort. Tony got in the truck and drove back to his trailer.

"You don't look so well," Tom Knowles said.

"A headache." Tony had walked across to Nan and Tom's, unsure how much he wanted to tell anyone about the incident with Franklin last night. He had an idea, though, that Tom would know something about the Marquesa family, perhaps something more than he'd learned from Kay Fulton's report, and he wanted to tap into that information. He had also decided to discuss having a room added to his trailer in the event that Jack ever wanted or needed to come down here.

Tom was alone in the house when Tony found him. Nan was in town shopping, while he'd been working on his in-

118

come tax. He invited Tony in, and they went into the front room. In the corner there was a large wooden table that served as a desk, piled with tax stuff. Tom sat down in the swivel chair behind the desk while Tony gratefully slouched on the couch.

"I've got to get some of these papers together," Tom said, "or I'll forget where I was and have to start over."

"Take your time," Tony replied. After the walk over here he decided he was still shaky. The room was cool, most of the house being in the shade of a huge broad-leafed almond tree; an overhead fan lapped the air. Two large windows looked out over the bay. It was comfortable sitting in the cool clutter of the darkened room.

"We can still talk," Tom said. "What's on your mind?"

"A couple of things. I'm thinking of putting a room addition on the trailer. I'd like your advice."

"Sure. When I'm done here we can walk over and take a look," Tom replied.

"The second thing is Ramon Marquesa."

Tom Knowles smiled. "Ramon has caused a lot of people headaches." He clamped a pile of receipts together and labeled them.

"You know him at all?"

Tom shrugged. "Oh, by sight," he said. "To say hello to if we ever found ourselves in the same place. Which wasn't often, since we didn't exactly run in the same circles. To tell you the truth, he wasn't somebody I much wanted to run into."

"What about the rest of the family, his parents?"

"Raimundo's dead, and probably just as well. He had never been able to get a handle on his son Ramon. Now his older son, Luis, was another story." Tom talked without looking at Tony, his fingers shuffling through the papers on his desk.

Luis had followed in his father's footsteps, Tom said. Raimundo was a Cuban immigrant who had come over in the early thirties to get away from the oppressive Machado regime in Cuba. He was poor, with little education, not much different from the boat people coming out of there today. Except he got out with his entire family—his mother, two

119

brothers, and his wife and Luis. He came to Key West, where the family fished and sold fruit on street corners during the Depression. No one ever called him Raimundo, though. He was always Mango. He loved mangoes, carried them door to door. People who didn't have a tree or friends to supply them could count on Mango seeking them out when the fruit came in season. Eventually Mango opened his own fruit and vegetable stand and built up a small business. Ten years after he arrived, by the mid-forties, he was well known and liked throughout town. He ran for political office and got a seat on the city commission even though he was a political novice and still considered a newcomer by the entrenched Conchs.

The business grew, his political base grew, and soon Mango was in county politics. Twenty years after he arrived on a boat from Cuba without a dime he was a force to be reckoned with. About that time Ramon was born. Probably a mistake; who knows? Or maybe because of his growing financial power Raimundo decided he could afford to increase his family. In any case, Raimundo was past forty and his wife was in her late thirties when Ramon was born. Before Ramon was in high school his father was elected to the state legislature and began spending much of his time in Tallahassee. Ramon was being brought up by his mother, who was fifty years old, and his brother Luis, who was by now a young man and looking after the Marquesa business interests in Key West and adding to them. Ramon was essentially on his own.

In high school Ramon ran with a wild crowd. Heavy drinking, carousing with girls, gambling, vandalism. Some of it minor kid stuff and some of it not so minor. The school attempted to discipline him—he was expelled more than once and was often on probation. Luis began passing money around to protect the Marquesa name. There were rumors of girls he'd raped and gotten pregnant whose families were bought off. Ramon never graduated from high school. Luis had gotten into the transportation business as Key West tried to build up its tourist market. He put Ramon in charge of running the cab company, presumably in the belief that a management job with a good salary would instill some responsibility in him. It didn't. Ramon just never grew up.

Mango had a heart attack when he was sixty, retired from politics, and returned to Key West. He died five years later. Luis, though he never ran for office, had a keen instinct for politics and kept the Marquesa power base alive. Until recently, anyway, he practically ran city hall from the sidelines. There were always rumors that Luis was also connected to the Cuban effort to overthrow Castro.

Tony listened, pleasantly distracted by the comfort of the surroundings and Tom Knowles's voice. "What about the mother—is she still alive?" Tony asked.

"If she is, she'd probably be in the convalescent center on Stock Island."

There was the sound of a car, its tires crunching over the pea gravel of their drive. Tom got up from his chair. "Nan," he announced. And he went to the front door to help her bring in the provisions.

Tony got up, too. When she entered and saw him her smile disappeared. "What happened to you?"

Behind her Tom laughed. "He had a run-in with Ramon Marquesa," Tom said. "I've just been giving him some family background."

Nan carried her bags into the kitchen. "A nasty piece of work," she said.

"It wasn't Ramon, but a cop named Franklin." Tony decided there was nothing to be gained by not telling them what had happened.

"Same thing," Tom said. "Franklin works for the city, but his loyalty's to the Marquesas, who probably supplement his salary."

Tony suspected as much. Mingo had no doubt called Ramon, or perhaps Franklin directly. The bartender at Bubba's could even have reported Tony's interest to Ramon. Whatever it was, Franklin hadn't hesitated to move.

"I take it you're working again," Nan said, putting canned goods on a shelf.

"I'm supposed to be finding Angel Lopez for the state attorney."

Tom whistled. He poured himself some coffee and offered

JOHN LESLIE

Tony a cup, which he declined. "That's about all I know of the Marquesas," Tom said.

"Thanks," Tony replied. "You've brought me up to date."

"Did you see this morning's paper?" Nan asked. "One of Marquesa's cabbies was killed."

"Yes," Tony said. "I saw that." He chose not to elaborate on his meeting with Scotty yesterday.

Nan paused and turned to Tony. "Please be careful," she said. She was always concerned, looking after everyone's welfare. Beverly had been like that, but by the time he'd come to Beverly he was in need of a father more than he needed a mother.

Tony walked back to the trailer with Tom, and they spent an hour discussing the possibilities for fixing up a livable room. Simply enclosing the already screened-in Florida room seemed to offer the fewest complications and the least expense. Tom offered to undertake the renovation, and they agreed on a price.

After Tom left, Tony thought about calling Kay. He had been putting it off, procrastinating while he tried to decide how to proceed. If he made an accusation against Franklin, it was going to be his word against the cop's. Tony had no way of proving that a city cop had driven fifteen miles out of his jurisdiction to blindside him. To call in Charlie Mingo or the bartender at Bubba's would be more damaging. Tony Harwood wasn't a cop anymore. They owed him nothing.

He decided to procrastinate some more by driving up the Keys to take a look at a drowning victim.

Marathon lay midway up the Keys, twenty miles northeast of Big Pine on the north edge of the Seven Mile Bridge. The town itself was spread out another five or six miles on either side of U.S. 1, along an odd collection of dilapidated and New Age gas stations, restaurants, resorts, bait and tackle stores, and shopping malls. The strip had a bleak and tentative look to it, like cactus growing in the desert.

Fisherman's Hospital was near the power plant and the Monroe County sheriff's substation. Tony parked in the hospital lot, went inside, and followed the directions given by one of the staff to the morgue.

122

An attendant at the desk listened to his request, then went into an office and reappeared a few moments later with a doctor who gave Tony a weak handshake and introduced himself as Felix Sanchez, the medical examiner for Monroe County.

Tony said, "I'm looking for a kid who came down here on spring break a few weeks ago and never went home."

"The boy who was pulled out of the water the other day?" Dr. Sanchez ran thin, scrubbed fingers through his hair.

Tony nodded.

"This boy's eighteen, nineteen years old," Sanchez said. "My guess is he's not from here because of the skin pigmentation. He'd been in the water for several days."

"And there was no ID on him?"

"None. We made dental impressions, which may be the only way we're going to identify him. Besides being dead, he's in pretty bad shape."

Tony followed Sanchez down a hallway and into the morgue, the medical examiner's rubber-soled shoes squeaking on the polished tile floor. There was a smell of chemicals. A body in a rubber sheet was laid out on a stainless table, apparently ready for autopsy.

Sanchez walked over to one of several drawers set in the wall and rolled out the shrouded body that was inside. He lifted a corner of the sheet and exposed the head and torso of a young male. He was dark-headed, his skin the color of warm wax. The facial features were distorted by the exposure to sun and salt water; fish had nibbled and sucked on his eyes, nose, and mouth. But Tony knew that if he were the boy's father, he would recognize him at once.

And he knew that this was not Wyatt Anderson.

"Is it the kid you're looking for?" Sanchez asked.

"No," Tony replied. "But he may have been traveling with a friend." He was trying to remember the name of the other boy Helen Anderson had mentioned. The name wouldn't come to him, but it was written down at home, along with the name and number of the boy's parents.

"What can you tell me about how he died?"

"We haven't done an autopsy yet. He may have drowned, but there's a gash on the back of his head indicating he fell or was hit with something. There are also bruises on his arms. Judging from the spacing and the lividity, I'd guess somebody had him in a tight grip not long before death occurred."

"What about his physical stats?"

Sanchez walked over to a desk and came back with a form. "Seventy and one half inches tall. Approximately a hundred and fifty pounds. Dark hair, green eyes. A birthmark on the inside of his right thigh."

"Did you take any photos?"

"Yes, some Polaroids. I have an extra one if it will help you identify him."

"Thanks," Tony said. "I'll check my connection and let you know what I find."

Sanchez nodded and pulled the sheet back up over the boy's face, then clanked the drawer shut.

THIRTEEN

There was a scrawled message from Randall Welch when
Kay came in from court asking her to stop by his office
before she went home for the day. It was almost five-thirty.
The rest of the office staff and most of the other attorneys
had gone. She'd had a court appearance that afternoon in
which Judge Grabill was adjudicating a dozen cases of parole
violation. She'd appeared in court at one-thirty and didn't
get out until moments earlier.

She planned to spend the evening going over the notes
Coral had given her that morning to determine if there was
something sufficient there to take before Grabill.

Randall Welch was in his office. The soft, sentimental
string sounds of Mantovani were coming from his CD player
as Randall leaned back in his chair, his feet on his desk,
reading from a fat file and sipping a cocktail.

"How did it go?" Looking up to see Kay standing in the
doorway, he pushed his glasses up on his forehead.

"Grabill doesn't like me," Kay said. She was still smarting
from the cheap verbal shots Grabill had fired at her whenever the opportunity arose. Then there was his way of stalling, almost as if he knew that by prolonging her time in
court he was robbing her of time on the Marquesa case. She
should have been out of court by four o'clock at the latest.

"Have a drink, relax," Randall said.

125

She thought about it. She would have liked a drink right then, but she didn't want to fraternize with Randall Welch. She was no longer sure she could trust him. "Thanks," she said, "but I've got to pick up my kid from the baby-sitter." She sat down in one of the comfortable leather chairs in front of his desk.

Randall shrugged and lifted his own glass. "Grabill's just testing you," he said. "Don't let him get under your skin."

She shook her head. "It's more than that. I'm sure that he doesn't want to see Ramon Marquesa come to trial, and he's doing everything he can to stonewall me."

"Come on!"

"I'm serious," Kay said.

Randall laughed. "Don't get paranoid on me."

She felt the anger rise, her cheeks coloring. But she checked herself before reacting. It was a mistake to have confided her thoughts to Welch, especially since she was beginning to wonder if he might not be on the judge's side, one of Grabill's drinking buddies. It was possible. She could see them now, the judge and the state attorney together, laughing over drinks and "Missy" Fulton's paranoia.

She should not have said anything to Randall about Judge Grabill. Smiling, she attempted to dismiss it. "It's been a long day. I'm just tired." Mantovani crescendoed, the timing seemingly a cartoonish orchestration of sympathy.

"You do good work, Kay. You take your job seriously. I like that. But you know the rules. Don't let it get to be personal."

"I'm trying," Kay replied.

"How's the Marquesa case coming anyway?"

"Slowly," Kay answered. She was more alert now, not willing to give anything away. Especially about her interview with Coral.

"Ramon was picked up by the Coast Guard yesterday."

Kay hadn't heard, but she was not surprised. Ramon Marquesa couldn't stay out of trouble. "Drugs?"

"No," Randall said. "He was rescued at sea. His boat went down. They think he was on his way back from Cuba."

Cuba. Kay had heard that Luis was linked to a political

group, the anti-Castro exiles in Miami. But she'd never thought of Ramon as political. She couldn't imagine him having any interest in Cuba. "Is he being held?"

Randall shook his head. "They questioned and released him."

"Was anyone with him?"

"A kid named Jimmy Santos, who apparently has been working for Ramon. He was on parole and not supposed to have left the county. He's in custody."

"Where were they picked up?"

"About fifteen miles from the Cuban coast. Ramon said they were fishing in the Gulf Stream when they ran into bad weather."

Kay was sure there was more to it but decided to pursue it through other sources if she could, still not fully trusting Randall, who had lifted his feet from the desk and, picking up a piece of paper, pushed it across to her. It was the preliminary invoice request for Tony Harwood.

"What do you know about this?" he asked.

"I asked him to investigate Angel Lopez's disappearance."

"He's not one of our regular investigators, is he?"

"No," Kay said. "He isn't."

"Seven hundred and fifty a week is more than we usually pay. A lot more."

"Colin Barker spent a few days on the investigation and couldn't come up with anything. He suggested that Lopez wasn't going to be found."

"You didn't believe him and hired Harwood?"

"I thought it might be prudent to have an outsider look into it."

They stared at each other across the desk, each trying to gauge the commitment of the other. Kay didn't waiver.

"I'll authorize five hundred a week, nothing more," Randall said. "And I'll want a weekly review of Harwood's progress."

There it was. She was going to have to come up with $250 a week of her own money. Marquesa was beginning to cost her financially now as well as emotionally.

She shrugged.

"We're on a tight budget," Randall explained, his tone softening, conforming to the music.

Kay stood up.

"You sure you won't have a drink?" Randall asked. He, too, stood up, crossing to the front of his desk to stand beside her.

"No," Kay said. "I really must go."

Randall put his hand on her arm. She hated it when men did that uninvited, when there was no intimacy between them. Kay gently but firmly eased away and started toward the door. Randall followed.

"I understand you've got a lot of personal problems right now," he said.

She paused in the hallway, turning back toward him. "Probably no more than anyone else in the office," she said.

"Well, I just want you to know . . . if there's anything I can do, you know, to help out, take some of the pressure off, all you've got to do is ask."

Kay studied him, unsure what he was volunteering. Was he propositioning her or being kind? It plagued her that she was becoming so suspicious lately. Everything seemed to have a double meaning. Always undercurrents swimming in her mind.

She tried to smile. "Thanks," she said, giving him the benefit of the doubt. "I'll keep that in mind." She continued on down the hall to her office, where she got her briefcase full of work for the evening and left the building.

Outside she saw Tony Harwood walking up the sidewalk from the parking area where she kept her Mustang.

"I saw your car," he said when she reached him. "I tried to get you at home, and no one answered the phone here. I took a chance and came by anyway."

He looked tired, as tired as she felt, and something else. There was some discoloration on the side of his face, as if it were bruised.

"Are you okay?" she asked.

"We need to talk," he said.

HAVANA HUSTLE

Kay looked at her watch. She was already nearly forty-five minutes late picking up Patty. The woman who cared for Patty after school was understanding about Kay's schedule, but Kay didn't like to press it except when there was an emergency. "I have to pick up my daughter from the baby-sitter's," she said. "If you want to go with me, or meet me at home, I should be there in fifteen minutes."

"I'll be there," Tony said. She nodded and went to her car. This would normally be time that she reserved for Patty, but Tony seemed uneasy, worried, which caused Kay even more anxiety.

Tony sat in his truck in Kay's driveway looking at the trim little Conch house with its wild, colorful tangle of bougainvillea that was trimmed to follow the line of the full-length porch. The cottage next door, the one where Tony had lived for six months, was smaller than Kay's and was lacking in similar details that made Kay's place charming and the other simply a house.

A car was in the driveway next door, and Tony wondered if it was Brad's.

Moments later Kay pulled in, and Patty scrambled out of the car, clutching some books in one hand, her other arm in a cast. Tony got out of the truck and met Kay at her car.

"You didn't mention the broken arm."

Kay sighed. "Just one of the traumas of parenting." She dragged her briefcase from the backseat.

They walked up to the porch, where Patty waited while Kay unlocked the door, then went running inside. They followed her in.

"Sit down," Kay said. "Give me a moment to get organized, and then we can talk. If you want something to drink, help yourself. The bar's in the corner there, and there's other stuff in the refrigerator. I'll be right back."

Tony sat down on the sofa and looked around the room. The coffee table was filled with legal documents and books. He picked up one of them. It was a book of poetry. He thumbed through the index and found Conrad Aiken's name. He turned to the page number and scanned the poems there until something caught his eye.

Shape has no shape, nor will your thinking shape it;
Space has no confines; and no borders time.
And yet, to think the abyss is to escape it.

Something to think about. Something Kay had been thinking about. He tried to imagine escaping the depression of
Nicki Costa's death by thinking about it. Or Ricki Lee. Or
Jack Dowd's old age, and his own future. Patty came into
the room wearing different clothes and carrying a bear.

"I broke my arm," she said, "but I didn't cry."

Tony put the book down. "Did you want to cry?"

Patty looked down at her feet. "No," she said. "But I did
when Orange got killed."

"Who's Orange?" Tony asked her.

"My cat. Mommy buried him in the backyard."

"When did Orange get killed?"

"Last night."

Jesus. It had been a busy night.

"Are you my mommy's boyfriend?"

He was about to answer her when Kay came into the
room. "Patty, this is Tony Harwood. He's a friend who is
doing some work for me, and I need to talk to him. Can
you play for a while?"

"Can I go see Daddy?"

Kay hesitated, then said, "Call him first and see if he's
home."

Patty ran to the phone.

Kay had changed into shorts and a man's button-down
shirt that was too large and slightly frayed at the collar. He
wondered if it was Brad's.

"She's at that age," Kay said quietly, pointing to her nose.
Tony laughed.

Kay came and stood in front of the coffee table. "Did
you get a drink?"

"No," he said. "I was reading."

"I think I'm going to have one. Do you want?"

"A beer, if you've got it, would be fine."

She walked into the kitchen, her legs just as he had imagined them above the dimpled ankles. The skin was pale with

130

the occasional filigree of light, almost imperceptible blue lines just below the surface.

He heard Patty talking to her father on the phone, then Kay took the receiver and spoke to him. When she hung up Patty went out the back door, and Kay returned carrying an open bottle of Amstel Light.

"I remember you don't take a glass," she said, handing him the beer. She walked to the bar, made a mixed drink, and returned, sitting opposite him in a padded antique rocker.

"Patty told me about Orange. Was it a car?"

Kay shook her head, then told him about finding the cat on the lawn early that morning.

Tony felt the way he had when Tom Knowles told him about the deer. "You think it was deliberate, something against you?"

"I don't know what I think anymore. Just before I left work my boss told me I was paranoid."

Tony shook his head. "I don't think so," he said. "You see, one of your cops followed me out of town last night. Stopped me on the highway and clubbed me with a flashlight."

Kay looked shocked. "Who was it?"

"A cop by the name of Franklin. Do you know him?"

She nodded. "I know of him. Off duty he sometimes moonlights for Luis Marquesa."

"That's what I thought," Tony said. "I got in the way of some of Marquesa's people last night, and I guess that's their way of showing their lack of appreciation."

"What will you do?"

"What can I do? I'm certainly not going to the police."

"I'm sorry," Kay said. She looked sad, tired, and genuinely troubled. "This is becoming a nightmare."

Tony shrugged. "Well, at least we now know what we're up against. We can start being more careful."

Kay finished her drink, got up, and carried her glass to the bar. He watched her mix another cocktail. He still had half a beer.

"I'm not sure I want to go on," she said, carrying the drink back to her chair. "I've got a child whose life is being

JOHN LESLIE

affected by this. I'm working twelve or more hours a day.
I'm being harassed by a judge, and I have no idea who I
can trust any longer."

"Quit?"

She leaned back in the rocker, her head against the frame,
looking at the ceiling. "I don't know," she said. "I just
don't know."

" 'Shape has no shape,' " he said. " 'Nor will your thinking
shape it. Space has no confines; and no borders time.' "

" 'And yet, to think the abyss is to escape it,' " she finished. "You found that poem."

"Yes," he said. "I think we're going to have to put our
heads together."

She lowered her head, looked at him, and smiled.

"I would like to take you to dinner," he said.

Once again he saw the fleeting hesitation in her eyes, desire masquerading as doubt.

"There's Patty—"

"Can't her father . . ."

"And the work I brought home—"

"You still have to eat."

She sipped her drink contemplatively. "I'll call Brad,"
she said.

FOURTEEN

Driving the Mustang with its top down to the restaurant up the Keys, Kay felt her mood alternate between merriment and misgiving. She felt carefree just getting off the rock for a while without Patty and without a sense of duty or work-related destination to impede her—something she had not experienced, it seemed, in months. It felt good, refreshing. Except when her mind would reel back to Patty, wondering if she was okay, if Brad could be responsible for the few hours Kay was away. Then she would think about the work that she had relinquished by coming up here and feel guilty.

She had made a thermos of margaritas to take along, illegally sipping a cocktail as she drove. She would let Tony, who was not drinking, drive back. She was not a regular drinker. The news of the attack on Tony and the emotional burden of the past several days, however, had left her depleted. She welcomed the instant relief that the tequila and lime juice provided.

"That's the spot," Tony said, pointing to the side of the road as they sped by.

"And you're sure it was Franklin?"

"I'm sure it was a black city cop in uniform. I got a brief glimpse of his face, which was familiar, and the only cop I've seen down here recently is Franklin."

"You said it was late. What happened earlier?"

JOHN LESLIE

Tony told her, described his ride with the cabbie, Scotty, now dead. And told her of tailing Mingo. Of Mingo's fear of the Marquesa family, and finally Tony's disappointing encounter in Bubba's.

Kay felt the same sense of panic she'd experienced when she picked up Orange and found his guts in a pile beneath him. "Scotty worked for Ramon?"

"Yes," Tony said.

Kay swallowed hard, lifted her glass from its plastic container on the door, and took a drink.

"Then it wasn't an accident."

"The paper said his brakes failed."

"What do you think?"

Tony hesitated, then said, "I think it's too much of a coincidence."

She felt a pressure against her temples.

"What about Angel?" Kay asked. "Do you think he's still alive?"

"If I had to guess, I would say it was a good possibility. He may be in hiding without the Marquesas even knowing where he is."

Something inside her did not want to hear that. After the previous night she realized that she was reaching the point where she would have been relieved if Grabill simply dismissed the case for lack of evidence. Even Coral's testimony now seemed skimpy and probably not worth pursuing. With the death of one of Ramon's drivers, the stakes suddenly seemed unacceptable.

She took another sip of her drink, beginning to feel slightly giddy on the alcohol and the moist air and fading light that surrounded them. The convertible top was down. There was almost a feeling of escape, and she began to understand how badly she was in need of deliverance.

The restaurant was a sort of screened-in shack just off the road at mile marker 25. It seated fewer than fifty people and had a bamboo bar, checkered tablecloths, a quiet jukebox that played country rock, and a view of the bay—everything you could want at the end of the day in the tropics.

134

The place was only half full, and they were able to get a corner table.

Tony ordered a bottle of red wine as they listened to a tape of Lyle Lovett singing about lonesome cowboys. It was almost dark; the edges of a couple of high clouds out over the bay still wore pink fringes reflected from the sun.

"Did you know that Ramon Marquesa was shipwrecked and rescued by the Coast Guard yesterday?"

"No," Tony replied. "Tell me about it."

Kay related what Randall Welch had told her in his office earlier in the day. When she was finished Tony watched her for a while without saying anything.

"What is it?" she asked.

"You're thinking about giving up, aren't you?" Tony asked. He could see it in her eyes, in the nervous movement of her hands as they strayed over the tablecloth.

"I've applied for some jobs in Tampa," she said.

"So you're running away. From Brad, or the case?"

She shrugged. "Maybe both."

"I've got some experience in that," he said, sipping the first of the wine.

"And?"

"The jury's still out."

"That's always the worst time, waiting on the jury." She smiled. *"Salud!"* She lifted her glass.

Tony lifted his glass and touched it to hers, and, studying her face, he held her eyes. "You seeing anyone?"

"Romantically?" She shook her head. "I've been avoiding getting involved right now." She laughed. "You want to know what they call me in the office, behind my back?"

"What?"

"The ice queen."

He smiled. "Somehow I don't see it."

"Good. Because it isn't true. What about you? Are you with someone?"

"No, no one," he said. "Not since the lesbian encounter."

There was a long silence. They both drank, looking out at the bay.

"It's a difficult time now, starting over," Kay said.

"Because of the big A?"

She nodded. "I haven't been tested. Have you?"

"No," he said, "I haven't." Not admitting that he'd never been asked, either.

There was another awkward silence.

"It's something people have to talk about these days," she said.

"Yes, I guess it is." Was this her way of signaling that she was interested in him? It felt bizarre, a clinical discussion of disease as a way of getting to sex. But he still felt drawn to her, stimulated by their talk. Even if they were tested tomorrow, he had no idea how long they would have to wait for the results. As soon as they came in, would the two of them then rush to the nearest bed, assuming the results were negative? So much for spontaneous sex in the nineties. His mind began to turn on some of the things they might do in place of the real thing.

Kay, as if sensing his mood, changed the subject. "I talked to a girl today who waits tables at the Bali Ha'i. She overheard Ramon plotting to kill Villareal."

"Can you use her as a witness?"

"I don't know. Maybe. But Judge Grabill will try to find some way to discredit her."

"What's her name?"

"Coral. She lives in an apartment on Simonton Street with her son and another waitress. I haven't subpoenaed her yet, and nobody knows about her testimony. Whatever happens with this case, I know I can't trust anyone in the system."

When their food arrived—grilled fish and vegetables with wild rice—they ate with simple pleasure while quietly exploring each other's past. Kay continued to drink wine and at one point laughed at something Tony said, a throaty laugh that suggested a side to her he had not seen before. A rich, pleasurable side.

When they finished their meal Kay leaned back in her chair. "That was good," she said. "I haven't done this in a long time. I've almost forgotten how to have fun."

"I know," Tony said. "You get dulled by all the pressure."

"The trouble is I don't want to go back, not to all that stress. Maybe that's why I've been suppressing it."

"Do you want to drive up to Big Pine? It's only another ten miles. I'll show you the homestead."

Her gaze was clouded. She said, "Yes, I would like that, but you'll have to drive."

They paid and walked out to the parking area, Kay weaving slightly, laughing; their hands touched, moved away, touched again, and by the time they reached the car their fingers were intertwined.

They took the boat out into the bay after Tony picked up a portable radio from the trailer. He headed out toward the mangroves at about half speed, the staccato beat of the motor savaging the still night air.

Throttling back to idle, he eased into one of the narrow mangrove channels, the twisted roots rising out of the water, ghostlike stick figures in a house of horror.

"It's like another world in here," Kay said, whispering as though someone might hear her.

"It's safe," Tony said.

"Yes," she said. "I feel that. I've heard about these channels, but I've never been back in any of them."

"I often come back here and just tie the boat off and go for a swim or sit here and look at everything."

"I imagine it's peaceful, meditative."

Tony cut the motor and let the boat drift into the mangroves, going forward to tie a line from the bow around one of the gray branches, securing the boat. He turned the radio on low, picking up the jazz station he'd had on the night before when he'd been driving down the Keys. Dexter Gordon was playing " 'Round Midnight."

They sat back in opposite ends of the boat. Kay sighed, staring up at the sky. They didn't speak, consumed by the silence, the darkness, and the liquid rush of air through Gordon's tenor sax.

"I needed this," Kay said. "I think I'd like to swim."

Tony didn't say anything, watching as she pulled off her shoes. Then she took her top off before slipping out of her shorts. Even though it was cloudless, there was hardly any moonlight, and with the overhang of branches the sky was nothing more than a dark ribbon above them. He steadied the boat as she eased over the side into the water. Then he shed his own clothing and joined her.

The water was deep. They floated, drifting in the current on their backs, then rolling over to swim back toward the boat, the water cool and salty against their skins. Flecks of phosphorescent marine life scattered before them. Kay could feel the tension drain from her body, the alcohol bringing a focus to the moment that she might otherwise have missed. In a way, she thought, this was a kind of deliverance.

Tony seemed to sense her state of mind and drifted nearby without speaking. He swam back to the boat and clung to the side with one hand. He could hear Kay but not see her, hear her treading the water, then silence, then the movement of the water again. He waited.

Seconds later he felt her, felt her hands touching his body as she broke the surface of the water beside him. He put his free arm around her, drawing her close to him, feeling the slick, smooth skin of her body as their legs touched beneath the surface.

She smoothed the hair from her face, and they kissed.

It was tentative at first, their lips brushing, then holding, transmitting a taste of salt and wine. He let his tongue explore her mouth, and she pressed herself to him, straddling his leg. One of her hands gripped the back of his neck, her fingers massaging him just below his ear.

The kiss deepened; moans, like echoes, escaped their throats until he let go of the boat, pulling her to him, their legs intertwined, and they went under, came back up, grasped for the boat and continued the kiss, the soft sounds of the jazz falling on them like rain in the dark.

They did not speak on the way in. The air dried their bodies as Tony headed the boat back on full throttle. Just before reaching the dock he idled back, then pushed the gear into reverse. The boat lurched over its own wake, then neatly slid into position. He shut the engine down and tied the boat off. Still they did not speak.

He took Kay's hand, helping her onto the dock. The touch was like a spark, and they grasped each other urgently, sliding to the smooth, worn boards of the dock. Her body was cool and excited. He touched her, running his fingers across her nipples and down her belly as she reached for him.

They explored each other, pushing, probing, rubbing, until finally, kneeling above her, he took her in his mouth while she lay on her back. She tasted mossy and slightly brackish.

She said yes, yes, and yes again.

Tony drove back to Key West. Kay lay with her head in his lap; the top was down, the radio on. When they pulled into the drive Kay got out of the car and asked him to wait. He watched her walk across the lawn to Brad's, returning moments later with Patty, who was half asleep, stumbling and rubbing her eyes. Tony looked at his watch. It was nearly ten-thirty. Kay took Patty into the house. Five minutes later she came back out.

"I'd like you to stay," she said. "But I have to warn you that I'll kick you out at six o'clock before Patty gets up."

Tony smiled and nodded. They went inside and closed the door. Kay pressed against him and began unbuttoning his shirt while he stood with his back against the door. He let her peel his clothes off, watched her hands begin to work on him. Safe sex offered a prurient kind of satisfaction.

Later, in bed, he said, "You've got an undeserved reputation in the office."

"I can live with it," Kay said.

"I wouldn't want to change it."

"Shall we get tested tomorrow?" she asked sleepily.

"Yes," he said.

RAMON

The Bali Ha'i had hired a new pianist to play medleys, quiet pop tunes from the sixties. Like "Moon River," always one of Ramon's favorites.

"What do you know about the death of that driver?" Luis's voice held its usual cool restraint, but in this changed atmosphere Ramon imagined that everyone was able to hear their conversation.

It was the first time he and Luis had been alone together since Ramon went to Cuba. "Nothing," Ramon said quietly. It was true. Stuff was happening that he had no control over. Franklin, for one. The incident with the state attorney's investigator, Harwood, for example. Franklin seemed to have taken things into his own hands.

"You had the car checked?"

"I talked to Datilla, who has been running things since Angel left. The car was in bad shape. The brakes failed. That's all anyone knows."

"The state attorney's investigating you. You don't think they're going to look into this?"

"I had nothing to do with it. Accidents happen."

"Conveniently for you."

"What am I supposed to do?" Ramon whispered in rage.

"Think. Start being careful."

The condescending prick, Ramon thought. "I'll tell you

something," he said. "You better rein in Franklin. You want my opinion, he's the one better start being careful. If you were spending less time in Miami, you might be able to see that."

Luis put his fork down, wiped his mouth carefully on his napkin, then took a sip of wine. "Don't push me," Luis said calmly. "You've pushed me all of your life, ever since you were a kid, and I've put up with it. But I'm reaching the end of my tolerance. There are bigger things to think about now than taking care of the trouble you get into."

Luis spoke in the same even tone. Ramon wondered if he made love to Lourdes in the same measured way, no emotion. He couldn't imagine his brother ever losing control.

"You don't take care of me, you take care of yourself," Ramon said. "Your image."

"You're not being careful."

"It's true," Ramon said. "All those fancy clothes, the house, the wife, the kids are a shield to protect you while you do your dirty work in Miami."

"You don't know what you're talking about."

"Come to think of it," Ramon said, "maybe I've just been trying to crack that shield all my life. Find out who you really are."

"Since when did you turn into a shrink?"

Ramon stared at his brother for a moment. "None of it matters," he said finally. "Besides, I've changed."

Luis nodded. "Lourdes tells me you're a believer now."

"Yes," Ramon said. "I have taken the Lord into my life." He tried out the line for the first time, liked the sound of it.

"What inspired that?"

Ramon told him. Luis looked at him, and for the first time Ramon thought he saw some small reaction in his brother's expression. Disbelief, amusement, some kind of mockery.

"You on the level, or is this just an act?"

"What difference does it make," Ramon said, "if the end result's the same?"

"Depends on who you're trying to screw. Like those TV evangelists."

"The world ain't a perfect place," Ramon said.

141

"Well, it doesn't make any difference, and maybe it will create some sympathy for you."

"You don't believe me?"

"I don't have to believe you," Luis said. "But a jury might."

"I'm thinking about deeding the island over to the church. Let them use it for a retreat."

Luis put his fork down. "You want to throw over half a million dollars away?"

"Would it get your attention?"

Luis stood up from the table. "You're a goddamned kook," he said. And he headed for the men's room.

Coral came by the table and took their plates. He hadn't seen her since the night he and Angel had eaten here. She seemed distracted, not her usual snooty self.

Ramon was aware that he had given her a rough time in the past, as he had many people. For the most part, he thought, those he'd treated badly, like Oreste, deserved it. But there were some, like Coral, who hadn't deserved his abuse. Maybe it was time to make amends.

"You okay?" he asked.

She stepped back from the table holding Luis's plate. She had a look on her face as if she expected him to jump her. "Fine," she said. And she started to turn away.

"Coral, I'm sorry."

Coral paused, looking over her shoulder as though she couldn't believe her ears.

"Yes," he said, "you heard right. I am sorry for the way I treated you, the shit you've taken from me." He surprised himself. He couldn't ever apologize to anyone in his life before now.

Coral actually took a step back toward the table. "You're sorry?"

Ramon nodded.

"Why?"

"I have Christ in my life," he said for only the second time in his life.

Coral shook her head. "A born-again," she mumbled.

"Well, I saw the light."

142

"And all that crap. I'm just supposed to forget because now you've got religion?"

"There's not much I can do to change that, but"—he reached in his pocket, took out a money clip and peeled off a crisp hundred—"consider it a tip," he said. "For the ones you didn't get."

"I don't believe this," Coral said.

"Take it," Ramon told her. "You earned it."

Coral took the bill with her free hand and tucked it into the front of her bra. "I'd say so, too," she said, then turned and walked away.

Ramon watched with some regret as she disappeared into the kitchen.

"Why did you leave Angel over there?" Luis ordered coffee and brandy, then pulled out one of his Churchill cigars and began fogging the place up.

"Who told you that?" Ramon asked. "Jimmy Santos?"

"What difference does it make? It was a stupid thing to do."

"Better than having him picked up and questioned by the state attorney's office," Ramon replied.

"Listen, things are happening in Cuba you don't know about."

"No," Ramon said. "Not that I don't know about, but that I don't care about. That's the difference. You've got all these kids playing weekend warrior in the Everglades while a few *jefes* from Miami run around thinking they're going to be the next president of Cuba. The next Castro. Liberators."

"You don't care about your country?"

"This is my country. I was born here."

"Your father came here from Cuba."

"So I'm supposed to go back there?"

Luis shook his head. "Next week we're sending men over there."

Ramon laughed. "You mean you're invading Cuba?"

Luis nodded solemnly. "A dozen men are going in."

"You're crazy," Ramon said. "Where's the support coming from?"

"The stuff you took over on the boat."

143

"Boxes of soap and razors?" Ramon asked.

Luis nodded. "There were enough guns and ammunition to arm them for a few days of quick strikes, enough to immobilize the country until a larger force that will be aboard boats in the Straits can come in."

"Who are these guys?"

"Cubans. Men with families back there who want to be able to return."

"Soldiers?"

"Men who have been training in the Everglades for a year."

"And Guillermo is your contact in Cuba."

"One of them. There are several groups of dissidents we've been in contact with there for more than a year." It seemed to Ramon there was a touch of pride in Luis's voice.

"And what about you, Luis? Where will you be?"

If Luis heard the tone of rebuke in Ramon's voice, he ignored it. "At home," Luis said.

Ramon brushed his hand in front of his face, clearing away the smoke. "Yeah," he said, "I guess you're right. The commander can't take any chances."

Luis smoothed his dark eyebrows and glared at Ramon.

FIFTEEN

A wide-hipped woman with heavy legs and hair the color of a peeled banana stood in Oreste Villareal's office. She held a cigarette lightly between her first and second fingers, her arm bent at the elbow and wrist so that the cigarette was never more than a few inches from her mouth. Smoke wound up through her bleached hair. With her free hand she carded through the thick Rolodex on Villareal's desk.

Tony stood leaning against the fake wood paneling. Mrs. Villareal had taken over the running of her husband's cab company. He asked her about Oreste. "Is laying up there in Miyami in Yackson Memoria. A veyetable." A vegetable in Jackson Memorial Hospital in Miami, Tony deciphered.

She was on her second cigarette, and he'd only been there fifteen minutes. It was eight-ten in the morning. He'd been prowling around since six this morning, when Kay, true to her word, had kissed him briefly, not letting it get charged, and sent him on his way.

He ate breakfast in a Cuban diner and dawdled over the paper and coffee, deciding not to drive back to Big Pine until later in the day. Shortly before eight he went to Villareal's cab company and was told that Mrs. Villareal would be in at any minute.

She walked in wearing tight stretch pants and a tuniclike

145

shirt, and after Tony introduced himself she invited him back to the office.

"You wanna know why that *bastardo* Ramon shoot Oreste, I tell you." She dragged on the cigarette.

Tony did want to know, although he hadn't gotten around to asking yet. Mrs. Villareal was looking for a name in the Rolodex, someone, she said, who might know something about Angel Lopez. Tony had told her he was looking for Angel.

"Is because Ramon is yealous."

"Why was he jealous?" Tony asked.

Mrs. Villareal seemed to find the card she was looking for. Tony watched while she put the cigarette in her mouth, leaned over the desk, and copied the name and particulars from the Rolodex onto a piece of paper.

"Is yealous because Oreste is better bidness man."

Somehow Tony found it hard to believe that Ramon Marquesa shot Oreste Villareal simply because Ramon envied the other's business acumen, but he didn't question her interpretation. She probably knew the motivation of Cuban men better than he. Or she was just guessing; it was equally possible that she knew nothing of Oreste's business dealings or his relationship with Ramon. One thing Tony had observed of Latin males was that they seldom communicated the details of their work to their women.

Tony took the paper Mrs. Villareal held out to him. "What about Angel Lopez?" he asked. "Did he and Oreste know each other well? Did they get along?"

Mrs. Villareal shook her head. Ash crumbled from her cigarette and dusted her tunic. "Talk to that man. He tell you everyt'ing you want to know."

Tony folded the paper and put it in his pocket.

"You know what I got to do now?" Mrs. Villareal asked, lighting her third cigarette.

Tony shook his head.

"I got to decide if I gonna let them pull the plug on Oreste."

Tony walked back through the outer office and out to his truck.

*   *   *

HAVANA HUSTLE

The fifteen-hundred block of Duval Street overlooked the Atlantic. Half the block was taken up by a sprawling wooden building with Victorian verandas wrapping around its three-storied southern exposure. Most of the glass windows were shattered on the upper floors, and its old wood had turned gray with age. It was like a fossilized dinosaur. The fact that the building had somehow escaped renovation made it even more of an anachronism.

Two or three stately homes occupied what was left of the block on either side of the street. A long wooden pier teed out from the shore a hundred feet into the Atlantic.

Tony parked the truck in the street and walked down the block looking for 1503, the number Mrs. Villareal had written down for him. Though there was no number on the dinosaur, after checking those on the nearby homes Tony came back to its entrance and walked through the wide double doors.

At one time the building had been a hotel.

The Cuban-tiled floors were dull; a couple of potted palms gathered dust near the mahogany counter that presumably had once served as a registration desk. From somewhere in the interior Tony could hear the whine of a circular saw. Perhaps renovation was claiming the place after all.

He walked along a hallway toward the sound of the saw. The place was cleaner than he would have expected for an abandoned building. Except for the broken windows, it had the appearance of having recently been vacated. There were even some framed photographs of the overseas railroad on the walls along the hall.

Tony found a couple of carpenters working in what at one time must have been a ballroom. One of them looked up when Tony came in.

"I'm looking for Addie," Tony said.

"Try the Birdcage," the carpenter replied.

The Birdcage was a bar, separate from the main building and tucked away among the interior grounds so that it escaped the tourist traffic—which it was apparently meant to do. It was shaped like a cupola, and the inside was covered in glass and mirrors and beaded curtains.

During the six months he had lived in Key West Tony

had visited the Birdcage once. He found his way through the maze of halls and pathways through the garden that had also been kept up. He stepped inside.

An overhead fan sifted the air. Billie Holliday was singing about a motherless child on a scratchy tape, and a man sat alone at the bar drinking beer from the bottle, talking to a young woman who couldn't have been much over the legal drinking age, standing behind the bar. The man didn't pay any attention to Tony when he sat down a few stools away. It was barely nine o'clock in the morning.

The girl came over, and Tony asked for a Rolling Rock, which she plucked from a cooler set in front of him on a tattered cardboard mat. "I'd like to buy him one, too," Tony said, motioning to the only other early-morning drinker.

When the girl put the beer in front of him the man turned slowly and looked at Tony.

He had stringy gray hair that fell to his shoulders. His face was gaunt, puffy around the eyes, and his frayed white shirt was open, revealing a butterfly tattooed across a hairless chest so thin that his bones were clearly defined.

"Addie?" Tony asked.

"Joseph K. Addison the third," the man said, plucking a Camel from the pack on the bar and lighting it.

"What does the K stand for?" Tony asked.

"Beats the hell out of me." Addie laughed.

"Oreste Villareal's wife gave me your name. Part of it, anyway."

"I didn't know that was your name," the girl behind the bar said.

"That's because you were born yesterday, honey. Thirty years ago when I came here I was J. K. Addison the third. Now look at me. A major improvement, wouldn't you say?" He laughed again, reaching across the bar, and stroked the girl's forearm. "Oreste's wife? What does Maria want?"

"She thought you might be able to help me," Tony replied. "I'm looking for someone."

Addie didn't speak, but something in his rheumy eyes changed. He took a swig of beer.

"Angel Lopez," Tony said.

Addie shook his head. He ground out the cigarette in an ashtray. "Honey, give us a six-pack to take up to my room."

The girl filled up a six-pack carton and set it on the counter. "I'll be back later," Addie said to her. And to Tony: "So Ramon's in trouble again." He grinned. "Follow me."

When he stood up and walked out of the bar Tony could see that both of Addie's skinny legs were deformed, which left him walking with a kind of stutter step.

Addie was the abandoned hotel's lone occupant. He had lived there, he explained to Tony on the way to his room, for more than ten years. The owners wanted a caretaker, someone on the premises to look after the building and keep up the grounds while they decided what to do with the place. When he first moved in Addie had expected to be out in a year, two at the most.

They rode up to the third floor in the service elevator, the only one that still worked. Addie was in room 313, for good luck, he said.

It was a room with an ocean view and not much else. A single unmade bed with grimy sheets that had once been white was pushed up against the wall. A table beside the bed seemed to hold the majority of his personal possessions; loose change, bottles of various drugstore remedies, packs of opened cigarettes, and an overflowing ashtray. On shelves beneath it were stacks of worn paperback books. Round the walls were snapshots of girls, most of them in bathing suits. Tony recognized in one of them the tall girl from the bar. Empty bottles gathered dust in one corner. Clothes were scattered around the floor, mostly shorts and sneakers, and there was a damp moldlike smell in the room despite the open windows.

Addie whipped some clothes off the one and only chair and invited Tony to sit down while Addie opened two beers, putting the other four in a room-service refrigerator.

"Not exactly home sweet home, but it's free." Addie sat down on the rumpled bed and lit another Camel. He blew out a ring of smoke and said, "I told Angel to get out from

149

under Ramon while he had a chance, but he wouldn't listen."

"You and Angel were friends?"

"We go back a ways, you might say. I had a notion some years ago to set up an independent company, one, maybe two cabs, not radio dispatched, keeping the overhead low. A job for me and one other person, someone like Angel."

"Let me guess. Ramon didn't care for the idea?"

"You got it, Toyota."

Addie got up from the bed and emptied the ashtray into a paper bag sitting in another corner of the room. He limped back to the bed in his peculiar gimpy walk.

"Joseph K. Addison the third," he said, by way of nothing. Shook his head and laughed. "You from up north?"

"Big Pine."

Addie laughed again. It was a rasping laugh that usually brought on a coughing attack, but there seemed to be genuine pleasure in it nonetheless. "That's far enough north. Some would even say a foreign country. You're out of the warp of this place, anyway. Me, I'm from Boston. Banking family. Winthrop and all that bullshit. Couldn't wait to get away from it. I came down here when I was twenty-one with a trust fund and a hard-on. A doomed combination."

"I take it you didn't start your cab business?"

"Yeah, I started it. It just didn't last long."

"Angel in on it with you?"

"No, Angel saw which way the wind was blowing. I was still a smart-ass Yankee. I was also learning how to drink and how to keep my friends drinking, which was an easier lesson. But never let it be said that we didn't have a good time." Addie smiled inwardly.

"How did he get you?"

"Ramon?"

Tony nodded.

"Put a hole through my kneecaps with a .22 or .32, I don't remember which. Something small."

Tony winced.

Addie shrugged. "The price you pay for an education."

"You didn't report it."

Addie shrugged again. "What for? I could still walk. What

was I going to do, let him cut my legs off altogether? That was twenty-five years ago. In those days the Marquesas ran the town. Ramon thinks he still does."

"What do you think?"

"You're looking for Angel, aren't you?"

Addie drank the remaining six-pack and smoked half a pack of Camels while he talked. Tony kept prodding him for information, but by the time Addie started on his fifth beer Tony could see he would get nothing more. Addie had talked at length about Ramon and Angel. And himself. He had become, in a sense, what he had set out to become. An eccentric, a local character. There was still a trickle of the trust fund left.

Enough, Addie said, to keep an abundance of beautiful young friends at his side.

As Tony was getting up to leave Addie said, "I hear Ramon's got religion."

Tony stopped at the door. "What do you mean?"

"A born-again," Addie replied. "The Coast Guard saved his life, pulled him out of the drink on Easter morning. He ascended."

Tony smiled. "You believe it?"

"Hey," Addie said. "A lot of guys have saved their skin with that shit. Who's to say?"

And this was the problem, Tony thought, walking out the door. Who was to say?

If Mingo had said anything about his encounter with Tony Harwood the other night, it didn't show on Angel Lopez's wife's face when she opened the door and Tony introduced himself. He told her he was looking for her husband. She smiled, said her name was Maria Elena, and invited him in.

The front door opened into the living room, and Tony stepped inside, following Maria Elena, who motioned for him to sit down on the couch. The room was carpeted, heavily furnished, and filled with framed photographs of children displayed on the coffee table in front of the couch, on the mantel over the fireplace, on the TV, and hanging on the walls.

A shrine with religious relics and a picture of Jesus was in one corner.

"Something to drink?" Maria Elena wore a pair of slacks and what appeared to be a hand-knit sleeveless sweater with a loose-knit weave through which her bra was clearly visible.

"I'm fine, thanks," Tony said. "I won't take up much of your time. Just a few questions."

"I'm sorry," Maria Elena said, sitting down in an armchair with frilly slipcovers. "Who did you say you're working for?"

"The state attorney's office," Tony replied.

"Someone from that office already called me."

"I understand. I just need more details."

Maria Elena nodded.

"Did your husband talk about going away at all, mention any trips he had planned?"

"Angel wasn't much of a traveler," Maria replied. "I doubt he's been away from Key West half a dozen times in ten years."

"He seem depressed? Did you notice anything unusual in his behavior?"

Maria seemed to give the question some thought. "No," she said. "He has ulcers, but he was taking his medication, so there was nothing unusual."

"What kind of medication?"

"Tagamet, I think."

Tony wrote it down in his notebook. Then Maria Elena started talking. She went through the history of the family, the kids, the grandchildren, and where everyone was living. It went on and on, a guided tour through banal family experiences. She seemed neither happy nor sad, simply incapable of shutting up. As though she'd been through this litany a million times. It was her life, and repeating it sustained her.

Each time Tony interrupted her she'd take off on a new tack, eventually, however, converging on the same conversation: family. He thought about asking how Charlie Mingo fit into this history but decided against it.

Thinking she might reveal something, he tried to give her his attention, but after half an hour he was having trouble staying awake. He stood up, looking at his watch.

Maria Elena laughed. "Oh. This is probably so boring."
Tony offered a compliant smile and said, "I'm sorry. I've got another appointment."

Tony sat through the waiting and the paperwork preliminary to his AIDS test, thinking about Kay and Addie. Angel and Ramon. It was a sobering moment. He could look up and watch the distinct click of the second hand as it ticked over on the quartz clock on the wall above the reception desk. It was like a jury trial. People came in and were never the same when they walked out, waiting for the jury to pronounce them free or condemn them to death.

He felt his innocence without being able to prove it. There were, after all, those first few early months in Big Pine when he'd indulged himself sexually with people he barely knew. His period of penance. Paying for his perceived sin of busting open Ricky Lee's skull with a nightstick. Hadn't he paid for that?

He wondered if Kay had already been in here.

Addie was an interesting guy, one of those kids who'd grown up with all the advantages, then decided to chuck it, but he'd hung on to enough loot to insure a measure of pleasure. Angel was something else. He was no angel, but an opportunist who was always going to be there holding your hat out to you, brushed and blocked, a big grin on his face. Just the sort of guy you didn't want talking to the state attorney when the chips were down.

It was all information. History. Connections, not unlike those kids' games where you had to connect the dotted lines to figure out the puzzle. Maybe something would lead to Angel Lopez, and maybe it wouldn't. He had no way of knowing. It was a process just identifying all the puzzles. Through Addie Tony had been able to connect some more dots, and the puzzle pieces were beginning to take shape.

His eyes found the second hand on the clock once more. It was eleven-thirty. He'd promised Tom Knowles he'd help this afternoon with the construction on the room addition to his trailer. Jack's room.

SIXTEEN

The cinder-block footings were in and the concrete had set up by the time Tony got back to Big Pine Key. He worked beside Tom and Nan, beginning the process of framing in the ten-by-eight-foot room. Tomorrow they would get the roof on and the floor down, Tom said. All that would remain would be the outside siding and the Sheetrock that was going up on the interior walls.

Nan, a worn rawhide nail bag strapped around her waist, finished nailing a two-by-four into place before holstering her hammer. "Break time," she announced. It was three o'clock. Tony went inside the trailer and came back with three cold beers. They sat in the shade and drank the beer.

"Another couple of days and you'll have a brand-new room," Nan said.

"We've got a jalousie window stored at home that will be perfect for here," Tom said. Most of the materials had come from Tom and Nan's stockpile. The entire project, they estimated, would cost Tony under a thousand dollars.

He hoped it would be worth it. His world of seclusion was coming to an end. He had put in a request with Southern Bell for phone service, which was scheduled to be installed tomorrow. Jack had agreed to come down for a few days once the room was finished, but only on condition that he had a phone. Tony requested an unlisted number.

"I also found a daybed at a yard sale," Nan said. "It would be perfect in here." She had agreed to give the room a little decorative touch when Tony told her Jack was coming.

Jack had not only taken an active interest in finding Wyatt Anderson, he had also managed to determine that Wyatt had come to the Keys. Now that Jack was coming down, however, Tony began to have second thoughts—especially after Jack told him that Helen, Wyatt's mother, was ready to follow Jack here. If she showed up, would Jack want her to stay with him in this room? If so, a daybed wasn't going to be enough.

"What does Jack like, what could we put in here that would make him feel at home?" Nan asked.

"Some cops," Tony replied.

Nan laughed. "Would a coffeepot and a small refrigerator for keeping drinks cold do?"

"Do you have one?"

"I know where we can get one cheap."

"Well," Tony said, "then in the absence of the Miami Police Department, it will have to do."

The next morning Tony drove back to Key West, stopping at the nursing home where Ramon's mother was institutionalized. An old woman with crippled fingers and palsy. Drool dripped from the side of her mouth, forming a puddle in the crease of her housedress when she was rolled out in a wheelchair to meet him. What a way to finish your life, Tony thought.

The nurse's aide who brought her out spoke to the woman as though she were a child. Which, in effect, she was. There was something luminescent about her eyes, and the skin on her face had begun to tighten against her skull; thin wisps of white hair were all that covered her head. She stared without recognition while a constant smile played across her thin blue lips—the expression of an infant. Berena Marquesa, the senator's wife.

He spoke to her, called her Mrs. Marquesa, asked how she was, and got only the bobbing head and the smile for a

155

reply. The nurse's aide left them. They sat and looked at each other, but Tony was unable to coax anything from her.

They were in the hallway of the convalescent center, Tony sitting in a plastic chair, patio furniture, while people moved through the hall. He was about ready to leave when another woman in a motorized wheelchair appeared. She came up and squeaked to a stop. Mrs. Marquesa turned and looked at the new arrival, her expression unchanged.

"Berena's not much company," the other woman said, looking at Mrs. Marquesa. "She was okay when she first came in here, but after five years ..." She let the thought go by.

"Does she get many visitors?" Tony asked.

"Not many. Once a month maybe someone from her family comes out."

"Her sons?"

"Her son Luis and his family. The other one came for the first time the other day."

"Ramon."

The old woman shook her head. "A shame, really. He hadn't been here in a couple of years. When he shows up Berena didn't know him. And her husband a muckity-muck in Tallahassee all those years."

Tony followed Mrs. Marquesa's gaze along the distant corridor, as if all those years as a prominent state senator's wife were simply waiting at the end of the hall to be relived.

"There was one person who used to come some and see her, but I haven't seen her in a long time," Mrs. Marquesa's spokeswoman said. "She looked foreign. You know—" The woman put her fingers to her temples and pulled back her eyes.

"Oriental?" Tony asked.

"Something like that."

"Did you know her?"

"I think she had worked for the Marquesas. She used to just sit and hold Berena's hand."

"You know her name?"

"They'd have a record of her, probably, at the desk."

Tony thanked her and left Berena Marquesa smiling and

shaking, the drool overflowing now down the front of her housedress.

The woman's name was Kim Morales, and she was dead. She had died six months ago, and she had been the Marquesas' housekeeper for more than fifteen years, a nurse at the convalescent center told Tony.

He drove to the courthouse and pored over records there, learning that Kim was of Chinese descent and divorced from a Cuban with whom she'd had a child, a daughter named Oona.

Tony wrote it all down in the notebook he carried.

There were a half dozen listings for Morales in the Key West phone book, but nothing for Oona. He called a couple of the Morales numbers and learned from someone that the last they had heard, Oona was living in Miami. Two more dots were connected.

From the same phone he called Jack in Miami.

"The room's going to be ready in a couple days," Tony told Jack. "You want, I could come up and get you tomorrow."

"I think I'll drive down myself," Jack said. "Get a rental car and take my time."

"Do me a favor, then," Tony said. "I'm looking for a girl by the name of Oona Morales. She's the daughter of Kim Morales, who was a housekeeper in Key West. Oona may be living in Miami. I'd like to ask her some questions about the case I'm on."

"Sure," Jack said. "I'll see what I can find out." Distinct pleasure in his voice.

Tony hung up and continued in search of Angel Lopez.

Ramon Marquesa's cab company was on the boulevard on the way in to Key West, sandwiched between an economy motel and a chain restaurant. The office was upstairs, a tiny cubicle where a dispatcher hunched over a microphone listening to the half-garbled messages of drivers calling in fares and destinations.

The place was a hovel, the grime of handprints smeared on doorways and tables; the thin carpet had been worn through to the plywood floor in several places. Waste cans were filled with the refuse from fast-food joints, and paper was scattered everywhere.

A bulletin board on one wall contained messages for drivers and an old picture of Scotty wearing his winged cap.

"Whatcha need?" The dispatcher stuck his head through a hole that had been cut in the wall.

"I'm looking for the manager," Tony said.

"Ain't here right now." The radio squawked, and the dispatcher turned to answer it.

When he came back Tony asked, "Who's in charge now that Angel's gone?"

"Datilla's the designated hitter."

"When can I catch him?"

The dispatcher shrugged. "Like the lady says, he's in and out."

Tony nodded and walked down the narrow stairs and out back to a garage where the taxis were serviced. There was a cab on the rack, a mechanic draining old oil into a funnel and tank that sat beneath the car's oil pan.

"How's it going?" Tony asked, stepping inside the realm of grease and oil.

The mechanic, a kid in dirty jeans and a blue shirt with the company logo over one pocket, inclined his head toward Tony. "The usual," he mumbled. He stepped from under the car, picked up an open-end wrench, and began probing at a nut on the oil pan while drops of oil ran down his hand and arm.

"Tough break Scotty had the other day," Tony said.

"Yeah," came the hollow reply from beneath the car.

"His cab back on the road?"

"You kidding?" The mechanic carted the funnel out from below the car. "The motor falls out of one of these things, they'll go down for a while. Otherwise they're patched and running."

"You do the repairs on Scotty's car?"

"Yep. Back on the road the next day."

"With new brakes?"

"Just put in a new hydraulic line. What are you, insurance guy? I thought someone went through all this."

"Just double-checking," Tony said. "Did the police ever look at the car?"

"Yeah, some cop came around." The mechanic lowered the car to the floor.

"Talk to you?"

"Asked a couple of questions. Filled out a report."

"You know him?"

The mechanic snorted. "Not personally."

"A black guy named Franklin?"

"That might be his name. Why?"

Tony shook his head. "Just curious. Did you like Scotty?"

"Yeah, he was okay. Better than a lot of them. Didn't complain if everything wasn't just right."

Tony nodded. "Maybe he should have," he said, and he walked back to his truck.

It was only ten o'clock in the morning. He was having lunch with Kay at twelve. She had an hour between court appearances. Since the night he'd taken her out in the bay he'd seen her exactly twice. Each time it had been in a public place for only brief moments. He could see that she was nervous, uncertain. That she was trying to step back and assess what was happening before she proceeded. Then, the last time they were together, she'd talked about the trip to Tampa, where she was going for a job interview.

Tony drove by the Laundromat with its coffee bar. Mingo wasn't among the men who lounged outside sipping their *buches*. He drove by the other place, the little corner grocery store that had an espresso machine, where Scotty had pointed out Franklin the other day. And there he was, clutching a grease-stained paper bag while getting into the driver's side of a patrol car. There was no one else in the car.

Tony turned at the corner and drove halfway down the block, watching the blue and white cop car in his rearview mirror before finding a lane in which to turn around.

He had cruised by these *buche* places more than once in the past few days, expecting sooner or later to run into Franklin. Now Tony watched as the blue and white pulled away from the curb, deciding only on the spur of the moment to follow the patrol car.

Franklin appeared to be eating a sandwich. Tony could see him through the rear window, Franklin driving one-handed while he ate. Tony dropped back, staying two or three car lengths behind Franklin. If he was spotted, Tony thought, it didn't really matter. It might even be good; just drive up beside him at a traffic light, honk and wave, and show that there were no hard feelings, but there was recognition.

There was little more that he could do, Tony thought. Any threatening move on his part and he would be hauled to jail, where, he was sure, Franklin and the Marquesa family, if not Florida law enforcement in general, would be delighted to see him.

A slight swelling still remained where Franklin's flashlight had made contact with Tony's head. The memory of that incident did little to predispose him to any friendly gesture toward the cop.

He wondered if Franklin was responsible for disemboweling Kay's cat. If, as Kay felt, it was all related—an effort to warn them off Marquesa—then it had been a busy night for the constable who was cruising along the four-lane boulevard.

When they hit the traffic light at the city marina Tony changed lanes, paralleling the blue and white. At the red light several cars were ahead of Franklin, and Tony had to stop well short of the car in front of him to remain beside the patrol car.

He lowered his window and honked.

Franklin looked around.

Tony grinned and pointed his index finger with the thumb raised, bringing it down in a bead on Franklin's unsmiling face.

It was a silly, adolescent gesture, one that Jack would not have approved. He could hear Jack now: "You don't provoke guys like that. All they need is an excuse."

The light changed. Traffic moved, and Tony caught up with the car in front of him, turning off at the next intersection. He kept his eye on the rearview mirror. He saw the blue and white go through the intersection. Apparently Franklin had decided to ignore the provocation or, more likely, would act on it in his own way and on his own time.

SEVENTEEN

There was a crowd outside the courthouse as Kay Fulton stepped out of the elevator and went down the sidewalk for the noon recess. A trial in another courtroom had just let out, and apparently a verdict had been reached, judging from the press who were filming and firing questions at the attorneys in the case.

It was another corruption trial. A couple of local firemen had been indicted on smuggling charges and, it would appear from what she heard on her way out, found guilty.

The firemen. Police. Politicians. Judges. She was beginning to wonder if anyone in this town was untainted. She also wondered if the prosecuting attorney had been intimidated in his effort to try the case. If so, apparently the intimidation had been unsuccessful. She didn't know the attorney very well—he was one of those who thought of her as an ice queen. She thought of asking him if he'd felt any intimidation, then decided he would only laugh at her.

Kay was about to cut through the parking area to her car when someone tapped her shoulder and said, "Ms. Fulton?"

She paused and turned. A reporter with the local paper stood facing her, someone who had questioned her once or twice at the conclusion of a couple of her trials. She tried to remember his name. Paul? Peter? She had noticed in the past few weeks that she was having a hard time with names.

She'd see someone she knew but be unable to come up with the name. Was it a sign of stress?

She gave the young man in front of her a smile of recognition.

"Peter Conway, with the *Herald.*"

"Of course, I remember."

"I'd like to ask you about the Marquesa case."

They were standing in the middle of the driveway in the sun. She could feel the heat reflected off the concrete through the thin-soled leather of her shoes. She was supposed to meet Tony for lunch, then go back into the courtroom for another round with Judge Grabill.

"There's not much I can tell you," Kay said. A car came through the driveway, and they stepped to the side of the courthouse.

"Has a trial date been set yet?" Peter had his notebook out, a pencil poised.

"No, not yet," Kay said.

"Is there some delay?"

Kay smiled. What a story she could give him. Yes, there was some delay. "Just the usual procedural entanglements," she said.

"When do you expect to go to trial?"

"I'll find out this afternoon."

"Judge Grabill?"

Kay nodded.

"Do you expect any difficulty?"

Kay said, "Off the record?"

Peter nodded.

"If I were you, I'd be in the courtroom," she said. "It might be interesting."

Interesting. She had interviewed Coral more—spent several hours with her, in fact—and was convinced she had enough evidence to present to Grabill to insure that he would set a trial date.

Until last night Kay had thought the problem was going to be protecting Coral. With Angel Lopez missing or dead it had seemed unlikely that Coral would be safe once her name was mentioned in court. Kay didn't want the weight of that responsibility. She thought of going to the police and asking for protection for Coral, but after the incident with Tony the other night the police seemed an unlikely source of help.

Then last night Coral had called. Ramon, she said, had been in the restaurant. Had even apologized to her. Gave her money, a hundred-dollar bill. Coral was, in her words, blown away.

Was Ramon threatening? Kay asked her.

No. The strange thing was he was sober, seemed genuinely sorry.

Ramon? This didn't track.

Did he mention the trial at all, like he knew she was going to testify? Kay asked.

No, not a word. Ramon told her he'd taken Christ into his life. He was born again.

No.

Yes.

Did she believe him?

Coral's laugh answered her.

Kay asked who he was with, and the man Coral described fit Luis's description.

So Ramon had been dining with Luis, working out a strategy, creating an image of a man who has made some mistakes but has been saved, his life turned around.

Coral was more willing than ever to testify.

Kay was wary. Tomorrow she was going to Tampa for a job interview. She would fly up in the morning and get back that night. If she got the job, she was considering resigning her position here and living on her savings while she made the move and got situated.

It was running away, a cop-out. But she couldn't help it. She would come back from Tampa and tell Randall Welch that she had to drop the Marquesa case. And what reason would she give him? She would tell him her family situation had deteriorated, something he already knew.

But it hadn't. It was more confusing, but it was not getting any worse. She could even see some improvement. Brad seemed more sober, claimed he was cleaning up his act, as he put it. And in fact, he'd been helping out with Patty more recently, not just demanding her at the times he wanted to see her, but actually taking care of her when Kay needed someone. She had begun to have a measure of trust in him again, knowing, of course, that things could easily swing back in the other direction.

Brad had even commented obliquely the other day on the possibility of their getting back together. A possibility she refused to consider, though she didn't say so to Brad for fear it might set him back.

. Then there was Tony. She liked him, was drawn to him in some feral way that was totally unexpected. It was like a part of her she didn't recognize and over which she had little control; it frightened her. She would be brought up short sometimes, in the middle of doing something, and have this wave come over her: desire that left her weak and shaken. What was going on?

Contradictions swirled around her. One minute she told herself she had to end it with Tony, that she wasn't ready for this kind of dizzying emotional ride. There were things she had to do, to get resolved in her life before she became involved with anyone. She had wanted to take a couple of years after splitting up with Brad to level out while she concentrated on her relationship with Patty, on being a good mother. But then another internal voice urged her on with Tony, to pursue her pleasure.

It was confusing.

Patty even sensed that there was some change in the atmosphere. Kay didn't think she felt threatened by it, but Patty had mentioned to Brad that Mommy had a boyfriend.

Brad had laughed about it when telling her the other day—Kay had made some offhand comment—but before leaving he'd asked her to keep her options open.

Kay got in her car and drove to the restaurant where she was meeting Tony for lunch.

He was seated at a corner table in a café, part of one of the newer hotels overlooking the harbor, when she came in. He stood up, leaning toward her, his arms open as she approached the table. She had decided that she wasn't going

164

to kiss him, then changed her mind, briefly touching her lips to his.

Despite whatever resolve she might have had for subduing her feelings, she felt her heartbeat quicken.

"It's good to see you." Tony held the chair for her as she sat down.

"You, too," she replied. And it was. A genuine pleasure to see him. Life was so complicated.

"I talked to Addie yesterday, and to a friend of Ramon's mother at the convalescent center."

"Addie?"

"Joseph K. Addison the third." Tony smiled. "He's got a room at the old vacant hotel at the other end of Duval Street."

"Oh, yes." She remembered now. He was a familiar sight, limping along Duval Street, although she wasn't sure she had ever known his name. Addie.

A waiter brought them menus and took their drink orders. Kay asked for iced tea; Tony ordered coffee.

"I didn't know he was linked to Ramon."

"Ramon shot him in the knees, crippled him," Tony said. "Several years ago."

Kay shook her head. Ramon Marquesa was literally getting away with murder. And she was running away from prosecuting him. She looked at her menu.

"What about Angel Lopez?" Kay asked.

"I'm working on some leads."

"Promising?"

"I don't know yet."

"I go before Judge Grabill this afternoon."

"With the other witness, right? The waitress who agreed to testify."

"Coral called last night. Ramon has got religion. He's been born again."

Tony smiled. "So I heard from Addie. You believe that?"

The waiter brought their tea and coffee, then took their orders.

"Cynically, no," Kay said. "But cynicism comes too easily in this profession."

"If Ramon has undergone a personality change," Tony

165

said, "then what? He comes into court and begs forgiveness, pleading he is one of God's innocents?"

"Or temporary insanity," Kay said, doctoring her iced tea. "I don't have any idea what he's going to do, but I'm scared to bring up Coral's name. I don't like taking responsibility for the girl's life just to get evidence I can't even be sure will convict him."

"What does she say?"

"She's not backing down."

"Then go for it."

Kay paused. "I've been thinking about asking Welch to relieve me of the case," she said.

Tony sat back in his chair and looked up at the ceiling.

"You can't do that," he said.

"I'm going to Tampa tomorrow for an interview for another job."

"Why?"

She couldn't tell if he was hurt or angry. "Because I've got a responsibility to my life, and my daughter."

"And what about Ramon Marquesa?"

She laughed. "If you're going to suggest that I've got a responsibility to see justice done, please don't. Look at Ramon's victims. I don't want another one."

He stared at her, and she felt that same wave of desire come over her.

"Then what about you and me?" he asked.

Kay shook her head. This was her chance, the opportunity to say bang, whir, thank you, sir. But she couldn't do it. Her emotional confusion reigned. In his presence she wanted to reach out, touch him, grovel even. Yes, she could grovel again in that swamp where lust had been rekindled the other night—little did anyone know, least of all her male colleagues, of the smoldering embers that lay beneath her cool exterior; there were times, however, when she could surprise even herself.

Nevertheless, she answered him indirectly. "I don't know," she said. "I'm just playing it by ear."

When their food arrived she welcomed the temporary distraction it provided, then changed the subject and asked him about life on Big Pine Key.

"I'm having a room added to the trailer, and my stepfather's coming down."

"Isn't he a cop? What's his name?"

"Jack Dowd. He's retired. But he's looking for that boy who disappeared."

Kay nodded. They talked about families, aging parents. Tony told her about Jack and Beverly taking him in when he was fourteen. She thought about her own parents, her father a lawyer, her older brother a lawyer back in New Jersey, where she had grown up. It was the only profession she'd ever considered. Now she was beginning to wonder if she was really cut out for it. But what else could she do?

"What do we know about Ramon's sudden conversion?" Tony asked.

"Not much more than I told you. He was having dinner with Luis last night in the Bali Ha'i. Coral waited on them."

"Luis," Tony said reflectively. "Maybe it's time to have a talk with Luis."

"Be careful," Kay said. "He's quiet, but don't underestimate him." She looked at her watch. In twenty minutes she was due in court. When the waiter came to take their plates she declined dessert; he refilled Tony's coffee cup.

Kay looked at Tony. "You could be interested in a woman with a kid?"

Tony smiled. "I don't know," he said. "I'm just playing it by ear."

Kay laughed. "Touché. I've got to be in court in a few minutes," she said, and she stood up. "I'll be right back."

He stood with her and held her chair. She walked down a corridor to the women's room and went inside. Another woman was there, standing at the mirror, powdering her face. Kay used the toilet. When she came out the other woman was gone. Kay washed her hands before running a comb through her hair. She felt a tingle of expectant excitement.

When she came out Tony was standing in the narrow, darkened corridor outside the door. She was glad he was there. He opened his arms, and she leaned into him, kissed him. The response was immediate; their bodies fit, clinging together like silk to skin. She pressed against his lips, the warm moistness of his mouth, and savored the taste of coffee on his breath. She could feel the urgency, the desire for connection. She ran her fingers through his hair, held his face, withdrew, looked at him, then kissed him again. Longing that seemed unbearable. With one hand she reached behind her and found the doorknob to the restroom.

She pushed open the door, and without breaking their connection they stepped inside. Kay closed the door, locking it.

Judge Grabill smiled rakishly. "So glad you could make it, Miss Fulton," he said from the bench. "It wouldn't have been the same without you."

Kay fiddled with the button on her suit jacket. She felt disheveled, and not just sartorially. She was emotionally wrung out. Still, she managed to give Grabill a smile as she stood before the prosecutor's table.

At the defense table Ramon's defense attorneys smiled, too, as though they all belonged to a secret club and shared a joke to which she would never be privy.

Ramon Marquesa, she noted, was absent.

Grabill put on his glasses and shuffled some papers in front of him. After a moment he said, "Miss Fulton, I believe you were going to present the court with evidence to show cause for proceeding in the matter of the state versus Ramon Marquesa. Are you prepared to do that?"

"Your honor," Kay said, "if it please the court, I have a witness in this case who wishes for obvious reasons to remain anonymous for the time being but who is prepared to give testimony against Ramon Marquesa—"

Grabill banged his gavel. He glared at her over the tops of his glasses. "Miss Fulton, would you and the defense attorneys come to my chambers? Now." He swept from the room.

Kay picked up her briefcase. As she went out the door she saw Peter Conway, the *Herald* reporter, seated in the back row of the courtroom.

She sat opposite the defense attorneys at the large conference table in the judge's chambers. Grabill stood, leaning over the table, looking like a shrike about ready to pounce.

"I warned you, Kay. Come up with something tangible or this case goes out the window. And the best you can do is present us with a mystery witness!" Grabill looked at the defense attorneys, who seemed unperturbed by this turn of events.

"Judge, we only request that a trial date not be set until we have clear proof that there's evidence to support it. Not innuendo."

"My thoughts exactly," Grabill said. He turned to Kay. "Name names, or I'm throwing this case out for lack of evidence."

Kay hesitated. Coral had given her assent. It was now or never. "Coral Hennessey," Kay said. "She's a waitress at the Bali Ha'i."

Grabill looked to Ramon's lawyers. "Will three days be enough time for you?"

They nodded.

"Then we'll reconvene at nine on Friday morning." As they all stood up Grabill shot Kay a dirty look.

RAMON

═══

One of the lawyers had gone back to Miami. "What do you need two of us down here for?" Lyle said. "It's open and shut." Lyle was in his fifties, Ramon guessed. He wore a rumpled suit with thick-soled leather shoes and walked as if he had fragile bones.

Ramon had on his Jesus Saves T-shirt tucked into his elasto-shorts, and a pair of flip-flops on his feet. They were in a room the Miami attorneys had taken in one of the law offices along Whitehead Street across from the courthouse. There was a desk and the boxed files the lawyers had built up on the case.

"You know this girl?" Lyle handed Ramon a sheet of paper with Coral Hennessey's name on it.

"Yeah, I know her," Ramon said. "She's a waitress at a restaurant I go to."

"Right. What's she got against you?"

Ramon shrugged. "I don't know. I gave her a hundred-buck tip the other night."

"A hundred bucks?"

"Well, she probably put up with some crap from me in the past. I don't know, it seemed like the right thing to do at the time."

Lyle shook his head and smiled. "Did you know this girl was going to testify against you?"

170

"No," Ramon said. "How would I know?"

"Well, she was. Is. Now I want to know what that crap was she had to put up with."

"Hey," Ramon said. "The usual kind of thing. I came on to her, gave her a hard time. You know, I was a jerk."

"What do you mean you came on to her?"

"Maybe I touched her in the restaurant, you know the kind of thing. I was drinking. I probably said stuff to her, too."

"She says you were talking about killing Oreste Villareal."

"She's full of shit."

Ramon snapped the rubber band he'd taken to wearing around his wrist to remind him of his language. He couldn't believe how hard it was to change the way he talked. Stuff just came out.

"So she's vindictive, then, out to get you?"

"How do I know?"

"Or maybe she was scorned. You were teasing, she responded, then you backed off. How about that? You ever see her outside the restaurant?"

"No, no way," Ramon said.

Lyle sighed. "Well, vindictive, then. We're running a background check on her. We'll dig up her past. Either way I'll destroy her on the stand."

"I don't want to see that happen."

Lyle stared, his mouth open.

"I'll talk to her," Ramon said.

Lyle seemed bemused. "You're different," he said. "You're definitely different."

Ramon conceded that he'd undergone some changes. He took out a crumpled envelope from his pocket and handed it to the attorney. "It's a deed to some property I own. I want to give it to the church."

"You mean you want to write it into your will?"

"No. I want the deed transferred to St. Stephens now."

Lyle now appeared bewildered.

"You can do that for me?"

Lyle took out the deed. "I suppose I can," he said.

"Good," Ramon said. He turned to leave.

171

"I wouldn't get anywhere near Coral Hennessey," Lyle said. "She's still a witness for the prosecution."

"Fuck that," Ramon said. Pop, pop. Snapping the rubber band twice as he went out the door.

From the law office Ramon drove to the bank and used his bank card to withdraw five hundred dollars from an ATM. He put the bills at the Beatitudes inside a copy of the New Testament that he kept in the car.

Her name and address were right there on the papers Lyle had shown him. Coral Hennessey, 712 Simonton Street. It was nine-thirty in the morning when Ramon parked, walked up on the porch, and knocked on the door.

"I'll call the police," Coral said when she opened the door. She had on a nappy bathrobe, and her hair was uncombed.

Ramon held up the Bible he'd brought with him. "What for?" he said. Through the screen, with its broken webbing, he could see that inside the house was a hovel. "I'm not going to hurt you."

"I don't know what you're doing, but I don't want to see you here. You're trespassing."

"I just talked to my lawyer. He's running a background check on you. They want to destroy you."

Coral stared at him. "You came around here to tell me that?"

"And to give you this." Ramon held up the Bible again.

"I don't believe in that crap."

"Neither did I. But you have to watch for signs in life, stuff that can change your life, help you."

"What kind of weirdo are you?"

"Check out the Beatitudes."

"The what?"

" 'The meek shall inherit the earth.' "

"Get out of here."

"I'll leave it in your mailbox." Ramon put the Bible in the basket that was tacked to the front of the house.

Coral didn't look so meek in that robe, her hair all frizzed out like she'd just gotten out of bed, Ramon thought. Well, at least he'd tried. Now he'd have to go and buy another Bible.

Ramon drove over to Luis's to comfort Lourdes.

Lourdes said, "I'm scared."

She looked scared, too. On the verge of tears, her eyes were swollen and startled. She looked as if she hadn't gotten much sleep the night before. Ramon put his hand around her shoulders. "Tell me," he said.

"Guys are calling here all hours of the night," Lourdes said. "Something is happening. I can feel it."

"Yeah, something is happening, all right."

"You know about it?"

Ramon hesitated. "Where's Luis?"

"Down at the docks in Stock Island."

"What's he doing down there?"

"Some guys showed up in a Ryder truck, and he went there with them," Lourdes said. "Tell me what's going on."

"I'll tell you if I were you, I'd take the kids and go away for a while. Go up and see your parents, or visit some friends."

"Oh, God!" Lourdes said.

"Yes, and start praying."

EIGHTEEN

Datilla, "the designated hitter" for the missing Angel Lopez, was an ex-jock whose sports activity appeared to be confined to pressing the channel changer for the large-screen TV in Angel Lopez's office.

"The trouble is they're all hotshots now," Datilla said. "You see that? Look at that on the replay."

Tony had distractedly been aware of the play, a ground ball hit hard to the shortstop, who bobbled it. Now he watched it again in slow motion, saw the ball bounce off the shortstop's outstretched glove.

"Get in front of the damn ball!" Datilla shouted. "See. They don't want to stick with the basics. They all play for the camera, mugging it up."

Tony nodded and unwrapped two sticks of gum, putting them both in his mouth. Baseball bored him. Datilla had played Triple A ball in Sarasota a couple of seasons, he told Tony, before an injury cut short his career ten years ago. He was lanky, his muscular arms flexing in his T-shirt as the next batter stepped into the box. Despite Datilla's perennially boyish face, fat was beginning to spread over the waist of the jeans that he wore low on his hips.

Angel's office was on the ground floor, a private cubicle with one window that was filled with an air conditioner. Besides the TV, the rest of the room was taken up with a desk and file cabinets and a couch along the back wall. There were framed photos, most of them of women, some minor TV actresses in bikinis giving product endorsements. Many of the photos were signed "To Angel."

Datilla clicked off the volume on the TV with his remote control and stood watching the players move soundlessly around the diamond. He shook his head, then sighed. "I guess you didn't come in to watch the game," he said.

Tony stepped away from the wall, where he'd been looking at the photos. "No," he said. "I just stopped in to see Angel."

Datilla's face went blank. "Jesus, where you been, on another planet?"

"Practically," Tony said. "I've been away awhile."

"Well, you missed Angel. He's not around."

"You expect him?"

Datilla raised his hands, palm up. "He could walk in the door today or next year. I don't know. All I know is the boss man said go in and keep the place running. That's what I'm doing."

"I'll stop in the next time I'm in town, then," Tony said. He walked to the door, his back to Datilla, palming the gum he had in his mouth.

"You want, you can leave your name. Angel comes in, I'll let him know you were here."

Tony opened the door and turned back to Datilla. "That's all right." He smiled. "He probably wouldn't remember me anyway." He deposited the gum in the recess of the strike plate. The door automatically swung closed behind him.

A coffee shop in a motel across from the cab stand afforded a view of Angel Lopez's office. Tony dawdled over another cup of coffee and the most recent image of Kay Fulton. He tried to imagine her now, in the courtroom, presenting her request to Judge Grabill. The two images collided, fought with each other, the one in the restroom winning out. Tony savored it the way he'd savored Kay's passion—a passion that was full of tenderness, yet one in which he could also taste her fear and anger. They connected on some primal level, and he tried not to think about her walking away from it.

Half an hour later Tony watched as Datilla left the office and got into his car. Tony waited a few minutes before walking across the parking lot. He knocked on the office door. When there was no answer he tried the knob; the gum had prevented the door from locking, and Tony went inside, retrieving the gum from its slot.

Tony walked over to the desk and sifted its surface before going through the drawers. There was nothing but the usual spill of paper and office hardware, a compilation of each cabdriver's weekly booking sheets. He quickly moved over to the file cabinets and rifled through them. There were plenty of items he thumbed through that he would have liked to give more attention, but not what he needed right now. He looked at his watch. It was almost two-thirty; he'd been there less than ten minutes looking for something, anything, that might point to Angel.

He found it in a trash can. A scrawled note that looked like a phone message; a list of supplies, mostly food, booze, and videotapes. Beneath it was the notation: Ragged Key.

Addie had mentioned that Marquesa owned some islands, but without naming them. Was Ragged Key one of them?

Tony dropped the paper back in the can and started to leave. He opened the door and saw Datilla twenty feet away, walking toward the office. Datilla paused a second, surprise showing on his face, then charged Tony, cocking his fists as he ran.

"I wondered about you, motherfucker," Datilla said.

Tony held the door open, and as Datilla reached for him Tony slammed it, jamming the jock's arm in the door.

Datilla grunted. Tony grabbed his wrist and pushed it against the doorjamb, then whacked his forearm once again by slamming the door on it. Then, opening the door, Tony gathered a handful of Datilla's shirt and, pulling him into the office, hit him twice, two quick blows to the jock's expanding midsection that dropped him to the floor.

Datilla da Hun, Tony thought. And he left the office.

*　　*　　*

HAVANA HUSTLE

Addie was in the Birdcage, drunk, when Tony found him. The same girl from the other day when he'd been there was tending bar. She arched an eyebrow in Addie's direction. A couple of other people were drinking at the bar. Addie had his head on the bar, his fist gripping a beer bottle.

"Addie," Tony said.

"Hmm?"

"It's Tony."

"Who?"

"Tony Harwood."

Addie lifted his head, peered through bleary eyes at Tony, then laid his head back down on the bar. "Never heard of you," he said.

The bartender came over. "We need to get him up to his room," she said.

"Come on, Addie," Tony said. "Let's take a walk."

Addie mumbled something but offered no resistance when Tony put his arm around Addie's shoulders, supporting him while he got to his feet and hobbled out of the Birdcage leaning against Tony.

Tony walked him down to the water. "Addie, I need your help."

"And I need yours. I'm legless, man."

"I'll get you to your room," Tony said. "But do you know where Ragged Key is?"

"Heard of it."

"Does Ramon own it?"

"Might. I told you he owns a bunch of islands around here."

"But you said nobody lived on them."

"Not that I ever heard."

"Could you get me to Ragged Key?"

"No, man. I'm strictly a landlubber."

"You know somebody who could?"

"Yeah, maybe. Tomorrow."

"Tomorrow?"

"When I sober up, man."

It was late afternoon when Tony returned to Big Pine. He kept a vigilant eye on the traffic in his rearview mirror, half expecting to see Franklin giving chase, a repeat of the incident a few nights before.

If Datilla had conveyed to Ramon what had happened at the office, then it was not an unreasonable expectation. Tony doubted, however, that Datilla would have said anything about it. First, Datilla didn't know Tony. Second, there was nothing missing, and Tony had deliberately not disturbed the order of Angel's office. Finally, Datilla was a man with considerable pride, Tony thought, unlikely to want anyone to know of the humiliation he'd experienced.

The setting sun had turned the high, puffy clouds in the west the color of molten rock as Tony drove up and stopped in front of his trailer. He got out and walked around back to the room addition to see what progress had been made.

Tom Knowles was still at work. The exterior siding was up and the jalousie window fitted. Tom was hanging the door.

"Hey," Tony said. "It's beginning to look like something."

Tom smiled. "You see Nan around when you drove in?"

"No, why? She quit on you? You working her too hard?"

"I had to go into town to get some supplies and was gone for about an hour. When I got back she wasn't around."

"Probably went home to make your dinner." Tony looked at his watch. "It's almost six o'clock."

"Yeah, maybe. We were trying to get the better part of this whipped today."

"Looks like you did a pretty good job." Tony stepped inside. Nan's nail bag was lying on the floor. Sheetrock covered the back wall.

"I guess I'll hang it up for the day."

"You want a beer?"

"Sure," Tom said. "I'll put away the tools and clean up around here."

Tony went around to the front of the trailer and stepped inside. He had left the door open for Tom and Nan so that they could get cold drinks and use the bathroom.

He walked into the kitchen and started to open the refrigerator when something caught his eye.

A throw rug in the hallway leading to the bedroom and bath in the back of the trailer was twisted up on the floor.

Tony walked down the hall to the bathroom and looked

inside. Nothing was out of place. Maybe Tom or Nan had stumbled over the rug coming out of the bathroom and hadn't bothered to straighten it.

He started to return to the kitchen, then turned, deciding to check the bedroom instead.

Nan lay on the bed, on her back, as if she was taking a nap. Except her eyes were open wide and fixed in terror on a point on the far wall; it was an expression he had never seen on Nan's face, and he knew even before he reached her that she was dead.

Her head rested awkwardly on the pillow. Her throat had been cut, the life drained out of her pooling in the darkening blood that stained the bedding and the floor.

Hearing Tom outside the front door, Tony turned and walked out of the bedroom, back down the hall. Tom was standing outside, smiling, about to say something when he saw Tony's expression. Tony stepped outside.

"What happened?"

Wrapping his arms around Tom Knowles, Tony, without speaking, held his friend to him.

Big Pine's rescue service transported Nan's body to Fisherman's Hospital in Marathon after a couple of Monroe County sheriff's detectives had initiated their investigation and the county coroner had made a preliminary examination of the body.

Tom and Tony were questioned separately by the detectives. The trailer was dusted for fingerprints. It was nine o'clock before Tony was able to drive Tom back home.

Tony went in with him, offered to make them something to eat. Tom said he wasn't hungry, slid to the couch, unnerved, and asked for a drink. Tony brought out a bottle of rum from the kitchen and two glasses.

They drank and talked for two hours, during which time the phone rang half a dozen times. Tony fielded the calls from reporters for the papers and friends from Big Pine and Key West. News of the homicide had spread quickly. Tom declined to talk to anyone.

By midnight they had finished the rum. Twice Tom broke down and wept. In his grief he talked about Nan, their life

179

together, their plans. They were planning a trip to Boca Grande after they'd finished Tony's project. They were looking for another place to live. Tom rebuked himself for not doing it sooner, for not taking her desire to leave here more seriously.

Tony listened and watched, looking for any sign that Tom blamed him for this tragedy. For the moment he didn't seem to, but he didn't have to; Tony was already blaming himself. There was no doubt in his mind that this was not a random act of violence, that Nan's death was in some way connected to him.

RAMON

"**W**hat happened to you? You look like you got run over by a truck." Ramon walked into the office and found Datilla punching an adding machine with his left hand, his right arm in a sling, his face bruised and swollen.

"A guy broke in the office yesterday," Datilla said. "I caught him."

"Yeah? If you caught him, then he must be dead. Who was it?"

"Some guy who'd been around earlier asking about Angel."

"He didn't give you a name?"

"Just said he was a friend of Angel's. From out of town."

Ramon shook his head. He felt pressure in his face and neck, and some hair on his wrist had gotten caught in the rubber band, causing irritation. Funny how that little thing could keep him focused; one way or another he was always aware of it. Before he'd accepted the Lord he would have blown by now, gone over and slapped the shit out of Datilla. Pop. He scratched his wrist.

"What did he look like?"

Datilla described him. Like that actor Al Pacino in *The Godfather*.

Harwood.

"So what did he find, what was in here?"

"Nothin'," Datilla said. "I looked through everything. Nothin' was missing."

Ramon didn't believe him. He'd go through the office himself, he thought, and he'd bet he'd find something that might interest an investigator with the state attorney's office.

NINETEEN

It was a grueling day. The early morning flight to Tampa, followed by a midmorning interview with two of the senior partners in the firm she had applied to, then lunch with a junior partner who had clearly set out to impress her with both the firm and himself. He never stopped talking about the cases they had tried and his own success rate. Anecdote followed anecdote as the young, handsome attorney attempted to enhance his reputation and succeeded only in boring Kay to death. He was so intent on stroking his ego, he hadn't even been able to flirt with any success. Fortunately.

During the interview she had been questioned about her personal life, acknowledging that she was a single parent raising a six-year-old daughter. The two elderly lawyers chuckled amiably and annoyed her by suggesting that no doubt in Tampa she'd have an easier time finding a man than in Key West.

Then they wanted to know, if she were offered the position, when she would be available to make the move. She was aware of her hesitation, trying to mask it as thoughtfulness when in fact it was fear; she was afraid that she was going to be offered the job and that, confronted with a decision, would be unable to make it. At least a month, she said. She would have to give the state attorney that much notice.

Understandable. They put their papers together and asked if she had any questions. She asked how many women they had in their firm. They smiled and said none. She might be the first.

The token, she thought.

Then they suggested lunch with the junior partner.

At two o'clock she escaped from the lunch, shopped for something for Patty, and at three caught a cab to the airport. She had a four o'clock return flight to Key West and was scheduled to be back there shortly after five.

At a quarter to four it was announced that the flight had been delayed.

Kay had not told her parents she was coming for an interview, knowing they would be disappointed if she didn't stop to see them. Now, with some time to kill, she decided to call them. She found a pay phone and used her calling card to dial them direct.

She spoke first with her father, who wanted to know the details of the interview; then her mother, who related her activities. Then she wanted to know all about Patty. After talking for twenty minutes Kay was saying good-bye when her mother said, "Wasn't that murder terrible down there?"

"What murder?" Kay asked.

"It was on the news. I thought you probably knew about it."

Kay repeated her question.

"Well, it was a woman killed someplace in the Keys. I don't remember where, but not in Key West."

Her parents had visited the Keys a few times but found it too hot and oppressive and had never really paid attention to its geography. They found too many strange people there, an atmosphere conducive to just this sort of thing. They would be more than happy to see Kay leave there.

"When did it happen?"

"Sometime yesterday evening," her mother said.

Well, she would learn the details soon enough, Kay thought. She said good-bye and went to the ticket counter.

There had been a mechanical problem with the plane, she was told. They were expecting to depart at five o'clock. Which meant it would be after six when she got home. She thought about calling Brad, then decided that was unnecessary. She would get there when she got there.

Brad wasn't home. His car was gone, and no one answered the phone. When she hadn't showed up at five he'd probably taken Patty out to eat, Kay decided. Brad had never been handy in the kitchen.

Kay took a shower, put on a pair of shorts and a T-shirt, and fixed herself a drink.

She sat down on the couch and picked up the remote control unit, flipping on the TV. She found a Miami station that was broadcasting the six-thirty local news. It was six-forty-five by the wall clock. A commercial was on. When the news program returned Kay only half listened as the anchor kidded around with the sportscaster leading into his segment. That would be followed by the weather.

Kay muted the volume, walked to the phone, and called one of the female attorneys at her office. "I heard there was a murder up the Keys," she said.

"Are you kidding? Where have you been?"

"In Tampa."

"Geez. A woman was killed in Big Pine. The guy who found her is the one you hired to look for Angel Lopez."

Kay felt as if she'd been punched hard in the stomach. She even bent at the waist slightly, feeling the contraction of a cramp. "Tony Harwood?"

"That's him."

"Tell me about it."

Kay listened to what details the woman could remember. Kay began to feel really ill, worried now. Even though she was sure there could be no connection, for some reason her concern for Patty mounted. Something was wrong. She tried to tell herself to keep calm, that they'd be home soon. Maybe Brad had taken her to the miniature golf course after dinner.

Tony had said he was getting a phone hooked up. Kay dialed information and asked for a new listing. She gave his name and waited until a recorded message announced that the number was unlisted.

She went back to the couch, telling herself nothing was wrong, to stay calm. Except that she wasn't very convincing. She tried to read but couldn't concentrate.

At a quarter to eight she began calling around to Patty's friends to see if by some chance she was with one of them. No luck.

Then Kay called Patty's teacher, and yes, Patty had been in school today, and her father had picked her up this afternoon. Hearing that, Kay felt somewhat relieved, if for no other reason than that she seemed to have made contact.

She went into the kitchen and fixed herself something to eat, more to be doing something than from hunger. She found some leftover pasta that she heated up, adding to the sauce with canned tomatoes, garlic, olive oil, and basil she picked fresh from a pot in her window.

By the time she'd eaten and done the dishes it was only eight-thirty.

Keys. There was a spare set of keys, she thought, to Brad's house. She found them in a drawer in the kitchen and walked over, letting herself into his house.

Everything seemed to be in order. Which was no order, the way Brad lived. Clothes and work-related stuff were strewn everywhere. It was impossible to tell if he had taken anything with him.

She could no longer suppress the nagging suspicion. She was afraid he had taken Patty, used this opportunity to whisk her away, his recent model behavior simply a ruse to quell Kay's fears. She couldn't believe she had been so gullible.

And as if to prove it, in the kitchen there were bottles of booze on the counter, and after poking around she even found a small bag of coke.

Kay ran back home, found the number of a lawyer in Brad's office, and called him.

"Brad?" he asked, sounding surprised. "He's on vacation, starting today, the lucky stiff."

Shit.

She went into Patty's room and looked through her clothing, but nothing seemed to be missing. Of course, it wouldn't be. Brad would have thought that all out. He could buy the stuff they needed temporarily until they got where they were going, thereby not alerting her to the fact that anything was desperately wrong. Then, when they got to their final destination, they could settle down and go about replacing their possessions.

Of course, it all made sense now. Kay bit her knuckles, attempting to push back the tears. She had to keep it together, to think where he might be going. She looked in Patty's bed. The stuffed animals lying there, all of them—

Except Pooh Bear. Patty wouldn't go anywhere for any length of time without Pooh Bear. It was a concession Brad would have had to make.

She could call his parents in New Jersey, but that would be too obvious. He was not close with them anyway.

It was nine o'clock. She could call the police.

First she called around to a few of his friends, casually asking about him. No one seemed the least bit nervous talking to her or gave any indication that anything was amiss.

Would he have driven out? It was a three-hour drive out of the Keys. If they'd left when school was out, they could have been in Miami by the time Kay arrived back in Key West. If they had flown out, they could be anyplace in the country by now.

Kay got in her car and drove to the airport, wheeling around the parking lot looking for Brad's car.

She went into the terminal and asked at the counters, giving a description of Brad and Patty, asking that the manifests be checked. There was no sign that they'd taken a plane.

Kay returned home, broke into tears, and called the police.

She didn't know the officer who came to the house. He filled out a report, asking endless questions. She gave him the make and model of Brad's car. She didn't know the license number, but she might be able to find it in his house. Or by calling his insurance company tomorrow.

Tomorrow. He could be out of the country by tomorrow. She tried to remember if Brad had a passport. Patty didn't have one, unless Brad had applied for one for her without telling Kay.

"Mrs. Fulton, we'll run a check, but there's still a good chance he'll turn up. If he doesn't, you'll probably want to turn this over to the feds. If it's kidnapping and he's crossed a state line."

Was it kidnapping? They weren't divorced, and they hadn't settled the custody dispute. Patty was his as much as she was hers.

Kay remembered the bottles in the other house. The bag of cocaine. God, she thought. Don't let this happen.

She had to do something. On impulse she called Randall Welch.

"Kay," he said. "You okay?"

"No." She told him, hoping that perhaps with his clout he would be able to do something.

There was a silence on the other end of the phone.

She said, "Are you there?" She hoped he wasn't drunk.

"Kay, I have to ask you something." She recognized the tone of voice, the gentleness he could get in his voice before a reprimand.

"What?"

"Where'd you have lunch yesterday?"

She was taken by surprise, expecting something else, and had to think for a second. Where—

Damn.

She told him.

"With Harwood?"

"Yes."

Another silence.

"Kay, you were seen."

She didn't have to ask where.

"It's all over town by now," Randall said.

Damn it! This was none of his business. Anger shot through her. "What's this got to do with my missing daughter?" she demanded.

"Maybe nothing. But if Brad heard about it . . . you know, it's possible—"

Yes, possible he got pissed off and decided I was an unfit mother?

"I'm calling in desperation," she shouted. "Asking for help."

"Don't get mad." Randall tried to soothe her. "I'll do what I can. I just wanted you to know what's what."

Because you're another asshole male, she thought, with a locker-room sense of humor.

TWENTY

―――

Rogue Cop Connected to Big Pine Key Murder.

Two days after Nan's murder Tony Harwood's isolation came to a screaming halt. As they played on the sensationalism of the killing the papers once again recounted Tony's background—his suspension from Miami-Dade over the episode with Ricky Lee; the murder of a prison informant shortly after Tony had interviewed him; and the discovery of Nicki Costa's body buried in the woods south of Tallahassee.

Death stalked him. And so did the reporters from the local papers now that he had a phone and an identifiable address. Wire services were even calling.

Hoping to dispel any rumors and the sort of innuendo that had dogged him since he'd retreated to the Keys, Tony talked. He kept his remarks concise, adding nothing to the known facts surrounding Nan's death, protecting as much as possible Tom Knowles, who did not want to be confronted by the press.

Tony had stayed at Tom's place the past two nights and worked with him during the day to finish the room addition. Tom insisted on working. He did not want to sit around the house in isolation. Yesterday they had put in a ten-hour day, the day after Nan was killed, the day Tony had cleaned up the trailer once the police had stripped away their yellow crime tape and allowed him back in his home.

In the evenings they took the boat out and caught fish, which Tony cooked for their supper. Tom was mostly silent now, working through the process of his grief, and Tony was there for him if he wanted to talk, and if not, he was comfortable with the silence. They drank their rum at night and sweated it out during the day. A kind of peacefulness seemed to settle over Tom, Tony thought, an even stronger composure that came with the acceptance of something that could not be changed. Nan's funeral was the day after tomorrow. She was being cremated; her ashes would be spread across the bay that had been her backyard for so many years.

The day after Nan was killed Tony had called Jack and suggested he come down as soon as possible. Jack was good at dealing with the press, and Tony hoped he would provide additional support for Tom.

"Jack, this is Tom Knowles. Tom, my stepfather Jack Dowd." The two men shook hands. "I'm sorry about your wife," Jack said simply. As a cop Jack had had to do this often, speaking to a grieving family member, and he knew how inadequate words were. "Tony has told me a lot about you, and Nan."

Jack's room, apart from being painted, was now habitable. It lacked the small domestic touches that Nan would have added, but the daybed she had found at her last yard sale was there, and the small refrigerator was plugged into an extension cord that Tony ran from one window of the trailer.

Jack put his bag inside the room and admired the work. "You did a good job," he said, looking at Tom.

"There's still some things left to do," Tom said. "But I'll get my tools out of here and let you get settled."

Tony walked around to the front of the trailer with Jack, whose car, a rented Plymouth that in its plainness resembled the police cars he'd driven before his retirement, was parked outside.

As they went inside Jack shook his head. "How do you figure this?" he asked. "She gets killed inside here."

"I'll tell you," Tony said. "I think someone connected her

191

with me, probably thought she was my wife or girlfriend. That's what I'm afraid of."

Jack seemed to mull that over. "Ricky Lee?" he asked.

Ricky had come to mind, yes, Tony affirmed. As had Ramon Marquesa.

"Jesus. Did you mention that to Tom?"

"No," Tony said. "I didn't think it was the right time."

"I suppose not."

They didn't say anything for a moment, listening to Tom outside gathering up his tools.

"What are you going to do?" Jack asked.

"Just keep going, keep working. About all I can do."

Jack nodded. "I found only one Oona Morales in Miami," he said. "She's a radiologist with Jackson Memorial Hospital. I've got her phone number." Jack reached into his wallet and took out a slip of paper, handing it to Tony.

"I'll call her," Tony said. "Can I get you anything? You want some coffee, a beer?"

"A beer would be fine."

Tony dragged two bottles of Rolling Rock from the fridge, opened them, and handed one to Jack. Jack looked well, as well as Tony had seen him in the past year. "How's Helen?"

Jack frowned. "She's worried sick, and she wants to come down. I've tried to convince her there's nothing she could do here right now. I doubt she'll accept that for much longer."

"Maybe you weren't trying that hard to be convincing."

"Maybe." Jack smiled. "But that room's kind of small for two, isn't it?"

"Depends on how close you are," Tony replied.

"You've got a point, and I'm not sure I know the answer to that."

"It's probably something you experience rather than know."

Jack laughed. "The son teaching the father. I like this."

Tony hesitated. Then he decided, what the hell, who was he to stand in the way of love? "You want to invite her down, she can stay here. We'll work out something."

"Maybe later."

"Anything on her son?"

192

"I've managed to track him to Key West," Jack said, looking out the window into the distance.

Tony shook his head in amazement. It was just the sort of thing he should by now have learned to expect from Jack, but it still took him by surprise. Jack always underplayed everything. Deadpan.

"Congratulations." Surprise aside, Tony took pride in the swiftness of Jack's accomplishment. And of course envied him.

"Well," Jack said, "congratulations may be premature. I know he was in Key West, but I don't know where he is now."

"How'd you track him there?"

Jack shrugged. "By telephone. Still not a bad tool if you can ever get through to a human at the other end, what with all the automated crap these days."

Tony smiled. "Still, you got a line on the kid. You're narrowing things down."

"We'll see. Wyatt was traveling alone, but while he was here he hung out with some other kids from his college. They got back, Wyatt didn't. There are scooter rental agencies, the hostel where he stayed that have got records of him. Tomorrow I'll go down and do some legwork."

"You make it sound easy." Tony remembered the kid who'd drowned lying on a slab of steel in the morgue.

"The luck of the draw. I take it you're not faring so well."

Tony thought about Kay. He hadn't spoken with her since they had had lunch the other day. Yesterday she'd been in Tampa, and his time had been taken up with Tom, Nan's murder, and Jack's arrival. He should call her right away. And call Oona Morales. He remembered that he was also supposed to have gone out to Ragged Key with Addie. Things were piling up.

Tony shook his head. "It's hard to tell. I keep running into roadblocks." He gave Jack a summary of the past few days' events.

Jack whistled. "I see what you mean."

Tom came to the door and announced he was going to take his tools back to the house. Jack offered to go along.

Tony was about to sit down to call Kay when the phone rang.

"I had to use a legal maneuver to get your number," Kay said.

"I was just reaching for the phone to call you."

"My God," Kay said. "What happened? I heard something the day I went to Tampa and saw the paper this morning."

Tony gave her the details.

"It's awful," Kay said. He heard her voice tighten, the knot of emotion.

"It couldn't be any worse," he said.

"I'm afraid it could."

Tony listened as Kay related her own difficulties.

"You're sure it's Brad?" he asked when she finished.

"It's been two days. They're both gone, and I haven't heard anything."

"Who have you called?"

"The police, and yesterday Missing Persons. I'm sure he's taken Patty out of the state by now."

"Brad will contact you," Tony said. "Sooner or later he'll have to. He's got to work, to do something. He'll want to bargain with you."

"There's no bargaining. I want Patty back. That's it."

Tony wanted to say: I think you'll get her back. But he knew how absurd that would sound to Kay. Brad was high, he was on the run. When the reality of taking care of a six-year-old day in and day out set in, he'd be back. "What do you think made him choose now to take off?"

"I was gone. He'd been working up to it. And—" He heard her hesitate.

"And what?"

"We were seen the other day, the last time I saw you."

Seen.

In the restaurant. At lunch.

Oh, yes.

In a clinch. Slipping into the women's room. Together.

Oh, yes, oh, yes. Just what he needed right now, something like this to leak to the press. Rogue cop caught copulating in women's room at local hotel.

194

Still, it was the first time he'd felt like laughing in a few weeks. He tried it to see what it was like. Nervous laughter.

"I'm glad you think it's funny," Kay said.

It was funny, and it felt good. "What about Tampa?" he asked her.

"I'm not going. How could I?"

"Good," he said. "I'm coming down. I'll take you to lunch."

Kay laughed.

Oona Morales spoke beautiful English. It was studied, precise, and only in its precision could he detect that it was a learned language and not her native tongue. Tony found Oona at home, her day off. She had a good job in the radiology department at Jackson Memorial—she did not pronounce it Yackson—where Oreste Villareal was a patient, a "veyetable," according to his wife.

Tony asked Oona if she knew anything about Villareal.

"No, I'm not familiar with him," she said. "But it is a large hospital."

Tony explained who Oreste was, what had happened to him.

"That's terrible," Oona said. Sounding like a woman who had seen her share of trauma.

"I spoke with a woman who remembered your mother coming in to visit Mrs. Marquesa in the convalescent center in Key West," Tony said.

"Yes," Oona said. "She worked for the Marquesas for many years."

"Did you spend any time there?"

"My mother and I had rooms in the big house from the time I was five until I was fifteen. That was all the time I wanted to spend there."

"You must be about the same age as Ramon."

"Yes," she said. But she hesitated, and Tony thought he detected fear in her hesitation.

"How well did you know him?"

"Much better than I would have liked."

"Why do you say that?"

195

Again the hesitation before Oona said, "Ramon Marquesa raped me when I was fourteen years old."

Tony hesitated now, letting that sink in.

"Mr. Harwood," Oona said, "it has taken me years to get to the point where I can talk about it. I never mentioned it to anyone, not even my mother. Especially not my mother. But it is behind me now, finished."

Ramon Marquesa. A kid who believed that there wasn't anything he couldn't have if he wanted it badly enough. Part of his American birthright, no doubt. The land of opportunity, where any kid could grow up to be president. Except he didn't want to be president. What he wanted always belonged to someone else, and it didn't come to him via the electoral process.

"Why didn't you report it?" Tony asked.

"Why do you think? My mother needed that job. And she was also devoted to Mrs. Marquesa. I was the housekeeper's daughter. Really, Mr. Harwood, think about it. We were kids. We played together. Who was going to believe me in that town where Ramon was the son of a popular state senator?"

Yes, he understood that. Just as he understood Addie, who believed he hadn't had a chance, an outsider being beaten down by the local mafia; Scotty, who never complained. And understood Kay, who couldn't bring Ramon to trial. Everybody was a victim of a punk kid who had never grown up, never had to learn that there were some toys he couldn't play with.

"Where did it happen?"

"The Marquesas owned some islands," Oona said. "Ramon was always hanging out on them with his gangs, taking other kids out there. It happened there."

"Ragged Key?"

"It might have been," Oona said. "I don't remember. It was a long time ago, and like I said, I've tried to put it behind me."

Tony was getting into his truck when he saw Jack walking along the path back from Tom Knowles's. He waited, watching him come out of the thicket of palms and walk across the open flat toward the trailer. A flood of memories swept over Tony; all the time they had spent together, and he couldn't remember ever seeing Jack in a wilderness setting. Jack belonged to concrete; he was rooted in the glass and tile corridors of a metropolis. He seemed so out of place walking here in his city slacks and khaki shirt.

Yet Jack was smiling when he approached the pickup.

"I like your friend Tom," he said. "A resourceful guy. He'll survive this."

Tony nodded, glad that Jack found Tom companionable despite the twenty-odd years of difference in their ages. He knew that Jack would be able to tap Tom for information when Tony wasn't around. "He plays cribbage, too," Tony said.

"Yeah, we're invited over tonight," Jack said.

"I probably won't be able to make it," Tony replied. "I'm going to be in Key West. I may not get back tonight." He was hoping that Kay would ask him to spend the night.

"I thought I'd drive by the sheriff's department, see if anyone I might remember from the old days is still around. Begin getting the lay of the land."

Tony smiled. He had little doubt that Jack would find a groove here to approximate, as best he could, his habits of a lifetime.

TWENTY-ONE

"What took you so long? I haven't had a drink in two days," Addie said when Tony showed up at the hotel a day late.

"I ran into some problems," Tony said. "I couldn't get away."

"I had a boat and a captain lined up to take us out to that island. I don't know if he's still available," Addie said.

Tony walked with Addie to the dock that teed off the end of the street from the hotel. Some boats were anchored, or on mooring buoys a hundred yards out in the still, shallow water.

Several people lay or sat on the dock. Most of them had the look of street people. Addie stopped beside a young man with braided hair. "You see Gabe?" Addie asked.

The guy with the braided hair motioned toward the anchored boats.

"Five bucks for you if you'll swim out there and tell him to bring the boat in."

The guy didn't look pleased but indolently slipped into the water and started swimming.

"You got an extra five, don't you?" Addie asked Tony, grinning.

Ragged Key, five miles west of Key West, was tucked back in a chain of mangrove islands that ran to the Marquesas, ending at the Dry Tortugas. The sea around them was thin and clear as glass, covering a sea grass and sandy bottom that at a distance reflected hues of green, from a murky pea soup to the delicate clarity of lime sherbet.

Gabe maneuvered the sixteen-foot boat with its old Evinrude hanging off the stern through the backcountry channels with practiced skill. Below the snarl of curly dark hair Gabe's eyes were ice blue, his face as rubbery as a Halloween mask. He was in his forties, a water sprite who hung around the docks and the bars of Key West, doing odd jobs and running his seagoing taxi.

It was a half-hour trip to Ragged Key, or rather the nearest approach to the Key, via what was known as the "lakes," a waterway more or less protected from rough weather by the surrounding mangrove islands. When Gabe suddenly cut the motor the silence was stunning.

"That's it," Gabe said. Tony looked to where Gabe was pointing. They were a couple hundred yards from the entrance to a series of privately installed stakes that marked a channel leading to a wooden dock built over the water. A boat was tied to the dock.

The island itself was unremarkable, a few acres of tangled mangroves, their gray roots rising like bones from the sea. Tony could see a pathway leading from the dock toward the interior of the island, which was on higher ground; the mangroves had apparently been cut back and fill added to allow construction of a house whose rooftop was just visible from the boat.

"What's to stop anyone from going ashore?" Tony asked.

Gabe laughed. "Some No Trespassing signs. Dogs. And a caretaker who probably wouldn't mind relieving his boredom with some target practice." Gabe fished around in a locker, came up with a pair of binoculars, and handed them to Tony. "He's probably got his eye on us right now."

"Why all the secrecy?"

"It's Ramon's hideaway," Addie said. "Rumor has it he throws some wild parties on the weekends."

Today was Friday, the beginning of the weekend.

Tony lifted the glasses to his eyes. He could see the No Trespassing signs, and as he scanned the pathway a Doberman came down to the dock and raised its nose to the air as if it had gotten a whiff of a foreign scent on the breeze. Tony turned the glasses on the house.

A cupola with wraparound windows overlooking the sea was built onto the roof. A modern version of the widow's walk that graced the roofs of so many Key West homes; built in the last century, those widow's walks had not only served the vigil of lonely wives of shipping captains but had also been a place where the captains themselves could search the seas for any wrecked vessels lying in wait for wrecking crews to plunder their cargos.

There appeared to be no one on watch in Ramon's cupola as Tony wondered what sort of dual purpose it might serve.

"What are the chances of you finding your way back out here at night?" Tony asked Gabe.

Gabe shrugged. "As long as you're paying, I can get you where you want to go anytime you want to go there."

"Pick me up at the dock at ten tonight," Tony said. "I want to come back out here."

Gabe raised his hand in a mock salute. "Anything you say, cap."

It was just after five o'clock when Kay Fulton opened her front door and stepped into her living room, glancing at the clock on the wall. Keeping track of time was something she did a lot these days, as if by knowing the time she could in some way know the future. Know where Patty was, and when she was coming home. It was a false sense of security, and ultimately this awareness of the passage of time served no other purpose than to deepen her depression.

Kay waited for things to occur, feeling powerless at her own inability to make anything happen. She would look at the phone frequently, as if willing it to ring. She would be doing something, working at her desk, or in court, when her concentration would suddenly be jarred, and out of the corner of her eye someone would pass a doorway, and Kay would look up expecting to see Patty, or someone with news of her daughter.

The lapses were getting more frequent. She was sure people were noticing her inability to concentrate. She kept to a tighter schedule. She came home for lunch now, taking an hour rather than bolting through a takeout meal at her desk. And here she was at home at five o'clock—following the parental schedule she had felt guilty about not following only a few days ago. When she had a daughter. The irony did not escape her.

Now here she was alone, with nothing to do except wait. When the phone rang it was usually her parents, or a friend calling to see if there had been any news and to attempt to hearten Kay. In a sense this was the worst, the endless conversations with others who were as powerless as she.

Kay walked into the bedroom and got out of her office attire. For a moment she sank down on the bed, thinking how easy it would be to take a sleeping pill and just crawl in here and sleep until morning.

But there was a campaign party this evening, the first this electoral year, for Randall, and all the staff members were expected to be there to show their support. Kay was not looking forward to it, but she got up, went into the bathroom, and took a shower.

She was toweling herself dry when the phone rang. Wrapping the towel around her body, Kay walked into the living room expecting to have to relate the day's events to her mother.

"Mommy, we're on vacation."

Kay's initial panic was suffused with relief, joy at the sound of Patty's voice. Three days had passed since they had last spoken, three days in which Kay had been expecting the worst. Now here was Patty, bubbling with excitement as if nothing more unusual than a surprise vacation had occurred. Kay marveled at the ability of kids to sublimate, while at the same time worrying, as she had for months, about how this parental tug of war was going to warp her daughter's future.

Oh, Patty. "Where are you?" Kay cried.

"In a motel. It's got a pool with a slide, and Daddy catches me so I don't get my cast wet."

Jesus.

"Where? What motel? What's the name of the town?"

Kay listened to dead air and the sound of Patty's retreating voice before Brad came on the line.

"Hi, Kay," Brad said.

"What do you think you are doing?" Trying to keep her voice under control, not to scream at him like she wanted to do.

"Look," Brad said, "Patty's fine. We're fine. I needed to get away for a while to sort things out."

"By kidnapping Patty?"

"She's my daughter, Kay."

Yes, she did not need to be reminded. It was that fact that had slowed her down, allowing him some time to come to his senses before she began aggressively pursuing him. Perhaps he had.

"Why didn't you talk to me?" She felt herself breaking now, the days of tension suddenly wilting, and she let out a sob.

There was a long silence from Brad during which Kay could hear the TV; Patty was watching some stupid sitcom with a designer TV family undergoing their weekly humorous conflict.

Kay waited, wiping her eyes against a corner of the towel.

Finally Brad said, "I couldn't. You wouldn't talk to me. Every time I came around you were checking me out to see if I'd been drinking. Looking for some sign I was high. We could never just talk. You were always suspicious."

"Do you blame me?"

"No," Brad said. "But I had to do something."

"Well, you did it. You've gotten my attention. Now what are you going to do?"

"I don't know." Kay heard him sneeze. "I've still got vacation time."

She could practically see him now, sitting on the side of the bed, trying to legitimize his act of betrayal to her by suggesting it was nothing more than a vacation lark, taking his cue from Patty. She recognized that childlike aspect of him, an endearing trait, she'd always thought, in the years when they'd been happy. Now it annoyed her.

"Patty's in school," Kay said, trying to appeal to some sense of responsibility in him.

"Her academic career isn't going to be ruined because she misses a couple of weeks of kindergarten, for Christ's sake." It was a whispered shout.

Kay backed off, realizing she had no leverage. "Will you tell me where you are?"

"No," he said. "Besides, we're traveling. We'll be gone from here tomorrow."

"I reported you as missing."

"I figured you would."

"Is that why you called?"

"No." Again Brad hesitated, as if he was holding something back. She had lived with him too long not to recognize these small traits of behavior. She waited.

"Kay, you're in trouble."

"What kind of trouble?" She remembered Randall suggesting that Brad might have heard about her peccadillo in a public restroom with Tony the other day.

"The Marquesa trial."

Was he playing on her fears, the anxiety she felt over trying to prosecute this case? Her paranoia, as Randall Welch called it. She couldn't believe he would stoop to this in order to relieve himself of blame. On the other hand, he was a lawyer, too; he heard the rumors, the gossip that swirled like smoke in this community, and he worked with some of the biggest sleazes in town. It was quite possible he knew something.

"What about it?"

"You're being set up."

"How do you know?"

"You don't want to know."

"Tell me."

"A client, someone I represented who isn't exactly on the social circuit, owed me a favor. I won't tell you who, so don't ask. But he knows what he's talking about."

"What did he tell you?"

"Luis Marquesa is up to his neck in Cuban exile politics. He's using Ramon."

"You're not telling me anything new."

"Ramon was coming back from Cuba when his boat went down. He knows too much. He could sink Luis's plans."

So much for paranoia. Her worst fears were being confirmed. "What plans? To overthrow Castro?"

"Yes," Brad said.

"So you're telling me you did this because you thought Patty was in danger?" she asked.

Brad coughed, and she heard the distant canned TV laughter. "Listen, Luis isn't going to risk letting Ramon go to trial."

"Why didn't you just say something instead of running away with Patty?"

"Would it have made any difference? What were you going to do, quit your job?"

"Maybe," Kay said.

"Is that why you went to Tampa?"

Kay didn't answer that question. "I might at least have have understood your taking Patty away from here for a while."

"Come on!" Brad snorted. "Don't be naïve."

No. She wouldn't have understood, and she wouldn't have allowed it. Still, she should have known.

"Will you call once in a while?"

"Yes," Brad said. "Be careful."

"Let me talk to Patty."

Kay listened as her daughter recounted everything that was happening on the sitcom. Kay tried to find it amusing, asking questions as though she cared. Then Patty said she had to go, they were going to get something to eat, pizza. And she hung up.

Kay had made a drink and was sitting on the couch, still wearing the towel, when someone knocked on the door. It was after six o'clock, and she was supposed to be at the fund-raiser for Randall at seven. She had been playing the conversation with Brad over and over in her mind, trying to decide what she should do with this information.

She looked out the window and saw Tony's truck before going to the door to let him in.

"Brad called," Kay said.

Tony smiled. "Didn't I tell you?"

"He isn't bringing her back," Kay said.

204

"You talk to Patty? She okay?"

"She thinks she's on vacation, living in motels, eating pizza."

"No idea where they are?"

Kay shook her head. "According to Brad, Luis is involved with the exiles movement to overthrow Castro."

"Do you believe that?"

Kay shrugged. "I can believe anything right now. And on top of everything else, my witness is backing down, and I have to go to a fund-raiser for my boss."

"What about Coral?"

"Ramon is killing her with kindness. Apologizing for his behavior, giving her money."

"That sounds like tampering with a witness."

"It is, but where do we go from here?"

"To a party," Tony said.

RAMON

Maybe, Ramon thought, he should have a talk with the woman attorney, what was her name—Kay Fulton. Just go in her office and sit down and talk this out. Or maybe go straight to Randall Welch. Except he didn't know how tight Randall was with Luis, if Randall would say anything to Luis. Not that Ramon cared. In fact, the idea had crossed his mind recently that with the information he had about Luis's activities he could just go to the feds and work a deal, plea bargain his way out of this. Never even go to trial.

Ramon tried to convince himself that it would also be in Lourdes's best interest. Lourdes had confronted Luis, telling him she was going to take the kids and go to Miami for a while, but Luis had refused to let her go, demanded to know who she'd been talking to, and when she wouldn't tell him, he accused Ramon of stirring up trouble.

Little Lourdes. Ramon needed a sign, some guidance here. He'd gone to the dock the other day and seen the boats, two of them, being loaded with various-sized containers that must have been the arsenal Luis had put together to launch his revolution.

Ramon thought of going to church, to confession. Forgive me, Father, for I have sinned. He would at least be protected by the sanctity of the confessional.

And what is the nature of the sin?

Attempted murder.

Penance.

Was an island house in the Gulf of Mexico worth half a million dollars too much to ask?

Father Mulvaney was coming to the island tonight. Perhaps Ramon would talk to him then about Luis and the sin of coveting his brother's wife. Then again, Ramon thought, maybe it was better not to say anything to anyone about Lourdes. He hadn't moved on her in any way, and the way Luis was going, the guy could be in jail any day now, or dead. It seemed like an un-Christian way to think of your brother, but there it was.

This business of being a Christian wasn't easy. It required constant vigilance, a habit Ramon wasn't exactly accustomed to. He had to begin thinking about what he was going to do with the rest of his life.

Jimmy Santos was getting out of jail this afternoon. And tonight was the Randall Welch campaign party. Luis would be there, and it seemed only right to Ramon, with his new identity, that he should be there, too.

Ramon would pick up Jimmy from jail, take him for a drink, and try to decide what they were going to do now that Ragged Key was turning into a religious retreat.

"You see a new man," Ramon said. He hoisted his glass, tapping it against Jimmy's beer bottle. Jimmy was wearing jeans and a T-shirt that looked like it had been laundered once too often; the fabric was turning yellow, it was stretched out of shape, and a tear was beginning around the collar. It was the first time Ramon had been alone with Jimmy since they were rescued at sea.

"You found God," Jimmy said. He looked hangdog, miserable.

"I know. Sounds bizarre," Ramon said. "But something happened, changed that day. It was Easter. Did you think of that?"

Jimmy swallowed some beer. "Yeah, I went back to jail."

"A bummer," Ramon said. "I've been doing what I could to get you out."

Jimmy nodded. "How're the dogs?"

"Nobody's on the island now, so I brought them in."

"Am I going back out there?"

Ramon ordered another drink and hesitated before saying, "I'm giving up the place."

"Selling it?"

"Turning it over to the church. St. Stephens."

Jimmy looked at Ramon in disbelief.

"The church?"

Ramon nodded. "Kind of like a commitment I had to make."

"Shit," Jimmy said. "I could think of better places to commit."

Ramon heard the frustration in Jimmy's tone, saw the look of awareness in his eye. Jimmy was just out of jail, without a job or a place to live. The old life would be tempting him back. Ramon felt a degree of responsibility. "You want a job at the cab company," he said, "there shouldn't be any problem."

Jimmy seemed stunned. "I don't know."

"Or," Ramon said, just now thinking of it, "there's a guy looking over my shoulder I need to start keeping track of."

"Who's that?"

"Guy by the name of Tony Harwood," Ramon said.

TWENTY-TWO

───

"That's Luis Marquesa," Kay said. "Walking away from the bar with my boss, Randall Welch."

Tony watched as the two men carried their drinks over to a group standing near the front door of the restaurant that had been privately booked for this party. They greeted newcomers.

Luis was sleek, his dark hair looking freshly scrubbed and perfectly coiffed; his skin was the color of old polished copper, with coal-black eyes that looked out from his round moon face. He wore an obviously expensive tropical shirt over linen trousers and loafers burnished nearly the same color as his skin. Rings, a gold watch, and a chain around his neck glittered in the muted light.

"Ramon coming?" Tony asked.

"He would have the balls to show up here," Kay said, "but I think Luis has enough sense to realize how inappropriate it would be and to talk him out of it."

"Ramon listens to Luis?"

Kay shrugged. "We'll find out."

Key West's power brokers were out in force. Kay pointed out the city's colorful mayor and most of the members of both the city and county commissions, along with a variety of politicos—even a state senator, who was just coming in, being greeted by Luis.

Money and power were in evidence here, a kind of easy familiarity among people who knew who they were, where they were going—and what they had done to get there.

A small combo was playing on the upstairs porch overlooking Duval Street, the tropical beat of a rhumba vibrating down, its rhythm mixing with the conversation, the sprinkle of laughter.

"Something I didn't tell you earlier," Kay said. "A couple of federal agents came to the office today."

"To see you?"

Kay nodded. "They were asking questions about Luis."

"Cuba?"

"They weren't forthcoming, but that would be my guess after what Brad just told me."

"Why would the feds quiz you?"

"Because of Ramon. Seeing if we'd uncovered anything in our investigation that would link him to his brother's politics."

"But you haven't, have you?"

"No. I don't think Ramon has a political bone in his body."

"What was he doing in Cuba, then, assuming he was there?"

Kay shrugged. "Maybe Luis was using him without Ramon even knowing it."

"Running guns over there to dissident groups?"

"If he was, it would be for money," Kay said. "Not politics."

"Money can buy politics."

A woman came up to Kay. "Any news from Patty?" she asked.

"Yes," Kay said. "She called me. She's with Brad. There was a misunderstanding. He thought he'd told me he was taking her out of town for a few days. She's fine."

"God, what a relief!"

Kay smiled. The woman chatted a moment longer, then walked away. "A colleague," Kay said. "Now I've given them something more to talk about for the rest of the evening."

"You exaggerated a little, didn't you?"

HAVANA HUSTLE

"A little. They don't need the gory details." Kay sipped
her drink. "Jesus," she whispered. "There's Grabill. He's
coming over here."

Tony turned just as the black judge reached them. He
wore a suit and tie, one of the few men in the room so
dressed. Tony would have bet anything that Grabill was that
rare species of black, a Republican and a political conserva-
tive who believed that as long as he had on a suit and tie,
even when no one else did, it somehow neutralized the color
of his skin.

"Well, Miss Fulton," Grabill said, winking at Kay, "hear
you havin' some troubles of your own lately."

"You may hear a lot of things, Judge, but if you ever
want to know the truth, don't hesitate to ask me."

Grabill's smile faded slightly, as if he wasn't sure whether
or not he was being rebuked. "By all means," he said, seeming to recover. "By all means." He turned to Tony and
offered his hand. "Bill Grabill," the judge said.

"Tony Harwood." They shook hands, the judge's grip
limp.

"Harwood. I've heard that name recently." Before Tony
could respond, Grabill's smile ballooned again. "Oh, yeah.
The murder on Big Pine Key. Sounds like you got some
trouble, too."

"We've all got trouble," Tony said. There was some nee-
dling quality in Grabill's manner that Tony didn't care for.
He could imagine what it must be like arguing a case before
Grabill if he didn't like you.

Grabill grinned. "Well, remember. A vote for Randall is
a vote for responsibility. Something we need in the halls of
justice, isn't it, Miss Fulton?" Grabill gave another wink,
then turned and walked away without waiting for an answer.

A buffet had been set up, catered by the restaurant, and
Tony wandered over while Kay talked with more of her
coworkers who had heard the news about Patty and had
come to quiz her about it. It was big news. It overshadowed
Randall Welch's run for re-election, the results of which
seemed to be a foregone conclusion anyway.

Tony was hungry. He hadn't eaten anything since breakfast, and the alcohol needed an absorbent. He put some Swedish meatballs on a plate, stabbed a couple of squares of jalapeño pepper cheese with a toothpick, and carried the plate over to a moderately quiet corner. As he ate he kept an eye on the crowd. Especially Luis Marquesa.

Marquesa was suave, debonair, giving off a wonderful sense of self-confidence that in other circumstances, with other people, Tony had no doubt, could be interpreted as arrogance.

People sought out Marquesa, angled to stand near him even when they weren't being included in his galaxy. It was interesting to watch the byplay. Other than shaking hands Marquesa never touched anyone, seldom smiled, listened intently as one after another approached him, chatted for a moment as if he were the pope dispensing blessings, then moved on.

"The guy could have been a politico himself, followed in his father's footsteps."

Tony turned. Randall Welch was standing beside him, following the Marquesa circus.

"I don't know," Tony said. "I hear his father had some integrity."

Welch looked as if he'd just eaten something that had gone bad. Then he tried to smile around the bad taste in his mouth. "So you're Tony Harwood," he said.

"And you're Randall Welch," Tony said. "That's what I like about small towns. You can know people without knowing them."

"Especially when they have reputations like yours."

"Oh? I imagine it's undeserved. Most of them are."

"A dead woman in your trailer?"

Tony wanted to say that had nothing to do with him, but he knew otherwise. It was irritating, to say the least, to have it thrown in his face in the same evening by two city officials he didn't even know. "A tragedy" was all he could say.

"Dallying with another woman in the public facilities of a hotel restroom?" Welch winked.

"Consenting adults."

"She works for me."

"She was on a lunch break. Is there some law against your staff members enjoying themselves?"

Welch grinned. "No. Not as long as they're doing their jobs." Welch grinned. "Speaking of jobs, how's yours going?"

"If I knew who you could trust in this town, it would be going better."

"Trust me."

Tony smiled. "All right. Why didn't you look into the death of that cabdriver the other day?"

"The car accident out on south Roosevelt Boulevard? The city investigated that and came up with nothing."

"A cop by the name of Franklin investigated it. Guess who he moonlights for when he isn't in uniform."

"You think the city pays these guys enough to do more than pay rent and buy groceries in this town?" Welch asked. "Sure, Franklin moonlights. So do half the other cops on the force."

"But if they're smart, they don't do it for a guy with an arrest record as long as Ramon Marquesa's."

"Nobody ever accused cops of being smart." Welch grinned again. "You were one once yourself, weren't you?"

"Once. Long enough to recognize a bad one when I see him."

"What I can't figure out is what any of this has got to do with you finding Angel Lopez."

"Maybe nothing and maybe everything. I don't think it was a coincidence that the cabdriver had given me some information the day before he died. In that accident."

"What sort of information?" The amusement on Welch's face disappeared.

"It will be in my report," Tony replied. "The one I'll write you when I find Lopez."

"And what if you don't find him?"

"I'll still write a report. That's what you pay me for."

"And without a witness it's too damned much."

Tony shrugged and was about to say something when Luis Marquesa walked up. Welch turned to him expectantly, as though he had been summoned. Marquesa glanced briefly at Tony, then spoke quietly to Randall, and the two men walked away.

Tony looked around the room and saw through the open windows Franklin standing on the porch overlooking the street. He was motionless, a cop on duty.

Kay was standing with some other women, and Tony watched her, the diffident way she talked. She wasn't evasive, just shy, withdrawn, and he felt a wave of tenderness for her. The music upstairs had stopped for a while, and there was just the street noise coming in the open windows, and the garbled sound of voices in random conversation.

Tony saw a bald guy come in the front door, an earring dangling from one ear. Ramon. He wasn't tall, maybe five and a half feet in shoes, but what he lacked in stature he made up for in bulk—the guy was built like a trash compactor. A thick chest and shoulders that would have made an offensive lineman on a pro football team proud. Ramon's center of gravity must be somewhere around his knees, Tony thought. He didn't envy the man who would have to move Ramon from his spot. Franklin, not small himself, paled by comparison.

A woman was with Ramon, petite, with dark hair and a nervous look about her. Tony watched Ramon guide her to the bar.

Kay touched Tony's arm. "Looks like he didn't listen," she said.

There was nothing of his brother Luis's suavity. Where Luis was combed and scrubbed and elusive, Ramon was pitted, scruffy, and direct. Where Luis would put a knife between your second and third ribs once your back was turned, Ramon would do his dirty work right in your face. Only in their eyes was there any indication of a relationship. Ramon, too, had the dark, distant Marquesa stare as he sauntered to the bar, slapping backs, punching shoulders on his way.

"Who's the woman?"

"Luis's wife, Lourdes."

"Things could get interesting."

"I'm ready to leave," Kay said.

Tony looked at his watch. He had half an hour before he was scheduled to be at the dock. He didn't want to leave right now, but Kay was showing signs of anxiety. "Let me make a pit stop," Tony said.

Kay nodded and walked to the restrooms with him.

"Separate or together?" Tony asked.

"I've created enough talk for one night." Kay smiled and went into the women's room.

Tony was standing at a urinal when Luis Marquesa walked in. He glanced briefly in Tony's direction, then headed for one of the two sinks along the opposite wall. Tony watched him wash his hands. Luis scrubbed them with the care of a surgeon, bending his fingers and massaging the nails in a thick lather of soap. Tony imagined him doing this several times a day. It seemed almost pathological, like Lady Macbeth washing away imagined blood.

Tony zipped up and flushed the urinal, sending a thunder of water rushing through the old pipes. Luis had dried his hands and was running a comb through his hair. Their eyes met in the mirror. Tony sensed that Luis was waiting for Tony to leave before he relieved himself, one of those men unable to pee while standing next to another man.

"Why don't you wash your hands of Ramon?" Tony said, holding Luis's eye in the mirror.

"What?" Luis shoved the comb into his shirt pocket and turned to face him.

"Ramon's nothing but trouble," Tony said. "Why don't you cut your losses?"

"Who are you?" Luis's voice was steady, his body maintaining the same rigid bearing, giving nothing away.

"You don't need this. Ramon's a punk. He'll always be a punk. How many times are you going to bail him out before he takes you down with him?"

One of Luis's tasseled loafers shifted involuntarily on the floor. "I don't know you," he said.

"You will. My name's Tony Harwood. I'm the guy bringing Ramon down even if it means running you through the muck. You're a class guy. Why put yourself through this? Ramon's not in high school anymore, forcing himself on girls like Oona Morales."

A nerve jumped in the flesh at the corner of one of Luis's eyes. "Ramon's reformed," he said.

"Prisons are full of born-agains," Tony said.

Luis started to move toward the door. Tony cut him off, leaning his back against it.

"You're not being very smart," Luis said. "Key West's judiciary is on the other side of that door."

Tony smiled. "Mostly your people. They don't much impress me."

Luis gazed at him with cold eyes. "What do you want?"

"Angel Lopez," Tony said. "I think you know where he is."

"You're wrong."

"You've got plans. You don't want Lopez to get in the way of those plans, do you?"

"What are you talking about?"

"Cuba."

Tony stepped away from the door.

Luis touched his hand to his hair, then pulled the door open.

"Think about it," Tony said.

Kay was standing with her back to a wood-paneled column. Ramon Marquesa hovered in front of her. The band was playing again, a female voice singing "I've Got You Under My Skin."

Ramon said, "You have any idea what it's like to go to the edge, look over, and see to the bottom?"

"I stay away from edges," Kay said. "I'm afraid of heights."

Ramon grinned. His teeth, Kay thought, were unusually large. They reminded her of horses' teeth. The gold snake dangling from his ear was distracting, and she had never trusted men who wore earrings.

"I'm glad to hear that," Ramon said. "Because it isn't pretty down there at the bottom."

"Thanks for reminding me."

He smelled of alcohol.

"I've been doing a lot of thinking recently," Ramon said. "Maybe we should talk, see if we can't work things out."

216

"You want to plea bargain here?" She couldn't believe him. It would have been funny except she knew she was talking to a psychopath who was capable of anything.

Ramon smiled. "Whatever you want to call it."

"I suggest you come to the office tomorrow. With your lawyers."

"I don't need lawyers anymore. I've got God on my side."

Kay couldn't help herself; she smiled. "I'm not sure God can adjudicate a plea bargain. Not in the lower courts, anyway."

"That's just the sort of cynical, smart-ass remark I expect from you lawyers."

"Forgive me," Kay said. "But we've earned our cynicism from people like you."

"Then you don't want to hear what I'm offering."

"I do want to hear it. But as an attorney, I'd have to advise you not to make a statement without your lawyer present."

"Fuck that."

Kay watched Ramon reach down and pluck a rubber band he was wearing against his wrist.

"Sorry," Ramon said.

She couldn't believe this guy. Was he serious? This religious crap wasn't just an act? Out of the corner of her eye she saw Tony walking toward them.

"What is it?" Kay asked.

"Luis," Ramon said.

"What about Luis?"

"Information about his activities."

Kay remembered the federal agents who had questioned her today. "You want to turn in your own brother? That isn't very Christian."

"I've thought about that," Ramon said. "It's for his own good."

"Let's get out of here," Kay said.

"What was that all about?" Tony asked.

They walked down a hallway, passing an open archway that led through the dining room to the buffet, on their way out. The rooms were packed now, the hum of conversation

217

notched up, driven by random energy. Randall Welch was getting ready to make a speech.

"Ramon wants to plea bargain," Kay said. "He's turning on Luis."

"Interesting," Tony said. "I had a word with Luis. He might be thinking about dumping Ramon."

As they walked down the street something made Tony turn and look back at the restaurant. Luis Marquesa was standing in the doorway, his hands on his hips, looking out at the night as if he were God—or the devil.

TWENTY-THREE

Kay felt shaken, disjointed. Ramon had unnerved her. She was totally unprepared for his change in manner and having a hard time reconciling this new Ramon with the man she thought she knew. Telling her she was cynical! By the time they got back to her car Kay didn't know whether to laugh or cry.

She drove down Duval Street, with its ridiculous T-shirt shops and blinding neon. Things had changed so much since she'd first come here. The funkiness was gone, having given way to a wave of tacky commercialism. She no longer recognized familiar faces on this street of lies.

Tourists ambled along, seemingly unaware of the sleaze, the fetid smell of sour beer and rotting garbage collecting in the gutters, the street hustlers lurking, ready to pounce and provide tomorrow's crime report for the local paper.

Tony had lived his life among these people, on these kinds of streets. She hadn't. And she didn't think of herself as cynical.

"That time in Miami," Kay said to him. "When you were suspended. What was it like? Tell me about it."

"With the drug dealer? Ricky Lee?"

"Yes."

He was silent, and she wondered if the memory revisited him in some ghostly way, the details shadowy, or whether it was permanently scored in his brain, his own private non-returnable video head game.

"I spotted Ricky downtown about two o'clock in the morning," Tony said. "It had been a slow night. One of those nights when cops start digging around old haunts just for something to do. I followed him."

"You knew Ricky," Kay said.

"I had arrested him once, but Ricky's a guy who keeps popping up like a bad smell. Come to think of it, he's not unlike Ramon. It's annoying, but you can't get to the source and stop it. You know what I mean?"

"I know exactly."

"Rick the Tic didn't have a place of his own. He spent nights with different women or stayed in abandoned houses, crack dens in Liberty City and Overtown. Which is where he went that night."

Kay wasn't ready to go home yet. She was still unnerved. Driving and listening to Tony seemed to calm her.

"Ricky was a guy we'd see almost every night. He was always on the hustle, but trying to catch him in the act was difficult. I spotted him coming out of a place we had tagged as a stash house, a pickup joint. I figured Ricky was carrying and was going to make a delivery, so I followed him. I waited until he went in the crack den. I called for backup, then went after him. He couldn't have been in there thirty seconds before I walked in. The place was a shell. Concrete floor where fires had been started, and everything that could be turned was a pile of ash. There were no lights, only some candles around. I had a flashlight and shoved it around the walls. A bunch of kids, all high, sitting there staring into the flashlight like rabbits."

"Sick," Kay said.

"Yeah, it does something to you, changes you when you see that. It's hard to explain."

"I imagine it's simple rage."

"Well, it's that, but also a depression that stays with you longer than the rage. A sense of loss."

Kay thought of Patty and nodded.

"I heard Ricky going out the back and knew I had lost him. He would be swallowed up in the tenements and projects. But when I went out he was there, standing in the rubble of concrete where kids had once played basketball. Ricky was grinning. He said, 'What is this shit, pig man?'

"I hit him with the flashlight, clubbed him, and when he got up to run I hit him again. The rage was turned loose, and I beat him senseless. When the backup got there they had to pull me off him. I would have killed him. He had about twenty dollars' worth of rock on him, that was all."

Kay reached across the seat and took his hand. "How did you feel afterward?"

Tony shrugged. "Nothing. I didn't feel anything right then. Maybe some satisfaction. The other feelings came later."

"Satisfaction?"

"Yeah, it felt good to get outside the uniform, the badge, the rules." Tony looked at his watch. "A guy's taking me out to Ragged Key at ten o'clock."

"What for?"

"Ramon's got a place out there. I want to look around."

"You didn't tell me."

"I haven't had much of a chance."

"Well," Kay said, "I'm going with you. I don't want to be alone tonight."

The moon had yet to appear, and though the sky was cloudless, away from the electrified nimbus of Key West the islands of the backcountry were bundled in darkness.

Gabe throttled his boat back in shallow water a couple hundred yards from Ragged Key, which was a mere shadow, rising slightly from the water, ragged in its outline against the sky. The dock where the boat had been tied this afternoon was no longer visible.

"How close can you get us to that dock we saw this afternoon?" Tony asked Gabe.

"I might be able to pole up there, but I sure as hell wouldn't risk going in by motor." Gabe cut the engine and picked up a long-handled paddle. Standing in the stern, he began to pole them across the flats toward Ragged Key.

It was still, the only sound that of the paddle as Gabe lifted it from the water and the boat's gentle rush across the

JOHN LESLIE

flats. "I hope you're not expecting me to sit around here waiting on you," Gabe whispered.

"We were counting on a ride back," Tony replied.

"Well, you'll have to get wet, then. I'll get you close to that dock, but I won't tie up to it. It's clearly marked No Trespassing."

"Anchor out and turn on a light. I'll find you."

In the distance there came the sputter of a motorboat whipping across the flats, the sound growing as it came closer. Gabe stopped poling. Moments later they saw the red and green running lights of a boat heading straight toward them.

"Now what?" Gabe said.

When the boat was a few hundred yards from them it suddenly veered, still at full speed, heading toward Ragged Key. Moments later its engine was cut, and the sound of voices could be heard as people disembarked. A couple of flashlights lit up the dock. Gabe waited until the newcomers had disappeared into the island before he resumed poling. They were still a hundred yards away from the dock.

Kay, who had been sitting in front of the steering console, came back to the stern. "I want to go with you," she said to Tony.

"No," he said. "Two of us doubles our risk. I'll go in, have a look around, and come back. If I'm not back in an hour or so, get somebody out here."

"Who?" Kay asked.

The question seemed to echo against the returning silence of the night.

Wading in less than six inches of water, Tony made it to the L-shaped dock that jutted out from the island. He carried a small pack on his back with the Beretta inside and a couple of sandwich bags containing raw hamburger rolled into bite-size balls around three Tylox capsules. The Tylox were leftover prescription medication from when he'd been shot by the lezzie. Three of them, he thought, would knock out any bothersome dogs he might encounter.

Tony was about to climb onto the dock when he heard the sound of another boat approaching. He stood behind

222

one of the pilings and waited as the boat thumped against the dock before its engine was cut. More people disembarked and walked, jabbering, along the dock.

Tony waded to the stern of the boat. No one seemed to be on board. He climbed up on the wooden dive platform attached to the stern, then stepped easily onto the dock. He could just see the new arrivals entering the pathway at the end of the dock leading to the island's interior.

He had anticipated that Ramon would be having a party tonight, and as he hurried to catch up with the others Tony hoped that a mob of people might work to his advantage, allowing him to lose himself in the crowd.

They were walking in pairs along the narrow path between boulders that had been placed there as riprap bordering the mangrove that grew beyond it.

At least there were no dogs barking, Tony thought, coming within twenty feet of the last person from the boat, and the only light came from the stars and some kerosene lamps attached to the end of bamboo poles that were stuck in the ground and staggered along the edge of the riprap.

Tony followed as they left the riprap and came into a small clearing where he could hear a distinct mechanical hum that sounded like a generator. Beyond the clearing were some dark palm trees that looked to be fanned out in a circle, and a house, dimly lit, the widow's walk he'd seen from the boat yesterday now only a shadow against the sky.

Tinny mechanical music reached his ears, the grunting percussion rhythm of a salsa beat enhanced by a marimba and rattlebones. A shout, then laughter erupted into the night.

Someone was standing at the end of the path where the palm trees began. Greeting or checking the new arrivals. Tony ducked out of sight behind a clump of mangroves and waited. He waited five minutes, and when he looked again no one was there. Rather than follow the path now he kept to the surrounding shrubbery, making his way toward the sound of the music.

He needed to get back in with a crowd; alone out here he was too exposed, at risk of being noticed, possibly recognized. Ramon, Franklin, Mingo, and certain guys from the cab company would be certain to recognize him. He needed to know if they were here.

The music came from a boom box on a table, an extension cord snaking along the ground, probably back to the generator he had heard earlier. Tony stood leaning against a palm tree, taking in the scene. People moved in and out of the house that was about twenty-five yards from where he stood. He didn't recognize anyone.

Following the circle of palms around the house, Tony glanced up at the sky. A thin cloud drifted across a particle of moon. Coming around to the other side of the house, he saw Christmas lights strung on posts around a small arena. The bulbs leaked harsh yellow light where the paint was chipped and cracked. More extension cords littered the ground. People milled around the arena, and cigarette smoke curled into the night air, seeming to hang just above the Christmas lights.

Tony recognized the familiar arena. Cockfighting rings were all alike. Planks surrounding a dirt floor. And someone had told him, Kay or Tom, that Ramon was known to raise birds for fighting, illegal in the state of Florida.

What he didn't recognize were the people here. They weren't the types he would have expected to find at a cockfight. Most of these people looked as if they would be more at home at a country club—or a campaign rally, although Tony didn't see anyone he knew from the Randall Welch party. A few women, all of whom were well dressed, were scattered through the mostly male crowd.

A woman who didn't fit in caught Tony's attention. He watched as she wandered around the edge of the crowd. She had on a denim vest over a T-shirt, a scarf knotted around her head. She held a beer can in one hand and a cigarette in the other. She was young, Tony thought. Too young for this crowd.

He followed her as she walked away from the arena and the house along a narrow, unmarked path toward the water. She stopped once and took a last drag on the cigarette, which he could now smell was marijuana, before tossing it down and grinding it out beneath the heel of one of her sneakers.

She came to a small beach, sitting down on sand that looked as if it had been imported. She was alone. Tony watched her for a moment as she drank the beer and stared up at the sky.

"That's a strange-looking crowd for a chicken fight," Tony said.

The girl casually looked up, hooked the beer can to her lips, then, lowering it, turned away from him.

"I never understood what people saw in cockfights. What about you?"

"What about me what?"

"You understand it?"

She shrugged. "Gets guys' dicks hard, I guess," she said without looking at him. "If that's what you're looking for, forget it. I'm not in the mood."

"Me neither," Tony said.

"Well, what'd you follow me down here for, then, just company?"

"That, and I've never been out here before. Thought you looked like a good guide."

She took another hit of beer.

"What's your name?"

"Darcy," she said without looking at Tony.

Tony sat down on the sand a distance from Darcy. He looked out across the water, listening as tide lapped quietly at the shore.

"I wonder why anyone would do this," Tony said.

"Do what?"

"Build a place out here so far away from everything, then invite a crowd in to overrun it."

"You're not with them?" Darcy asked.

"That gang?" Tony motioned toward the arena. "No."

"Then what are you doing here?"

He had trapped himself, Tony thought. Walked right into it and closed the gate. But Darcy was stoned, and maybe he could talk his way out of it. "Ramon told me to drop in sometime. I happened to be in the neighborhood."

Darcy looked at him without expression. "Well, those people aren't here to watch chickens fight," she said.

"No. I didn't think so. Who are they?"

225

"Church people."

Of course. "I heard Ramon got religion."

Darcy scoffed. "Yeah, he's giving the place away."

Tony couldn't believe what he was hearing. "What place?"

"The island, the house, everything."

"To the church?"

She nodded. "The jerk."

Tony heard bitterness in her voice. "You stay out here?" he asked.

"No, but Jimmy does. He took care of the dogs. He loved those dogs, and now Ramon's taken them off the island."

So he was safe from that threat, Tony thought.

Jimmy. The kid who'd been picked up on the boat with Ramon. "Jimmy's your boyfriend?"

"Yeah. He's on parole, and this was a good job for him."

"Jimmy the only one who stays out here?"

"I don't know. When I've been here he's the only one."

"When was the last time you were here?"

"I don't know. It's been a while."

"Makes it tough on a relationship, I guess."

"You could say that." Darcy took a drink.

"I thought Jimmy was in jail."

"He just got out. Ramon got him in trouble on that trip, and now Jimmy's got his parole extended, and Ramon's kicking him off the island," Darcy said.

Tony sympathized. This had been a safe place to wipe the slate clean. If you weren't working for Ramon Marquesa, Tony thought. Tomorrow he would have to talk to Jimmy Santos. But right now, without Ramon around, it seemed like a good time to take a look inside the house.

TWENTY-FOUR

The house was built on concrete stilts. Various sliding glass doors gave access to the house from a balcony that wrapped around three of its sides. From where he stood he looked up into the kitchen. The doors were open, and lights were on throughout the house. The constant hum of the generator could be heard above the human babble.

When he walked by the arena on his way to the house he noticed a priest in conversation with several of the people gathered there. A few people moved in and out of the house from the living room, but Tony still didn't see anyone he recognized. He kept to the shadows as he walked around to the kitchen entrance.

He could easily walk away from here, he thought—just continue back down to the dock, use his flashlight to signal Gabe and Kay, then wade out and be back in Key West in half an hour.

Instead, compelled by instinct, he walked up the outside stairs and entered the kitchen. The voices from the adjacent room were more distinct now, speaking mostly Spanish. Some glasses and plastic cups littered the tiled counter next to a double stainless sink containing ice in which beer bottles were buried. Catholics were nothing if not good drinkers.

A large plastic garbage can with a trash bag in it stood in the corner. Tony looked inside it. There were empty bottles, remnants of food, paper, and plastic, and cigarette butts. He wondered how they disposed of garbage here, if Ramon bothered to haul it back to Key West or buried it at sea.

He opened cupboards and found stacks of plates, cups, and glasses. Ordinary flatware. Enough to feed at least a dozen people. Canned food, a lot of soup and tuna fish and boxes of spaghetti. The refrigerator was full of more beer. Two large coffee urns sat on the counter.

Someone came into the kitchen as he was holding the door of the fridge open. Tony looked up as the guy went to the sink and pulled a bottle from the ice. Tony took a bottle from the fridge.

"Colder in here," the man said.

"Too cold," Tony replied. "Hurts my teeth."

The guy grinned. "You a member of the parish? I don't recognize you."

Tony thought of the hitchhiker he'd picked up coming back from Miami Easter Sunday. "No," Tony said, "I'm a faith healer."

"No kidding. I'm Catholic, but I love watchin' you guys work."

"It can be inspiring," Tony said.

"You know Ramon's deeding this place to St. Stephens. Tomorrow it will be official. You talk to Father Mulvaney, he might let you use the place once in a while. He's open-minded about that stuff."

"I'll talk to him," Tony said.

They shook hands, and the guy left the kitchen. Tony opened his beer and walked into the hallway leading to the living room. Halfway down the hall was a stairway. He walked up to the second floor.

A couple of doors leading off another hallway. Then a shorter set of steps that he guessed would go to the widow's walk. Tony opened one of the doors and stepped into the room, with only the light illuminating the interior. It was a bedroom. A pair of single beds.

Tony was aware of the risk he was taking by being in here, but he needed a quick look around, a couple of minutes to find something, anything, that would lead to Angel Lopez.

Two minutes. Then he'd get out, walk down to the dock, and be out of here.

It didn't take two minutes. The closet was empty. Magazines were stacked on a table between the beds, subscriptions to *Playboy* and *Time.* Current issues. Little white stickers on the front of *Time* with Angel Lopez's name and the address at the cab company.

The door to a small bathroom was open, and Tony went in. Clean. No sign that it was regularly used, which made him think it must have been a guest room. There was a wicker container between the sink and the toilet. Tony picked it up. A few tissues, and under them a prescription medicine vial. He read the name. Angel Lopez. Twenty-five tablets of Tagamet for gastrointestinal problems to be taken twice a day. The prescription was two weeks old.

The guest, Tony thought, would have been Angel Lopez.

Tony put the vial in his pocket and walked out. He went downstairs and out of the house, where he found the riprap bordering the path that led down to the dock. He was just about to start down when Ramon came into the clearing and saw Tony.

Ramon did a double take, a look of surprise on his face before he broke into a grin. "Look who we have here," Ramon said. "You do get around, don't you?"

Tony considered his options; Ramon, with his trash compactor build, was no movable feast. Insult was added when Franklin came up behind Ramon, followed by a younger man. Jimmy Santos?

"Glad you could make it," Ramon said. "I wanted to talk to you at the party this evening, but you took off with the lady lawyer before I got a chance. She here with you?"

"No," Tony said. "She couldn't make it."

"No problem," Ramon said. "You know Franklin?"

"I think we met once."

Franklin glared at Tony without saying anything.

"And my young friend here, Jimmy?" Ramon asked.

Tony didn't offer his hand, and Jimmy seemed slightly bewildered.

"This is Tony Harwood," Ramon said. Jimmy seemed to perk up. "He's been showing an interest in my affairs recently," Ramon continued. "You also interested in church affairs?"

"I guess it never hurts to have God on your side," Tony said. "Just in case."

Ramon kept smiling. "Cynical," he said. "Just like the lady lawyer. But the thing is, this is a private party. By invitation only."

"I don't mind leaving," Tony said.

"Well, as long as you're here, why don't we see if we can convert you?" Ramon turned to Jimmy. "Why don't you and Franklin show him up to the guest room?"

As he was led back upstairs Tony heard someone say, "It's the faith healer."

Kay looked at her watch again. She seemed to be checking it by the minute now. It was after midnight, and they'd been out here for more than two hours. Gabe was getting restless, and she didn't know how much longer she would be able to persuade him to stay. She had doubled the fee he was charging Tony, but he'd made it clear he wasn't going to stay out here all night.

She didn't know what to do. Boats were returning to the mainland, and she had no idea who was left out there. She didn't want to leave Tony stranded. On the other hand, if she went onto the island looking for him and encountered Ramon, then they were both in trouble.

If Tony had been caught, her only recourse, she supposed, was to report him as missing. Another missing persons report! And the only ones she could report to were the police. And tell them that he'd come out here. On private property. Trespassing. Who could she trust?

"How much longer?" Gabe asked. "There's only one boat left at the dock, and that's probably the caretaker's."

"You want to go over there with me and look for him?"

"I told you, I'm not setting foot on Ragged Key."

Kay felt hope fade. She scanned the shoreline looking for some sign of Tony. Instead the faint illumination from the house was extinguished, and Ragged Key became even darker.

Half an hour later Gabe started the motor. "That's it," he said. "I'm going back to Key West. With or without you."

Franklin was the sort of man who always knew what was expected of him, Tony thought. And never failed to deliver. He was expressionless, his features ironed into his milk chocolate face; Franklin betrayed no emotion.

Tony sat on the edge of the bed. Franklin stood by the door.

"Am I being charged with something?"

"Could be trespassing."

"Could be, or is?"

"Depend on you," Franklin said. "And the boss."

"Like the other night on the highway."

Franklin shrugged his broad shoulders in a way Tony understood meant that he was finished answering questions. Tony could hear party sounds, someone singing: "He's got the whole wide world . . . in his hands."

There was a knock on the door. Franklin opened it. Jimmy came in and handed Franklin the drink he'd sent him to get. Franklin took a sip, then put it down on the table by the other bed across from where Tony sat.

"I talked to Darcy," Tony said.

Jimmy turned from the door. He was young, a sullen expression on his face. Tony recognized the look—it was a look that attempted to ward off contact. Don't fuck with me, it said. Tony had carried that look himself for many years. A product of desperation and hopelessness.

"She says your luck's running bad."

"No complaints," Jimmy said.

Of course not, Tony thought. Keep it bottled up. Go along and get along. Franklin was moving around the room. He picked up a magazine without noticing Angel Lopez's name on the cover and thumbed through it. Jimmy the caretaker would have been here with Angel.

"Maybe I can help," Tony said.

Franklin looked up from the magazine and scoffed. "Can't help your own damn self," he said. And he told Jimmy to move it. Santos went out the door.

"How long you going to hold me?" Tony said.

231

"Hold you?" Franklin asked, putting the magazine down. "Nobody holding you. You a guest of Mr. Marquesa. I think he wanta talk to you when he gets a moment."

"The party's over. I'm ready to go home."

"Uh-huh. Why don't you just go, then? You see how easy the door opens. Give me great pleasure to shoot your ass on the way out, all the trouble you been causin'."

Yes, and Tony had little doubt how that would be played. The suspended ex-cop, his neighbor's wife found murdered in Tony's bedroom one day, shot while trespassing, breaking and entering a religious retreat another day.

Tony settled back to wait and picked up one of Angel's *Playboy*s. He looked at the perfect airbrushed skin tones of the models, then tried to concentrate on an article despite the monotony of religious hymns now being sung outside. Under other circumstances it would have been laughable.

Franklin got up and went into the bathroom, leaving the door open.

Tony reached into his jacket and took out one of the bags of meatballs he'd carried here for the dogs. Listening to the heady stream as Franklin peed, Tony clawed through to the fatty centers of the hamburger and dug out the three Tylox capsules.

Franklin had finished about half of his drink, the cup still sitting on the table across from the bed. Tony broke open the capsules, spilling their contents into his hand, then reached across and dumped the powder into the remaining dark liquid of Franklin's drink.

The toilet flushed. Franklin came back into the room, looked at Tony, picked up his drink and took a swallow, then sat back down in the chair with his magazine.

The Tylox, Tony remembered, had worked quickly and effectively against pain. One capsule left him lightheaded. On the street these things would go for three or four dollars a pop for people who had no pain, just wanted the high. Three of them and Franklin should be staggering like a drunk in a matter of minutes.

Franklin read, taking occasional sips from his drink. At one point Tony was aware of the cop's glance. He appeared

puzzled, then went back to the magazine. A few minutes later Franklin started to stand up.

Tony got to his feet.

Franklin took a step in Tony's direction and staggered, fumbling behind him for something at his waist. The big man grunted, shaking his head like a wounded animal.

Tony drove his fist into Franklin's belly, then dropped him with a chop to the neck. Franklin tried once to get up, struggling to his hands and knees. Tony plucked the gun Franklin had been reaching for from the clip-on holster in the small of his back.

Holding the short barrel, Tony smacked the butt against Franklin's head just behind his right ear. Franklin dropped back to the floor and did not move.

Tony took some satisfaction in knowing just how bad the guy was going to feel when he came to.

Ramon was outside talking to the priest, his back to the house, when Tony came down the stairs, Franklin's gun tucked in the waistband of his pants. He walked back through the kitchen, where the guy he'd talked to earlier was helping himself to another beer.

"The faith healer's back. I saw you goin' upstairs. What's happening?"

"I was needed," Tony said.

"No kidding. How'd it go?"

"The patient'll recover."

"You don't say. I'm impressed."

"Do me a favor," Tony said.

"You got it."

"There's a kid around here, the caretaker of this place."

"Jimmy."

"Yeah. If you can find him, tell him there's somebody looking for him down at the dock."

"Will do." He popped the top of his beer and left.

Tony left the house and headed for the dock.

Two boats were still tied to the dock when Tony got there. He scanned the darkness for Gabe's anchor light but didn't see it. After signaling twice with his pocket flashlight Tony paused, then signaled twice more, waiting for a return signal that never came. He was standing at the edge of the mangroves near the end of the dock when Jimmy Santos arrived. He was alone. Tony watched him walk out to the opposite end of the dock and look over the boats.

Tony took out the snubnose he'd taken from Franklin and climbed onto the dock. "Jimmy," Tony called, turning the beam of the flashlight on him.

Jimmy turned, captured in the light as though poised for trouble, the same sullen expression on his face. Tony even thought he saw the young man's nostrils flare.

"It's all right, Jimmy." Tony tried to calm him. "I meant it back there when I said I might be able to help you." He focused the light on the dock now, walking toward Jimmy, holding the gun by his side but pointed down at the dock.

"Where's Franklin?"

"Taking a nap. He got tired reading." Tony stopped ten feet from Jimmy.

Jimmy looked down at the gun. "What's that for?"

"So you can tell Ramon you were forced at gunpoint to take me back to Key West."

"How's that gonna help me?"

"You got your parole extended when you got picked up by the Coast Guard the other day on your way back from Cuba, right?"

Jimmy didn't say anything.

"I think I can get that lifted for you."

"For the price of a boat ride?"

"And some conversation."

"About?"

"Angel Lopez," Tony said.

Jimmy's face flinched visibly. "I work for Ramon," he said.

"Look where that's gotten you. You don't owe him shit."

"I don't know nothin'."

"We'll talk about it on the way back," Tony said. "Let's go." And he raised the gun in case there was any doubt about his resolve.

*　　*　　*

Kay couldn't sleep. It was like a misty rain that wouldn't stop, the despair that came from her helplessness in finding her daughter. And now Tony. She had waited for an hour once she got home, hoping he would show up. He didn't. Finally she called a detective she knew in the sheriff's department and gave him an abridged version of what had happened at Ragged Key.

Then she was left with the shame she felt, the full force of it finally hitting home, blaming herself, as she was sure that others would be blaming her, for the loss of Patty. The humiliation of having people talking about her, about why Brad might have whisked Patty away like that; it was unreasonable, she knew it was unreasonable, but she was still unable to step away from her feelings.

She mixed herself a drink. Then a second. The TV was on, without the sound. At midnight she called her mother, waking her, hearing the alarm in her mother's voice. Kay wanted to cry, had to work at holding the tears back.

"Think of all the places he might go," her mother said, trying to sound reassuring.

"I have," Kay said.

"Then call people he might know there, tell them what's happened.

Kay hadn't gotten to that point, and she now knew why. It sounded as if she was not responsible, that it was her fault that Patty was in this situation. Which, of course, it was.

"Then hire a detective, someone like that to look for her," her mother said.

Yes, but he was missing, too. God. If only—if only. A sob escaped her throat. And someone knocked on the door. She left her mother on the line and went to the door.

Tony Harwood stood on the porch beside a young man she'd never seen before.

"I think we've located Angel Lopez," Tony said.

TWENTY-FIVE

After all the false starts, Tony thought on the ride back to Big Pine, the probing questions, it came down to a pissed-off punk kid named Jimmy Santos whose character was formed like a moon crater, constantly imploding and re-forming itself, fine granules of dust drifting away in the dark, unaffected by gravity. Ramon would not have been aware of such subtlety of character, accustomed as he was to imposing his own orbital system on the personalities around him.

Jimmy had saved Ramon's life, and the thanks he got was to watch God get the credit while Jimmy went to jail, got his parole extended, and lost his job!

Tony had recognized immediately the expression in Jimmy's eyes even without knowing his story, because it had once been Tony's own story. Jimmy Santos was a spy looking for a master. Tony left him with Kay, who in the morning would see to it that he got legal protection.

The trailer was dark when Tony drove up, parked, and climbed out of the cab. It was after one o'clock in the morning. Jack would be in bed unless he was over at Tom Knowles's place having a marathon cribbage game.

The night seemed endless, and Tony welcomed the nearness of his bed, the first night he would spend here since he'd discovered Nan's body. He thought of sleeping on the

couch, but he was so tired that he hoped sleep would over-power whatever evil spirits might still linger in the room.

He might have stayed at Kay's except that he did not want her—or anyone, for that matter—to know of the plan he was hatching for getting Angel Lopez out of Cuba.

Tony went into his trailer and closed the door behind him. A distantly familiar smell greeted him at the same time a voice he knew and had hoped never to hear again said, "You want to keep the old man alive, Harwood, just glue yourself to the floor."

Rick the Tic. The smell, the scratchy voice like a worn-out record, he would recognize anywhere, even in the dark, before the light came on and Tony saw Ricky standing over Jack Dowd, who was seated, his hands and feet bound, a rag in his mouth.

Ricky was skinnier than Tony remembered him, his spiky blond hair thinner, the Adam's apple prominent as a wish-bone in his throat. Were these the ravages of crack? He held a gun to Jack's head while Jack's stoic expression fixed on Tony.

"Hello, Rick." Tony tried to gauge Ricky's state—he wasn't wild-eyed and shaky, which meant he probably wasn't high. At least not crack high. "Sorry to keep you up so late waiting for me," Tony said.

"Fuck you!" Ricky said. "Enjoy what air you've got left, because it's about to run out."

"You carry your grudges right to the end, don't you, Ricky?"

"You know it. The way you should have, asshole, when you had the chance."

"I think I found some of your work in my bedroom the other day."

"She got in the way. I thought she was your wife."

"You made a mistake," Tony said. "Another one."

Ricky shook his head, showed a mouthful of bad teeth. "You made the mistake, asshole. Now shut up."

Franklin's gun was in the waistband of Tony's pants, but there was no way Tony was going to get his hands on it while Ricky had his own gun to Jack's temple. Jack never took his eyes from Tony.

"It's just you and me now," Tony said. "Isn't that what you wanted, to settle the score? Let him go, and we can do that."

A nerve jumped at the corner of Ricky's eyes. The tic. "We'll get to that. But killing you is too easy. I want you to feel something, know what it's like when you're trapped and somebody beats the piss out of you for no good reason."

Ricky brought the gun back and slammed the barrel against Jack's face.

Tony winced, remembering his own pain and the blow he'd recently given Franklin; he had not expected this, though in truth he should have expected anything from Ricky. Tony watched a trickle of blood seep from the corner of Jack's mouth. Jack's head bobbed on his chest, but the blow hadn't been hard enough to knock him out, which Ricky would not want.

"Feel that?" Ricky asked Tony.

"For God's sake, he's an old man."

"Old, young—what difference does it make once you start beating on someone?"

Tony's eyes were scalded by tears. Jack was going to pay for the sins of his son, as if he hadn't already paid enough.

Ricky dug the barrel of the gun into the loose flesh of Jack's cheek. "How's that, old man? How's that? Feel your life crawling out of you?"

Tony leaned against the door, humiliated, unable to move, feeling Franklin's gun pressed against the doorknob.

"Maybe we get him to eat it, huh? Whachoo think? You want to watch your old man suck on some steel?"

Jack's eyes watered, his face disfigured, but he continued to look at Tony.

"Please," Tony said. "Stop."

"Stop? I don't understand. You get all this juice going, all that frustration, you know. You know about that, doncha, cop face? And you know how hard it is to stop. Something just keeps on hammerin' at you, won't let you stop."

Ricky pulled the rag from Jack's mouth and replaced it with the gun barrel.

"Your old man," Ricky said, "sucks the big one." He jerked the barrel up.

Tony could practically feel the front sight ram into Jack's soft palate. "No!" Tony began to slide down the door until he felt the butt of Franklin's gun catch on the doorknob.

"What, motherfucker? You want me now, doncha? You really want to do me. You can taste it, cancha? Huh? Huh?" The gun ripped up into Jack's mouth once more. Tony heard teeth break in Jack's mouth, and blood began to leak out around the gun barrel.

Tony was breathing hard, his breath coming in gasps, trying to get control, trying to hold on to himself, unable to watch this senseless torture. He slipped further down the door, the gun in his pants being lifted now from his waistband.

He stopped. It was his only chance.

Stay with me, Jack, he thought. Just stay with me.

Ricky brought the gun out of Jack's mouth and lifted it to strike the old man in the head once more.

Tony watched the arc, screamed just as Ricky brought his gun down, Tony dropping to the floor, Franklin's gun now free and falling; he grabbed it one-handed behind his back, brought it around as Ricky was turning, sensing something wrong.

There was a roar in the trailer as Ricky fired, firing as he swung.

Tony brought Franklin's piece up and shot Ricky in the chest, blowing him back against the wall of the trailer, glass breaking as he shattered a window.

Tony crawled on his knees, holding the gun out, ready to shoot again, but Rick the Tic didn't move. The trailer stank of cordite, the deafening echo of the gun blasts reverberating in Tony's ears.

Jack's head lolled on his chest, blood smearing his white shirt and seeping from a wound in his leg where Ricky's bullet had struck him as Ricky, turning toward Tony, had fired too quickly.

Tony laid his head against Jack's chest, listening to his heartbeat, the labored, wheezing breath. "Hang on," Tony said. Then: "I am sorry."

Tony put a mattress in the bed of the truck, then picked Jack up in a fireman's carry, put him in the truck bed, and

239

wrapped him in blankets. He had fixed a tourniquet on Jack's leg and now drove the fifteen miles to Fisherman's Hospital in Marathon in ten minutes.

At two o'clock in the morning the emergency unit was relatively quiet. While Jack was being treated Tony found a public phone and called Tom Knowles.

Tom answered on the second ring, his voice sounding as if he had not yet been asleep, a slight whiskey edge to his words.

"What's happened?" Tom asked.

"I'm in Marathon," Tony said. "At Fisherman's Hospital. Jack was shot, and I just brought him up here."

"Jesus! Is he going to be okay?"

"Yes," Tony said, "I think so. He's in the emergency room right now with a bullet in his leg, but I think he's going to make it. Now listen to me. The man who shot Jack killed Nan."

There was a silence at the other end of the line before Tom said, "Who was it?"

"His name is Rick Lee," Tony said. "You don't know him, but I do. It was me he was after, not Nan, and I will carry the burden of her death for the rest of my life. I'm sorry." For the second time tonight he was apologizing.

"No," Tom said. "I won't have that. There is no blame." Tom's voice was firm, and Tony could have hugged him; he needed to hear that. "Now what can I do?"

"Call the cops," Tony said. "Rick is in my trailer, dead. I shot him. But I can't get involved right now. You know the cops would lock me up this time."

"What about Jack?"

"The hospital will report the shooting, but by that time I'll be out of here. Don't ask," Tony added, sensing Tom's next question. "The less you know right now, the better."

"Anything you say, Tony."

"Just don't let them browbeat you. Rick has got a record as long as your arm. It will come up in the computer once he's identified."

"No problem," Tom replied. "I can handle myself with these guys. Anything else you want?"

"Yes. Call Kay Fulton and tell her what happened. Tell her I'll be back here as soon as I can, maybe even tonight."

Tony hung up and called Wayne Costas.

Unlike Tom, Wayne sounded half asleep, which gave Tony some measure of satisfaction. For a couple of years Wayne had been an insomniac, and only a few months ago these calls were routine at this hour. The middle of the night was when Tony would report in on what was going on in his search for Wayne's daughter, Nicki.

"Tony, I wasn't expecting to hear from you."

"I've got a problem," Tony said. "You may be the only person who can help me right now."

"Whatever you need," Wayne said.

"You still flying?"

"Sure."

"I need a plane and a pilot."

"You've got it. When do we leave?"

"Right now," Tony answered.

Wayne yawned. "It's after two in the morning."

"I wouldn't ask if I wasn't in need," Tony said.

Wayne seemed to consider that, then said, "Where are you?"

"Marathon. I'll be at the airport here in one hour," Tony said. "Oh, and bring your passport."

Jack was in the intensive care unit—intensive scare, he had always called it. A nurse informed Tony that he was recovering, had regained consciousness, and would be taken to his room shortly.

Twenty minutes later Tony stood at Jack's bedside in the private room. Jack was hooked to an IV; he looked wan, shrunken, his lips pocked and indented where he was missing teeth. Nevertheless, Jack opened his eyes when Tony touched his shoulder and gave his son a diffident smile.

"A close encounter with the worst kind," Jack mumbled.

Tony gripped Jack's hand. "It's over," he said.

"But what's Helen gonna think she sees me like this?"

"She won't."

241

Jack shook his head. "She's coming in today," he said. "I got a lead on her son."

Tony stared at Jack in amazement. "Guess she'll just have to put up with you on a cane for a while."

Jack tried to smile again, then closed his eyes.

"Cuba?" Wayne Costas said. "It's off limits."

They sat on the runway at three-thirty in the morning, ready to take off. "Our government says it's off limits," Tony said. "You ever hear of the Cubans refusing anyone entry?"

Wayne seemed to think about it. "No, I guess I haven't."

"There's an air corridor for aircraft flying over the country, isn't there, a kind of DMZ?"

"Yeah, it's on the charts," Wayne said.

"Then let's take it and see what happens."

"You want to tell me why we're doing this?"

"It's a ninety-mile flight. I'll tell you on the way."

Wayne shook his head. "I wouldn't do this for just anyone," he said.

"Like I said, you're the only one I could count on."

Wayne pushed the throttle forward to begin takeoff.

RAMON

Just after dawn Ramon went into the big house on South Street. Luis was up, dressed as usual, looking as though he'd never been to bed. A New Age revolutionary who wore silk shirts and Cole-Haan loafers and had his nails manicured. It made Ramon laugh, but not this morning. Luis was pissed.

The morning edition of the *Herald* was on the kitchen table when Ramon walked in, the Keys section. A picture of Ramon with a bishop down from Miami to receive the deed to the island, and the story of Ramon's conversion and baptism.

"Why didn't you tell me about this?" Luis asked, his gold ring glittering as he tipped a cup of coffee to his mouth.

"I told you the other night at dinner."

"I didn't think you were serious. Or that you would move so fast."

Ramon smiled. "Well, hell, you should know when I say I'm gonna do something, I do it. The place is in my name. I can do what I want with it."

Luis shook his head. "I need to be out there tomorrow. I've got things to do there."

"What, run your revolution?"

Luis stared at Ramon over the top of his cup. "I'm going to be out there tonight, and I don't need the pope looking over my shoulder."

"No problem," Ramon said. "I'll arrange it."

"What happened to Franklin?"

"What makes you think anything happened to him?" Ramon had hoped Luis had not heard about last night.

"It was his day off. I had him scheduled to work for me. I called him a few minutes ago, and he said he couldn't make it. Told me you had Harwood out on the island last night."

"I didn't have him out there. He showed up uninvited. I just wanted to question him, but he sapped Franklin and took off."

"With that kid who works for you," Luis said. "What's his name?"

"Santos."

"He went to Cuba with you, right?"

Ramon nodded. He'd spent the rest of the night looking for Jimmy after finding the boat at the place where they kept it in town. There was one place he hadn't looked, and he was going over there as soon as he left Luis's. "Jimmy's cool," Ramon said.

"You've become so trusting in your new life. I hope you know what you're doing."

Ramon shrugged. If not, he thought, Luis was going to be on the same sinking ship.

"By the way," Luis continued, "stay away from Lourdes for a while. You've been putting things in her head that don't belong there."

Ramon popped the rubber band a few times before he said something he might regret.

From his car parked half a block down the street Ramon watched Kay Fulton come out of her house a few minutes before eight o'clock. She walked across the lane to the house next door, three houses from where Ramon sat.

He saw Kay knock on the door, wait a minute, then knock again. The door opened, but she didn't go in. She stood talking to someone Ramon couldn't see, then walked back to where her car was parked in the driveway and drove away.

Ramon waited five minutes, then drove around the block and parked. He walked back to Kay's house, making sure he stayed out of view of the neighboring home on the other side of the lane. Across the street was the cemetery.

Ramon walked up on the porch, knocked, waited, then sauntered along the narrow side yard, shielded by the thick, spiky pendennis that grew there, to the back of the house.

The French doors that gave onto the kitchen from the back were closed. A six-foot fence with staggered siding on either side enclosed the backyard. A gate door in the fence was closed, but when he reached over the top and pulled a string the latch clicked open and the door swung in.

Ramon stepped up onto the enclosed deck and walked to the back of the house. French doors gave onto the kitchen, and Ramon peered in one of the glass panels. Not a tidy housekeeper; dishes were piled in the sink, the countertops littered with appliances, and papers scattered everywhere.

Interesting, Ramon thought. Get in there and take a look through those papers. The doors were locked, but it would be easy enough to break one of the glass panels near the lock and open them. Not the Christian thing to do, but it was too tempting to pass up.

Ramon picked up a plastic patio chair and, using one of its legs, broke out a pane of glass. The noise probably wouldn't have carried beyond the fence, but he paused and listened for a moment before removing the glass shards and sticking his hand in the opening to unlock the door.

He made a quick inventory of the house to make sure no one was hiding anywhere. Empty. There was a kid's room, but Fulton hadn't come out of here with a kid. Where was the kid? Ramon examined some of the papers that had been left lying around, but none of them made much sense.

Ramon pawed around in the drawers and the closets looking for something, anything that might give up some information about the case against him. Other than the kid, Fulton seemed to live alone. There was no sign of a man around, neither in the bathroom nor in the main bedroom. Divorced? In the living room Ramon picked up the phone book and looked under F. There were three Fultons listed. Brad Fulton on Francis Street, and Kay on Francis. A third Fulton was in another part of town.

Brad and Kay on Francis next door to each other. Interesting. Husband, brother—what? Easy enough to find out, but what difference would it make? Ramon walked back into the kid's room and looked out the window, one that looked next door to the house where he'd seen Kay knock on the door.

From this window he could see the backyard, smaller than the one here, a picket fence around it not as tall as this one. The yard was bathed in morning sun; a kid in shorts, his shirt off, was sitting in one of the two lounge chairs.

Not a kid, but a young man by the name of Jimmy Santos.

The phone rang a dozen times at Brad Fulton's while Ramon, the phone cord stretched to the max, watched Jimmy Santos through the window. Whether or not he could hear the phone, Jimmy didn't even bother to open his eyes.

Hanging up, Ramon went back to the kitchen and opened one of the drawers where moments before he'd seen a bunch of keys. One of them was clearly labeled with the number of Brad Fulton's house.

Ramon left Kay's by the front door and casually walked next door, carrying the key that opened the other house. Ramon quietly strolled to the back, through the kitchen to a utility room, where a door opened onto the backyard. He stepped outside. Jimmy still didn't open his eyes.

"Morning," Ramon said. "Get yourself a good night's sleep?"

TWENTY-SIX

———

Another one of Randall Welch's scrawled notes was on her desk when she came in, this one more peremptory than ever: See me! This day was definitely not getting off on the right foot.

First Tony arriving in the middle of the night with that kid from Ramon's island, asking her to put him up overnight, then disappearing without telling her anything about his plans. She'd put Jimmy Santos in Brad's place, thinking it was the safest place for him. If he wanted to run, he could, but she got the sense that he was frightened and not unhappy to be there.

Then, at seven-thirty this morning, Tony's friend Tom Knowles called to tell her about another shooting in Tony's trailer. A man was dead, and Tony's stepfather was in the hospital.

"Who was killed?"

"A guy named Rick Lee," Tom Knowles told her.

Rick Lee, the man who was responsible for Tony's suspension. They'd just been talking about him last night.

And where was Tony?

Tom didn't know.

Where was Patty? Kay didn't know.

Now she had to face Randall. And tomorrow Grabill.

247

Wondering how bad it was going to be, Kay fixed herself a cup of coffee, then started down the hall to Welch's office.

Randall was at his desk. No Mantovani strings were coming from the stereo. His face seemed to have aged overnight; the lines along his broad nose down to his mouth were deepened furrows. He was staring straight at her when she got to his office.

"Come in and close the door," Randall said.

She did so, then walked over and stood behind one of the chairs in front of his desk, taking a tight grip on the leather back with one hand, holding her coffee cup in the other.

Randall didn't ask her to sit down.

"What was that business with Ramon last night?"

"What business?"

"C'mon, Kay, you know very well. You were practically tangoing at the fund-raiser."

"Hardly. Ramon was trying to plea bargain."

"Plea bargain! With you?"

"That's what I said. I told him to talk to his lawyers, then have them talk to me."

Randall nodded. "Ramon must be feeling the heat if he wants to bargain. You go before Grabill tomorrow, right?"

"Yes," Kay said.

"How's it looking?"

Kay thought for a moment. She wasn't sure, but Tony at least had given her some hope. "Promising," she said.

Randall chewed on his upper lip. Finally he got around to asking what he really wanted to know. "Ramon have anything of interest to offer?"

"Luis," Kay said. Then she watched for his reaction.

Randall twisted his shoulders once before picking up a pencil from his desk. "Details?"

"Not from him, but I get the impression it's connected to Luis's politics. Cuba specifically."

Randall shook his head. "We're not walking down that road," he said.

Luis had no doubt written out a check for a thousand bucks last night, the maximum legal contribution, for Randall's campaign war chest. It put Randall in a compromising position. Perhaps he thought that Kay would be too intimi-

dated now to prosecute this case with any authority. If so, he was underestimating her. Again.

Kay smiled and loosened her grip on the chair. "Yesterday I had federal agents in my office asking about Luis and Ramon."

"They were in here, too."

Kay waited, then realized Randall, too, was waiting.

"Apparently Luis was mixed up in the Bay of Pigs invasion in the early sixties."

"A lot of guys around South Florida were involved in that. It's ancient history."

"I get the feeling history may be repeating itself," Kay said.

"If it is or if it isn't, it has nothing to do with this office. We're prosecuting Ramon, not Luis." Randall's face was set, the corners of his thick mustache pulled down. "There won't be any plea bargaining," he added. "We convince Ramon or we don't. Either way, our job's done."

Kay had the feeling that it wouldn't much matter to Randall one way or the other.

Kay went home for lunch. She wanted to check on Jimmy. She parked the car, walked to Brad's, and knocked on the door. There was no answer. She was surprised, because he'd seemed glad to be there, and she didn't think he would run. Apparently he had fooled her.

Kay went over to her home and walked into the kitchen. She saw the broken glass on the floor; a chill actually came over her. Oh, God. For some reason she thought of Orange—was it only a week ago—and the fear of knowing that someone was watching her, lurking around. Was this Ramon's work?

She went to the drawer and looked for the key to Brad's. It was gone. Walking into Patty's room, she felt sick. She looked out the window. The back door was open. Kay walked back over to Brad's, going down the lane and in through the gate in the fence to the back.

The house was empty. It didn't look any different to her than when Brad was there. Jimmy must have slept on the couch. She locked the doors, then returned to her home and called someone to come and replace the broken pane.

Unable to eat anything, Kay returned to the office.

"Did you know about the shooting at Harwood's?" Randall demanded.

Kay was back in Randall's office.

"I heard about it this morning."

"You heard about it this morning," Randall said with some sarcasm. "But you didn't say anything."

"We were talking about other things."

"I'm beginning to wonder."

"What does that mean?"

"Harwood was out at Ragged Key last night."

Kay tried not to let her expression betray her. "What was he doing there?"

"Trespassing," Randall said. "And causing a city cop some discomfort."

"Franklin?"

"He's pressing charges," Randall answered, nodding. "Assault."

Kay didn't say anything. Was this why Tony had disappeared, or had he really gotten a line on Lopez?

"When did you last see Harwood?"

"Last night." Not really a lie, but if Randall quizzed her further, she knew her face would definitely give her away. She tried to ward Randall off. "What about Ramon? Where is he?"

"Nobody knows. He hasn't been seen since last night either. And he's supposed to be out at Ragged Key turning over the deed to the church this afternoon. Luis is looking for him."

Kay shrugged. She really had no idea what could have happened to Ramon and frankly didn't really care, except for how it might relate to Tony. There was still the matter of Jimmy Santos and the break-in she'd discovered earlier. She decided it was best not to mention Jimmy, aware that she was going to be in deep trouble if Randall found out about him.

"Someone broke into my house this morning."

One of Randall's eyebrows arched upward, giving his face a puzzled, cockeyed expression. Like a Picasso painting, Kay thought.

"What'd they get?"

"As far as I could tell, nothing."

Randall lifted his hands. "Then what do you think it was all about?"

"I think it was Ramon, and he was looking for something connected with this case," Kay said.

"But he didn't find it."

"I don't think so."

"Did you report it?"

Kay shook her head. "What for, if nothing was missing? You know the number of break-ins around this town that never get solved."

Randall paused. "I'm still trying to decide if I should remove you from this case." He looked at her as if soliciting her own opinion.

"Isn't it a little late for that?" Kay said.

"Why, because you're carrying a grudge now?"

"No. Because Ramon is a creep who belongs in jail. And tomorrow I'll be in court anyway. Like you said, this thing is going to be decided one way or the other tomorrow."

Randall nodded, reflecting a moment before saying, "Kay, I know you're under stress. But if you're withholding information that would have a bearing on this case, you'll be finished. Not only here, but in any other prosecutor's office where you might look for employment. Understood?"

Kay nodded her assent, then turned to leave as she felt color rush to her cheeks.

TWENTY-SEVEN

Half a dozen men in shabby olive uniforms sat or lounged against the cinder-block walls of the small office at the airport outside Havana. Tony and Wayne sat at a table answering questions, filling in forms, against the background sounds of conga drums and marimbas coming from a Soviet-built transistor radio on the table.

Some of the men were from the Secretaría de Gobernación, some the Guarda de la Frontera, according to the labels on their uniforms. One man, in a somewhat better tailored uniform, was Aduana—Customs. They were all efficient and without hostility.

When they had landed a couple hours earlier a female doctor, a beautiful mulatta, looked over the plane with an agricultural inspector to make sure there were no fresh foods on board.

It had been a relatively easy matter, landing in Cuba, despite some anxious moments in the cockpit when they made initial radio contact and requested permission to land.

The Cubans sent a military aircraft—it looked like a MiG—up to identify them before guiding them to the airport. From then on they were definitely a curiosity, but they had been treated as tourists, not as enemies.

The taxi driver who drove them into Havana just after dawn spoke English. "Hey, you guys Americans?" he asked.

"Yeah," Tony said. "All the way from Key West. How'd you know?" He and Wayne sat in the back of the Soviet Ladra, their knees wedged against the front seat.

"The hills are alive with the sound of music," the cabbie said. "And strange planes landing in the night."

"And which part of Cuba do you live in?" Tony asked. "Southwest Eighth Street?"

"Where's that?"

"Miami."

The cabbie laughed. "No, man. I grew up in Cincinnati. Folks went there when I was a kid. My dad was in telecommunications, got a job there with the phone company. We came back here when I was fifteen."

"You don't say." Tony nudged Wayne. "And you went into the cab business?"

"No, man. Got a degree and taught English at the university for ten years. Then I started driving a cab. Pays about the same, but I like this. Meet a lot of interesting people."

"I hear you," Tony said. He was thinking of the last cabdriver he'd had in Key West. Scotty. Cabdrivers, it seemed, were the last adventurers.

"Where you guys going?"

"I'm looking for someone," Tony said.

"Who's that?"

"A Cuban-American who got left here by mistake."

The driver actually turned around in his seat to look at them, and before he turned back Tony imagined him with wings on his cap.

"That's what I like about you Americans, always joking."

"You think so," Tony said. "How far is it to Santa Fe?"

They stopped at the Habana Libre, formerly the Havana Hilton, for breakfast. Carlos, their cabdriver, told them he would be in front whenever they were ready.

At this hour only half a dozen people were in the restaurant, which was the size of a ballroom. They sat at the American-style counter and ordered scrambled eggs, toast, and coffee. From the preparations going on in the kitchen you'd never know there was a food shortage in this country, Tony thought.

253

He was physically and emotionally exhausted after last night's turmoil and gratefully accepted the cup of coffee put in front of him, dumping in two packets of sugar.

"You want to explain what's going on now that you've got me here?" Wayne said.

"The guy I'm looking for," Tony said, "is a key witness in a trial."

Wayne looked different from when Tony had last seen him. He had gained some weight and lost the empty look that had been a part of him during the months Tony worked for him. Life was returning, although Wayne had told him on the flight over that he'd become a workaholic; the most excitement he had in life now was watching stock market transactions. That could change today, Tony had said.

"What makes you think he's in Cuba?" Wayne asked.

"He was shanghaied on Easter," Tony replied. "From Key West to Cuba by boat."

"And you're just going to fly in here and take him out. Easy as that."

"Maybe not," Tony said. "But if I have to, I think I can broker a deal."

"How's that?"

"The exiles are restless. They're plotting a coup."

"No shit!"

Tony nodded. Their waitress, a woman with skin as translucent as flower petals, put their food in front of them, then moved away.

"Out of Miami?" Wayne asked.

"And Key West."

Wayne shook his head. "Who do you talk to?"

"I'm not sure. I think the first thing to do is find out if the guy I'm looking for is still around."

"Santa Fe's where your man is?"

"It's where he was dropped. One of the people on the boat described the house there along the shore. It's a small town. I think I can find it."

"And then what?"

"I'm not sure. What I think is that the guy was probably left in the care of a dissident, someone who would be sympathetic to conquering exiles from the north."

"You know, something's always bothered me about the Cuban situation," Wayne said. "Remember Mariel in 1980? All the Cubans coming across on boats to the states? Castro supposedly let anyone who wanted to leave go. Then he opened up his prisons and palmed off some of the dregs of this society."

"A lot of them in our jails now," Tony said.

"Don't you think he's smart enough also to get some of his own people among the twenty thousand people who left here? Mix them into the exile community so he'd know when and where the threats were coming from?"

"Spies?"

"It seems only logical to me."

"So if there is a coup coming from the exiles, Castro probably knows about it."

"Look at those three guys from Miami who were picked up a few months ago trying to get in here. One of them was shot. They barely got their feet on Cuban soil."

Tony nodded. "If Castro knows something's coming, then I don't have much of a bargaining chip."

"Maybe you've got some specifics they don't have," Wayne said.

"Let's see if we can find Angel Lopez first."

"What about the cabbie? Can we trust him?"

"At least to get us to Santa Fe," Tony said.

The blue and white cabs were lined up along the hotel ramp when they came out of the Habana Libre. Carlos, their driver, honked and motioned to them. They walked over to his cab. Tony got up front beside the driver, Wayne sat in the back.

"You guys want to hire me for the day, your own guide?" Carlos smiled.

Tony agreed and sat sideways in the seat so that he could look back and carry on a conversation with Wayne but also watch the traffic behind them as they turned west on the wide boulevard.

Several cars seemed to follow them off the ramp. One of them, a white Ladra with two men in it, turned onto Twenty-third Street with them.

"Let's take a look at the *malecón*," Tony said. "Do some sight-seeing on the way."

"Sure," Carlos said. "Whatever you guys want." He drove a few blocks, then turned north on a side street. No other cars made the turn behind them.

The sloping street was tree-lined, shaded, the gutters clean, and large colonial-style homes graced either side of the street. People walked along the sidewalks or bicycled, and going downhill, the sea was briefly visible in the distance. It was not what Tony had expected.

Coming in from the airport, he hadn't seen the usual cluster of shantytowns and signs of poverty that were predominant features in the rest of the Caribbean, and elsewhere, for that matter.

People here were dressed well; he had seen no beggars lying in doorways or other obvious signs of the inequities of class in their short parade through Havana.

"This the sanitized tour you give the tourists?" Tony asked.

Carlos smiled. "Something else about you guys—you're all suspicious."

Maybe you're right, Tony thought.

Carlos parked along the curb at the *malecón*. The seawall curved along the broad sidewalk high above the sea like a stone fortress. Tony and Wayne got out of the car and looked down at the sea where it frothed and pounded below them.

Some distance away early morning lovers sat on the wall's ledge, a boy lying with his head in a girl's lap while she stroked his hair.

"Beautiful, no?" Carlos joined them.

"Magnificent," Tony said.

There was little traffic—bicyclists, some buses, but only a handful of cars traveled along at what should have been rush hour—the effect of gas rationing.

"Changed your mind about going to Santa Fe?" Carlos asked.

A couple of cars were parked along the *malecón*, unoccupied.

"No," Tony said, "I haven't changed my mind. Let's go."

* * *

Santa Fe was half an hour's drive west of Havana. The road went past Embassy Row, at the end of which Carlos pointed out the Soviet embassy, a large, modern building that bore more of a resemblance to a grain elevator in the Midwest, the way it dominated the scattered buildings around it, than it did to any diplomatic edifice.

Tony commented that it looked deserted. Carlos shrugged as if to suggest that it was the Soviets' loss, not Cuba's. He then launched into a discourse on the plight of the Cuban economy, and how, in this special period, Cubans were responding with the same consensus that had gotten them through tough times in the past.

"What about the people who are leaving, crossing to the States?" Tony asked.

"*Gusanos,*" Carlos replied. Worms.

Tony turned to Wayne, who winked from the backseat. They sped by open fields and the turnoff to the Marina Hemingway, originally meant to have been a gambling resort belonging to Meyer Lansky, Carlos said.

Santa Fe was a village with cluster housing, concrete houses built side by side with American autos from the fifties sitting in dirt yards. "Where you guys want to go here?" Carlos asked.

"What's special about this place?" Tony asked. He was trying to figure out why Ramon would have chosen Santa Fe to drop Angel.

Carlos wrinkled his nose. "It's where the *gusanos* leave from," he said.

Tony gave Carlos some money and told him to let them off on the beach road and come back around noon. They were going to take a walk.

TWENTY-EIGHT

The beach road was narrow, a potholed street with houses, some of them only bungalows, but in better shape than the concrete dwellings they'd seen further inland. After a five-minute walk the asphalt street gave way to dirt, and the houses became farther apart and larger, not dissimilar from the less grandiose houses in Key West, Tony thought. A long, empty beachfront suddenly stretched before them, and at the end of it a house with a long wooden dock that fit the description Jimmy Santos had given him.

"That looks like it," Tony said. He turned and cut across the beach, then began walking toward the house with Wayne until they got to within fifty yards.

"What are you going to do?"

Tony paused, stared out to sea. The house didn't look lived in. There was nothing on the windows, no sign of anything on what he could see of the porch, and no boats tied to the dock. It had a look of desertion about it, but that didn't mean anything.

"Sit here a minute and see what happens," Tony said.

They sat down on the soft sand, Tony so he could look out to sea but also have a view of the house. He asked Wayne about his life since he'd last seen him, when they'd flown back from Tallahassee with the burden of his daughter's death, not that long ago.

An hour passed, and no one came in or out of the house. Occasionally a car went by along the road some distance from where they sat. The sea was loud, the waves busting up as they hit the shore, unlike in Key West, where the sea lapped the shore with the calm of a lake, except during a storm.

Tony looked at his watch. It was eleven o'clock, and he was hungry again. They'd been sitting here for a couple hours. He said, "I'm going to walk over there. You just hang here and watch the back in case anyone goes out that way."

"What do I do if they do?" Wayne asked.

"Keep an eye on them," Tony said. He began walking, his feet sinking in the sand, which spilled over the edges of his loafers.

The house, which had appeared deserted from a distance, now took on an eerie lifeless quality as Tony approached; it had the feel of a summer house on the beach that had been closed for the winter. A place in disintegration. The exterior had lost most of its paint, and what adhered was weathered—lusterless, dry flecks on the old wood. The windows were dirty, uncovered; some kind of political slogan he couldn't read was finger-written in the dust on one pane; the corner of another pane had been broken out.

Tony noticed the debris accumulated in the corners of the foundation and the spiderwebbing along the railings as he went up the steps to the porch.

Through the dirty windows he could see some odds and ends of furniture, but nothing that looked as if anyone could actually be living here. Still, he knocked on the door and waited, listening. No sounds came from inside.

He looked around him. From this angle he could not see where Wayne sat on the beach. Down the road several hundred yards was another house, with more houses back in the direction they had walked; but directly across from him was a large lot, overgrown with weeds. Nobody was walking or driving along the dirt road.

Tony tried the door. Locked. He could have kicked it in, but he had to remember he was playing in someone else's park now. He went down the steps and around to the back. There was a boardwalk down to the dock. Tony walked out

259

there. From here he could also see Wayne sitting where he'd left him on the beach. The dock was worn where boats had tied up and rubbed against the wooden rail.

Everything looked just the way Jimmy Santos had described it. There was a back door opening onto two steps that dropped down to the boardwalk.

Tony walked back there. He looked in the window to the kitchen, knocked, and, after waiting again, tried the door, which, like the front one, was locked.

The windows were intact, but, using a chunk of crumbled cinder block lying on the ground, Tony broke out a section of the window and unlocked it. He pushed open the window, dusted broken glass off the sill, and scrambled inside. Breaking and entering. In the States he knew the penalty; here the law was foreign.

Unlocking the back door, he told himself to be quick.

The tiled floors were dirty, but foot tracks had been left in the dust. The refrigerator was on, but nothing was in it except a jug of water. Upstairs in two small rooms, one of which had a bed with a bare mattress, there was nothing except some newspaper and a few discarded garments. The newspaper was more than a week old.

Tony went back downstairs. He was turning the corner into the hallway that led back to the kitchen when he saw them. Half a dozen young men—boys really; the oldest couldn't have been over nineteen—most of them probably no more than fifteen. Kids. Their eyes carried that look of despair he'd seen so often—kids without a future.

One carried a piece of wood, a section of a tree limb, hanging from his hand like a club.

The front door was locked, and probably swollen from moisture and lack of use, even if he could get to it. He could throw himself out a window, risk cutting himself, and they would still probably swarm on him before he could run.

Which left the only other option: taking them on.

He flexed his knees and began to move slowly back into the larger space of the front room. The kids surrounded him. The one with the club lifted it to his shoulder.

"No trouble," Tony said in Spanish.

The circle tightened.

"Bueno." Tony crouched, moving in a tight circle of his own, then shot a foot out, catching the kid with the club unexpectedly in the stomach. The boy dropped to his knees, the club falling from his hand.

Tony lashed out with another kick, but the teenagers had widened their circle. He tried to get to the club, but another kid danced in, beating him to it.

Tony kept trying to maneuver closer to the front door. He feinted in one direction, then moved in the other, trying to kick the biggest of the boys. The kid stepped out of range, and Tony felt the sting of the club as it came down on his knee.

He stumbled. Five kids swarmed on him, grabbing at his hair, punching him, trying to hold him down as he bucked and kicked to throw them off. Their hands were like crabs, prodding and poking; their adolescent voices grunted, squawking directions to one another.

Tony was on the floor, on his back, when someone kicked him in the nuts. Pain and nausea shot through him. He retched and tried to bundle up in a fetal position only to be struck in the small of the back with the tree limb.

Others began kicking him in the back, in the ribs, while two boys held his arms. Then someone kneed him in the face, and he felt his nose cave in.

And then it was over. Someone shouted, *"Vamos!"* and they were gone.

He lay there on the floor tasting his own blood as it leaked into his mouth while listening to the approaching sound of a siren.

There were three cops and their cabdriver, Carlos. Someone gave him a handkerchief, which Tony held to his nose. Carlos asked him questions about his health. Anything broken? Did he wish to go to the hospital? He felt a little foggy, Tony said, bruised, but other than his nose he didn't believe anything was broken. He listened as Carlos translated for the cops.

Could he make it out to the car?

With pain, and some help from Carlos, Tony sat up, then stood. The cops watched, unsmiling. He limped outside, leaning against the porch rail, and looked along the beach. Wayne was not there. He started to ask about him, then decided it would be better to wait until he could speak to Carlos alone.

The cab was parked in the street behind the police car. Tony began walking toward it. The cops intercepted him and escorted him to their car. He was in too much pain to protest. There was a dull ache around his kidneys, and his ribs were so bruised the pain forced him to walk stiffly and take only shallow breaths.

Tony sat cramped in the back between the two cops; the third drove.

They sped back into Havana, passing along the *malecón* where he and Wayne had stood hours earlier.

They turned off, bumping through narrow brick streets past the thick fortified stone edifices of the old colonial city before turning in through open double gates and driving across a cobbled square, stopping before an imposing building.

Someone opened the door. One of the cops got out, laid a hand on Tony's shoulder, not unkindly, and held him as he got out of the car. His guards flanked him as they walked into the building and led him down a dim hallway to an office with an old scarred wooden desk with a phone on it and a globe lamp suspended from the ceiling.

The door closed, and Tony was alone. He sat down on a chair in front of the desk—besides file cabinets, the only furniture in the office.

Tony searched his pockets. His passport was gone, along with his watch and wallet. The punk kids had cleaned him out, robbed him of his identity. He shook his head as if to clear it. The nosebleed, thankfully, had stopped.

Where was Wayne? Carlos would have mentioned him, surely, and it would be easy to track down their arrival this morning.

He thought of Jack, a hundred miles away lying in his hospital bed, or perhaps by now he'd been discharged and was back in the trailer. And Ricky Lee. And Kay, who was going to court tomorrow, waiting for a miracle.

They hadn't filed a flight plan, so no one knew he was in Cuba. Tony leaned forward, holding his ribs.

Moments later the door opened, and two men came in. They both wore slacks and *guayabera* shirts. Dark hair, dark eyes, dark looks—neither one of them offered a smile. One of the men dropped a file on the desk and sat down behind it; the other moved behind Tony, out of his vision.

"Su nombre?" the man behind the desk asked.

"Anthony Harwood," Tony said. It was the way his name appeared on his passport.

The man behind the desk did not look at Tony, keeping his eyes on the documents in front of him as he fired questions in Spanish.

Where did he come from?

Marathon.

When?

This morning.

How?

Private plane.

Who with?

Wayne Costa.

Who is he?

A friend from Miami.

Why do you come to Cuba?

To find someone.

Who?

Angel Lopez.

Pause. Shuffling through papers. Who is Angel Lopez?

A witness to a crime.

Where?

In Key West.

Another pause.

Why the house in Santa Fe?

Looking for Angel Lopez.

Why in Santa Fe?

Heard that he was left there.

Who left him?

Ramon Marquesa.

Pause. Shuffle, shuffle.

Who is Ramon Marquesa?

The guy on trial in Key West.

Who do you work for?

No one.

What is your name?

It went on. The same questions repeated over and over without the man in the *guayabera* once looking at Tony. An hour, two hours went by—Tony lost track. His nose was swollen; he had to breathe through his mouth, think about each breath, to avoid causing pain to his ribs.

Finally his interrogator stood up and walked to the door, the man he'd come in with following him.

Tony said, "One question."

The men paused.

"Where is Wayne?"

They went out the door without answering.

For the next few hours the routine was similar—someone would come in, question him, and leave. Tony would then be left alone, sometimes for as much as an hour, before the next inquisitor appeared. The questions were familiar, more often than not repetitive. Sometimes he would ask to expand his answers. Occasionally a question would be framed in broken English, but more, or so it seemed to Tony, for the practice of his examiner than for him. There was always the file on the desk, but beyond the questions no one showed any sign of personal interest in Tony.

It must have been midafternoon—he'd waited well over an hour since the last man had left—when the door opened. Tony turned his head expecting to see the familiar shape of a young man in a *guayabera* or a sport shirt in the doorway.

Instead it was an older man, in his fifties, Tony guessed. He had thick white hair and glasses, and he wore a suit and tie. He took a seat behind the desk and looked at Tony. Smiled.

"My name is Manolo," he said in nearly unaccented English.

"Tony Harwood. Have you got any aspirin?"

"Pain?" Manolo asked.

"A broken nose, ribs that feel like they've punctured my lungs. Yeah, there's some pain."

"Would you like a doctor? Aspirin is in short supply right now. But we have plenty of doctors."

"Thanks," Tony said. "I could use a doctor."

"I'll arrange it when we're finished here." Manolo looked down at the file he'd dropped on the desk, the same one the others had used, and pushed it aside. "Maybe you have some questions."

"Where's the guy I came here with, Wayne Costa?"

Manolo nodded. "He's here. We're questioning him, too."

"He's okay?"

"He's fine. He told us that you worked for him, about the tragedy of his daughter's death."

Tony nodded. Manolo's face carried a lifetime of sadness; something about his expression reminded Tony of Jack.

"He is in your debt," Manolo said. "He will always owe you."

"That debt was paid in full," Tony said.

Manolo shook his head. "Not a question of money. This is something we Cubans understand. Those of us like me who have lost family."

"To America?"

"I have a sister," Manolo said, nodding absently, "who I have not seen in thirty years. I don't know if she is even still alive. We were very close."

"The ugly side of politics," Tony replied.

"This is what you do," Manolo said. "You find people."

"I was a cop once. I found it frustrating, disappointing. I work for myself now."

"Tell me about Angel Lopez," Manolo said.

Tony described in detail his search for Angel. How he'd come to believe that Angel might have been staying in the house in Santa Fe.

"If you found him, just how were you going to get him out of Cuba?" Manolo asked.

"I was hoping to trade for him."

"Trade?" Manolo removed his glasses and wiped the lenses on his tie.

"Information about a raid on Cuba."

Manolo put his glasses back on. "Which one?" he asked. "The exiles plot at least one a month."

"You know about them?"

"Many of them."

"Then I guess I don't have anything to trade."

"Well, perhaps you have details," Manolo said.

"But I don't have Angel Lopez."

"We picked up one of those kids who attacked you this morning," Manolo said.

"What about my passport? You get it back?"

"We're working on that. The house is used by dissidents."

"I'm not surprised. I figured that's where Angel would be."

"It's where he was," Manolo said. "Two days after he was dropped there we picked him up."

Tony stared at Manolo, who said, "I'll get a doctor in here. Then we'll talk details." Then he added, "Do you think you could find my sister for me?"

Wayne, Manolo, and Tony had dinner in the restaurant of the Victoria Hotel. With his ribs taped, his nose packed to hold the cartilage in place, and some pain pills the doctor had given him, Tony felt like a piece of freight packaged for shipment.

He spent two hours talking to Manolo and another official. Manolo did not say, but from the look in his eyes when Tony mentioned Luis Marquesa, it was clear the name was not unfamiliar.

Tony's description of what he knew of the Marquesa operation came from everything he'd learned from Kay, Tom Knowles, and his own investigation.

Afterward the three of them went to dinner. Wayne's treat. Wayne, trying to chill out after the questioning, during which the cops were looking for inconsistencies in their stories, was still tense despite Manolo's reassuring manner.

Angel Lopez would be escorted to the airport later tonight, Manolo said. Also, the police had recovered Tony's passport. It, too, would be at the airport.

With their coffee Manolo passed out cigars. "You know," he said, "whatever happens here, Cuba's going to be run by Cubans. Not exiles."

TWENTY-NINE

There was a plane off their starboard wing, just above them, its white strobe on the underbelly of the fuselage winking like a star. "Looks like we've got an escort," Wayne said. He had reported radio contact with the phantom plane a few minutes ago, and here it was.

"Narcs?" Tony asked.

Wayne nodded. "They must have spotted us coming out of Cuba."

The narrow island chain of the Keys was clearly visible, like the back of a giant alligator basking in moonlight.

"What's the procedure?" Tony asked.

"We're twenty-five miles from Marathon. I told them we would be landing there. They seem happy with that. Said they'd have a welcoming committee to meet us."

Which meant they'd spend the rest of the night in jail, Tony thought.

Angel Lopez sat in the seat behind Wayne. He had said nothing since being turned over other than to ask if Ramon knew he was coming back. Tony told him not to worry about Ramon, Ramon was a Christian now. Angel had stared at Tony as if he was out of his mind.

"Kay, I'm not coming back."

Kay felt weak, the sort of weakness that would sometimes

267

suddenly come over her when she was first getting her period. She was standing now, the eleven o'clock news just coming on TV, and she sat down in the rocker beside the phone table, feeling her legs go shaky.

She lived daily now with the hope, and dread, of Brad's next call; but tonight she was unprepared for it. When she answered the phone she had been expecting to hear Tony's voice.

She said, "Brad, don't do this." Her own voice thin, almost a whisper. "Where is Patty?"

"Asleep. She's fine. I just wanted to let you know."

"Bring her home. Send her. I'll come and get her." Kay heard herself begging and wondered for a moment if that was what Brad had wanted all along.

"I'm keeping her." There was a finality in his tone.

Kay tried to think of something. "You can have her in the summer," she said. "We'll draw up an agreement. I'll sign it."

"I'll call you once in a while. You can talk with Patty. Later on," Brad said, then he hesitated before adding, "Well, we'll see what happens."

Kay felt an impotent rage come over her. After the years she'd spent with him she recognized the tone of voice and knew there was nothing to be gained by trying to reason with him or begging. She said, "I'm coming after you. You can't hide forever, and sooner or later I'll find you."

She heard the click as Brad hung up the phone.

Kay was late getting in the next morning. She showed up at eight-thirty with about an hour to get her stuff together and appear before Judge Grabill at ten o'clock.

About the time it was getting light she'd finally fallen asleep, and she didn't wake up until eight o'clock. She knew she looked a mess; she was going to have to spend some time putting on makeup, trying to cover up what the stress and a sleepless night had done to her face. Thankfully, there were no notes from Randall Welch.

The phone rang, and Kay picked it up, annoyed.

"I decided to make you my one phone call."

Tony.

"Meaning what I think it means?"

"Yeah, I'm in jail in Marathon."

"I suppose it's a long story."

"I'll give you the condensed version."

"Good, it's all I've got time for."

"We got picked up flying back from Cuba by a narc surveillance plane."

"Cuba!"

"I brought you a present."

Kay looked down at her desk, the open file on Ramon Marquesa. Angel. "You found him there?"

"Yes. Wayne's got one of his high-powered attorneys working to get us out of here. Then it will take an hour to get down there, less if we can fly."

"Who's Wayne?"

"Costa, the pilot. It was his plane. His daughter, Nicki . . ."

Oh, yes. So many questions. "You sound funny."

"Sinus problems. I hope to see you in court."

Ramon stood on the third-floor balcony overlooking the courthouse lawn. He lit a cigarette and watched the traffic go by on Whitehead Street. He didn't have to be there; this was supposedly the last of the preliminary hearings, but his lawyer had pleaded with him. "Grabill's probably going to dismiss this case. You should be there." Ramon decided, why not? He didn't have anything better to do today. Then, almost as soon as the Fulton woman started—she looked like hell—some technical wrangle broke out, a lot of legalese being spoken that Ramon didn't understand, and he walked out to have a smoke.

Thinking about Jimmy Santos and Luis. Both out on Ragged Key right now. Ramon had told the church yesterday there was going to be a slight delay in turning over the deed; then he'd taken Jimmy out there along with the dogs. Asking Jimmy if he believed in the power of Christ and the forgiveness of sins.

Jimmy, never looking at Ramon, mumbled something that Ramon couldn't hear.

"I can't hear you."

"I guess so," Jimmy said.

"I hope you do," Ramon said. "I hope you do." Then he sent Jimmy to get the generator started and feed the dogs. Ramon went to get a couple of planks of wood from what remained of the pens where they'd kept the fighting cocks, carried them around to the shed where he kept his tools; he found the power nail gun, plugged it in, and quickly nailed the planks together in the form of a cross.

Then he waited for Jimmy. Saw him come out the door of the house with a new bag of Ken-L-Ration, pour the dry nuggets in two big bowls on the table, and add water. The dogs were barking, hungry, prancing around Jimmy's legs.

Ramon shouldered the cross and carried it over to the house, dragging the nail gun and its air cord with him.

"What's that for?" Jimmy asked when Ramon leaned the cross up against the house.

Ramon lifted the nail gun, held it against Jimmy's side, and pulled the trigger. "Redemption," Ramon said. He had done his best for everyone, but they wouldn't accept the new man, kept fighting against him until he was left without choice.

Jimmy looked down, saw the blood leaking from him, put his hand down to stop it. Ramon grabbed him by the wrist, pinned his hand up, and nailed it to the cross.

Jimmy screamed, but other than the dogs and Ramon there was no one out there to hear him.

Ramon finished the crucifixion, then smeared the dog food that had turned to chunky gravy over Jimmy's body. When he turned and walked back to the shed with the nail gun, listening to the dogs, he thought: Just goes to prove some animals will bite the hand that feeds them.

Ramon ground out his cigarette on the balcony rail and dropped it over the side. He was about to go back inside and see if the lawyers had worked everything out and he could get out of there when something caught his attention. Two guys hurrying along toward the front of the courthouse. He looked again and couldn't believe his eyes. Angel. And the other guy, Harwood, coming into the building like he knew right where he was going and was in a hurry to get there.

*   *   *

HAVANA HUSTLE

Tony stepped off the elevator on the third floor onto the outside balcony and started down to courtroom B, his hand on Angel's arm. He felt Angel freeze; Tony looked, and there was Ramon, leaning against the rail fifty feet away. He tightened his grip on Angel's arm.

"What's the matter, Angel? You look pale," Ramon called. "Cuba didn't agree with you?"

"Just keep walking," Tony said. "Nothing he can do to you now."

They were almost an hour late as it was.

Tony wondered what Ramon was doing out there, if Kay had said something in court to let him know that Angel was on his way and Ramon had come out to provide a welcoming committee of one.

But somehow he didn't think Kay would do that, would give them any warning until Angel actually walked into the room. So Ramon must have just stepped out for some air or a smoke and been just as surprised to see them as they were to see him.

"You're not going to talk to an old friend?" Ramon asked. He was standing in the center of the balcony, blocking it like a truck. They would have to pass him to get to the door of the courtroom.

Tony could feel Angel trembling beneath his hand. "We're going in," Tony said. "They're expecting us."

"Hey," Ramon said, "I'm not stopping you. It's just that Angel looks a little sick. Maybe he needs some time to think about it, some fresh air."

"I don't think so," Tony said.

"Angel? You want to go in there?"

Angel found his voice, a quiver in it. "Ramon, this ain't my doing. They came, they got me. I had no choice."

"I'm giving you one," Ramon replied, smiling. "Showing some Christian charity."

"I heard you got religion," Angel said hopefully.

"That's right. I'm God-fearing. You should try it."

"A little late for that," Tony said, and he tried to push Angel around Ramon. "Let's go."

Angel balked. And in a motion swifter than Tony would

271

JOHN LESLIE

have expected, given Ramon's size, Ramon reached out and grabbed Angel by the shirt.

Just then the door to the courtroom opened. Ramon's lawyer stuck his head out and said, "Ramon, the judge is going to rule."

Ramon dropped his hand. "Think about it. Vengeance is mine, saith the Lord. But He works in mysterious ways. You just never know what His instrument's gonna be." Ramon turned and went through the door that was still being held open.

Tony had to urge Angel in.

As the procession came down the aisle toward the front of the court Grabill looked up over his half glasses. Kay turned to look. Ramon joined his lawyer at the defense table as Kay stood up.

"Your honor, I believe the witness for the prosecution has just arrived."

Grabill took off his glasses and massaged the bridge of his nose. "Is this the elusive Mr. Lopez?"

Kay glanced briefly toward Tony, who winked. "It is, your honor."

Ramon's lawyer rose. "Your honor, these last-minute theatrics are fine for the movies. But I don't have to remind you that we haven't had an opportunity to depose Mr. Lopez, nor do we even know if this witness has relevant testimony."

Grabill twirled his glasses. "Well, we can soon find out, because I can tell you we're not leaving here today until we've got a court date set or this case is dismissed. Mr. Lopez?"

Angel stood up. Tony could see the steady tremble in Angel's hands.

"Would you come forward here, approach the bench?"

Angel stepped up between the attorneys' tables.

"Mr. Lopez, you have been listed as a primary witness for the prosecution, but for some reason Miss Fulton here has been unable to bring you to court until now. I'd like to cut through some of the crap, if you don't mind, and find out if what you have to tell us was worth this wait."

272

Ramon had turned his stare on Angel, who held his hands clasped firmly behind him.

"It has been stated, Mr. Lopez, that you were a witness to the charge brought against Mr. Ramon Marquesa of the attempted murder of Oreste Villareal. Is that correct?"

Tony watched Angel tug at his fingers, his knees beginning to shake.

"I was with Ramon in Bubba's that night," Angel said.

"And so were a couple hundred other people," Grabill replied. "What I want to know about is after Mr. Marquesa left Bubba's. Were you with him then?"

Angel stared straight ahead, hesitated a moment, then said, "No, Judge, I went home from Bubba's."

Silence. Kay looked down at the floor.

"That'll be all, Mr. Lopez," Grabill said.

Angel turned and slipped into a seat.

"Unless you have any more surprises hidden away there, Missy Fulton, I'm going to dismiss this case as of now."

Grabill banged his gavel. Kay stood up and began packing her briefcase.

THIRTY

Tony drove up to the hospital in Marathon with Kay that evening. Jack's expression was beatific, Tony thought. His stepfather was sitting up in bed, beaming, when Tony walked in with Kay. Helen Anderson stood beside Jack's bed; she'd arrived yesterday evening, less than twenty-four hours after Ricky Lee had shot Jack.

"That bullet belonged to you," Jack joked to Tony after introductions were made.

"I had that experience," Tony replied. "I turned in my cane, remember?"

"The first time in forty years as a cop I was ever shot, and it wasn't even meant for me. By the way, I talked to the detectives investigating the shooting. They may have some questions for you, but they're ready to close out that case."

Helen laid her hand on Jack's shoulder. Jack smiled. "I tell you we found Wyatt?"

Tony shook his head, looking at Helen, who didn't seem to be grieving. Wyatt had been missing less than three weeks. "Where is he?"

"He fell in love. He's been shacked up—"

"Jack!" Helen said.

"Living with a woman—an older woman, it turns out—in Key West. He was afraid to call home. Seems he was having some problems in school and trying to decide what to do."

"When did you find him?"

"About twelve hours ago," Jack said. "He talked with Helen on the phone this afternoon."

"How'd you do it?"

Jack smiled. "Legwork," he replied.

Tony looked with pride at this phenomenal man, his stepfather.

"I'm getting out of here tomorrow," Jack said. "Helen's going to drive me back to Miami."

"What about Wyatt?"

"I'm just relieved to know that he's okay, but as Jack reminds me, Wyatt is nineteen years old. He's on his own now. He knows where I'll be if he needs anything or wants to see me."

"What about you?" Jack asked.

"I've got a court appearance to settle up the Cuba trip and a little girl to find," Tony said, glancing at Kay.

"So the end is just another beginning."

"So it seems," Tony replied.

He and Kay drove back toward Key West, stopping at the restaurant on U.S. 1 that was tucked back in the palms overlooking the Gulf, where they'd eaten together one other time. They sat at the same corner table, with Lyle Lovett serenading them from a tape.

"I'm turning in my resignation tomorrow," Kay said.

"Taking the job in Tampa?"

"No," Kay said. "I'm finished with being a lawyer. At least for now."

"What will you do?"

"Look for Patty. I'm ready to get out of here."

"Together?"

He watched her pause and look out the screened porch to the wispy clouds over the Gulf as if searching for the answer.

When she turned back one tear tracked down her cheek. "We'll try it," she said. "Together."

The next morning Tony got up, squeezed orange juice, made coffee, and brought it to Kay in bed. With the paper that had been tossed onto Kay's porch. Carrying the story of another attempted raid on Cuba—a dozen heavily armed Cuban-Americans captured on boats off the Cuban coast.

In an apparently unrelated story, the Marquesa home on Ragged Key was reportedly destroyed by an unexplained explosion. Luis Marquesa was believed to have been in residence at the time.

ENJOY SOME OF THE MYSTERY
POCKET BOOKS HAS TO OFFER!

SAMUEL LLEWELLYN
__BLOOD KNOT 86951-5/$4.99
__DEADEYE 67044-1/$4.99
__DEATH ROLL 67043-2/$3.95

ANN C. FALLON
__DEAD ENDS 75134-4/$4.99
__POTTER'S FIELD 75136-0/$4.99
__WHERE DEATH LIES 70624-1/$4.99

AUDREY PETERSON
__DARTHMOOR BURIAL 72970-5/$4.99
__THE NOCTURNE MURDER 66102-7/$3.50

TAYLOR McCAFFERTY
__BED BUGS 75468-8/$4.99
__PET PEEVES 72802-4/$3.50
__RUFFLED FEATHERS 72803-2/$4.50

JUDITH VAN GIESON
__NORTH OF THE BORDER 76967-7/$4.99
__THE OTHER SIDE OF DEATH 74565-4/$4.99
__RAPTOR 73243-9/$4.99

DALLAS MURPHY
__APPARENT WIND 68554-6/$4.99
__LOVER MAN 66188-4/$4.99
__LUSH LIFE 68556-2/$4.99

POCKET
B O O K S

Simon & Schuster Mail Order
200 Old Tappan Rd., Old Tappan, N.J. 07675
Please send me the books I have checked above. I am enclosing $_____ (please add $0.75 to cover the postage
and handling for each order. Please add appropriate sales tax). Send check or money order–no cash or C.O.D.'s
please. Allow up to six weeks for delivery. For purchase over $10.00 you may use VISA: card number, expiration
date and customer signature must be included.
Name _____
Address _____
City _____ State/Zip _____
VISA Card # _____ Exp.Date _____
Signature _____ 958